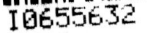

ChangelingPress.com

Stripes/Ram Duet
A Dixie Reapers Bad Boys Romance
Harley Wylde

Stripes/Ram Duet
A Dixie Reapers Bad Boys Romance
Harley Wylde

ISBN: 978-1-60521-893-9

Publisher:
Changeling Press LLC
315 N. Centre St.
Martinsburg, WV 25404
ChangelingPress.com

Printed in the U.S.A.

Editor: Crystal Esau
Cover Artist: Bryan Keller

The individual stories in this anthology have been previously released in E-Book format.

Table of Contents

Stripes (Devil's Boneyard MC 12)
A Dixie Reapers Bad Boys Romance
Harley Wylde

Melina -- Men have never given me a reason to trust them. The Bratva taught me men are brutal. Selfish. They take what they want. Death would be better than tying myself to one ever again. Then a Russian biker dives in to save me. As much as I want to believe everything he says, how can I? I've only known pain at the hands of men. I want him to be different... but any hope I had died long ago.

Stripes -- She thinks she's broken. I see a survivor. A strong woman who's still standing despite what's been done to her. It will take time, but I'll help her heal. Prove not all men are evil. I'll give her a reason to keep living. Never again will someone cause her pain. If they do, they'll answer to me. My hands are already stained with blood. What's a little more?

Prologue

Melina

Marriage to Ruslan had been nothing but pure hell since day one. He'd given me two beautiful daughters, and I wouldn't wish them away for anything, but every other moment of our lives had been only pain and humiliation. I'd learned early never to speak back, and to never ask questions. If he told me to do something, I did it, regardless of whether I should.

Which was how I found myself in trouble.

I bowed my head, refusing to make eye contact with Feliks Sobol. The higher-ups had left him in charge for some reason, not that it mattered. When Ruslan forced me to aid him in his thirst for power, I'd known it wouldn't end well for me. But I'd done it, because the alternative would mean letting him kill me, and leaving my girls vulnerable. I'd have done anything to keep Yulia and Oksana safe. Although I had a feeling Ruslan had embellished my involvement. One last chance for him to make my life hell.

"Melina Romanov, do you know why you're here?" Feliks asked.

"*Nyet*, Mr. Sobol." No one had told me outright why I'd been brought in. The fact my husband hadn't returned home had left me uneasy. They had to have caught him, and now I'd pay the price as well. Ruslan wouldn't go down without a fight, and nothing would delight him more than knowing the Bratva would destroy me.

"Your husband is guilty of breaking multiple laws. He tried to cheat the Bratva, and he's failed. At this very moment, he's being tortured to gain more information on those who aided him." He tapped his fingers on the desk. "Your name came up."

I clenched my hands. It didn't surprise me. Anything Ruslan had asked me to do could have tied into his human trafficking ring. I wouldn't have known since he told me very little. Although I did know what he'd been up to. He hadn't kept it a secret. In fact, I thought he got off on letting me know about the women and children who would suffer at his hands. If I'd gone to anyone without proof, they wouldn't have believed me.

"Nothing to say?" Feliks asked.

"Will it matter?" I doubted it. If my husband hadn't cared what I had to say, why would this man? In the Bratva, women were to be seen and not heard. We were merely a decoration, or a means to gain power through political marriages. Nothing more. Except in my husband's case, we were meant for twisted forms of entertainment. The louder we screamed, the more he got off on the pain he inflicted.

"For your crimes, you'll spend the rest of your days in one of our brothels. Seems fitting, doesn't it? You're guilty of helping Ruslan Romanov steal women and children and selling them into sexual slavery. Now you'll be in the same predicament. Just so we're clear, it won't be one of our upscale places."

I swallowed the knot of fear lodged in my throat and gave a short nod. Pleading for my life wouldn't do me any good. Telling him I was innocent would only fall on deaf ears, or perhaps anger him. The thought of being used by countless men made me sick. I'd been a dutiful wife, and I'd been a virgin when Ruslan married me. I'd never been with anyone other than him. Of course, being in his bed had been far from pleasant, but I had a feeling my life would be much worse now.

"This is rather disappointing," Feliks murmured. "I'd hoped for some sort of reaction. Do you enjoy being a whore? Is that why you aren't crying and begging for me to spare you?"

Bile rose in my throat when I contemplated what my life would be like moving forward. I hadn't liked my husband touching me. The thought of strangers paying to use me made me want to throw up. All my choices had been taken from me. I hadn't had many to begin with. As long as they could pay, they'd be permitted to do whatever they wanted with me.

"Still nothing?" Feliks asked, pursing his lips.

"I don't know what you want me to say," I admitted. "Begging won't do me any good. Saying I'm innocent won't either. Whether I speak up or remain silent, my fate will remain the same."

"Smart woman." Feliks smiled, but the sight chilled me to the bone. "Someone will escort you to your new home, Melina Romanov. As for your daughters…"

My gut clenched. No! Not my precious babies. They wouldn't be so cruel as to do the same to them, would they? Yulia was still a child. A teenager. And my sweet Oksana… she'd never harmed anyone in her life.

"Yulia will finish her schooling at an all-girls' academy here in town." Feliks steepled his fingers. "We've received word Oksana helped her father by luring in victims. Because of her involvement, and her age, she's been tried accordingly. Her fate will be the same as yours."

"No!" I fell to my knees. "Please! Spare my daughter. She didn't do anything! I don't know who claimed she'd helped Ruslan, but it was all lies. She'd have never done such a thing."

His jaw tightened, and anger flashed in his eyes a moment before his expression went blank. I'd heard of Mr. Sobol before and knew his reputation of being hard. Cold. A killer without regrets. It seemed my family would now suffer at his hands.

"Not her, but you would, hmm?" Feliks peered down at me.

"I did whatever my husband commanded." I swallowed hard. "It was the only way to survive. If I disobeyed, he'd have killed me, then my babies would have been alone with that monster. I survived for them."

My words didn't seem to move him. Not even a little. *Not Oksana. Please don't let them do this to her!* I'd have given anything to spare her.

"I'm sorry, Melina, but everything was already decided. Their fates are sealed."

The door behind me opened, and two men grabbed my arms. They clenched down hard, leaving bruises as they dragged me from the office. Tears streaked my cheeks as I realized the short life my sweet Oksana would live. It would destroy her to be in such a place, and I knew she'd been a good girl and hadn't been with a man before. I'd have endured anything to spare her.

What had Ruslan told them? Why had he turned on our daughter? I'd known he was a monster. I'd never thought he'd lie about our daughter's involvement, though. Selling her in marriage for political gain was one thing. This was something entirely different. What did he get out of this?

Instead of going straight to the car, the men shoved me into a small room. I stumbled but caught myself against the wall. One of them started to unfasten his belt, while the other cracked his knuckles.

The darkness in their eyes told me enough. My torture would begin now. They'd break me before taking me straight to hell.

The taller man's fist slammed into my side, then my thigh. I fell to the floor, the wind knocked out of me. As I struggled to breathe, I saw the other one shove his pants down his legs and reach for me. He tugged at my skirt, and I pushed at his hands, trying to fight him off. The other man's fist slammed into me again and again. I coughed up blood as they tore my clothes from me.

They took turns beating me. Violating me. When I thought I couldn't handle another moment, everything started to dim. At least I wouldn't be awake for whatever happened next. It was a small blessing, but one I'd gladly take.

Please spare Oksana from this treatment! It was my last thought before I gave in to the darkness.

Chapter One

Stripes

"What intel did Wire send us?" I asked.

Gator shrugged, which meant he'd been as pissed as I was and hadn't paid close attention. We'd parked about a block away and observed the place from a distance. I leaned against a building, smoking a cigarette, in the hopes people wouldn't be suspicious. So far, we'd seen a few customers go in and come out not too long afterward. I highly doubted they were getting their money's worth.

"I wish Specter would show the fuck up," I grumbled.

"We'll be lucky if he does." Gator scanned the area. "Can I ask you something?"

"If I say no, will it stop you?"

He snorted and shook his head. As I figured. I motioned for him to go ahead.

"Why did you agree to this? Breaking the woman out of there, I understand. But letting them marry the two of you? Why the fuck would you take a whore as your wife?"

I fought for control, knowing he was genuinely curious and didn't mean it the way it sounded. Otherwise, I'd have already put my fist through his face. I took my time, trying to figure out how I could word it.

"The woman in there didn't agree to become a whore. They beat her. Raped her. Forced her into that way of life. If we don't get her out, she'll only suffer more. Grimm and the Dixie Reapers are concerned the Bratva will try to take her back. Marriage is the only way to protect her."

Gator stared a moment before giving a slight

nod. "Fine. As long as they didn't coerce you into this shit. I know how big your heart is, Stripes, even if others don't always realize it."

I grinned and put out my cigarette. "Let's get this out of the way. If Specter shows, great. If not, we'll handle it."

Breaking into a brothel wasn't exactly difficult. I'd expected security, but I hadn't seen a single man watching over the place. If they'd had electronic surveillance, I knew one of the hackers would have disabled it by now. We walked through the front doors and a woman, most likely the madam, smiled at us broadly.

"Gentlemen, what's your pleasure today? We can cater to any and all of your needs."

I curled my fingers into a fist, fighting to maintain control. I wanted to rip this place to pieces with my bare hands. Instead, I took in my surroundings. At a quick glance, I saw the frightened women nearby. A few of them looked completely destroyed. They no longer cared what happened to them, and the woman in front of me was the deadest of them all. Despite her smile, her eyes were vacant. She was little more than a puppet. I doubted she had any real control. The Bratva owned her, same as the other women here. Her greeting us only meant she'd been here the longest. They'd broken her long ago and had no reason to doubt she'd do exactly as they commanded.

I didn't think any of these women came here voluntarily. Someone had possibly trafficked them. At the very least, they were being disciplined like Melina. I didn't want them to get hurt, which meant I needed to be careful. And yet, I'd have to get my point across. The thought of scaring them soured my stomach. But fear and pain would be the only way to get their attention. At first, anyway.

"Do you want easy way or hard way?" I folded my arms. I didn't need them to know I was a pushover when it came to a damsel in distress. With my accent, they might even think I had Bratva ties. And I knew it was thicker than usual right now. Even I could hear the difference. "I want Melina Romanov."

The woman flinched slightly. So, she at least knew who I'd come for. The question was whether she'd hand her over, or if I'd have to destroy the place searching for her. I noticed Gator eyeing the women huddled together in the corner. Something told me Gator would prefer it if we took more than Melina with us. The Bratva was going to be pissed as fuck if we did, but I knew how he felt. I didn't want to leave these women here, either. Hell, some of them didn't look old enough to be legal. But Melina was my priority.

Shit. The madam said they catered to *all* needs. Did that mean those girls were underage? It made me want to throw up, but I needed to keep my cool at least a little longer.

No one came forward or gave up Melina's location. Reaching for a vase on a table nearby, I threw it against the wall, watching it shatter all over the floor. The madam flinched again, but still didn't give in. The others seemed frightened, and I hated being an asshole to them. But there were times it couldn't be helped.

Next, I picked up the table itself and hurled it against the wall. The plaster cracked, and the table broke before it fell to the ground. Someone nearby whimpered. The madam only pressed her lips together and still refused to speak. This bitch wasn't going to crack easily. I really didn't want to fucking hit her.

I took a step forward and raised my hand,

bracing myself to deliver a slap I knew I'd feel all the way to my soul. A soft voice stopped me.

"She's downstairs," one of the women said. "There are rooms in the basement. That's where she is."

The doors opened behind us, and I tensed a moment until I saw it was only Specter. The man had said he'd meet us here, and it looked like he'd kept his word, even if I'd had my doubts. He gave me a nod, and I pushed past the madam and found the door leading to the basement. All the rooms were empty, except for one. However, the bloodstains in the vacant ones made me wonder if those women had died. The madam's words made me freeze. *All* needs. Holy fuck! This wasn't just a brothel. It was a slaughterhouse. The twisted fucks who got off on killing women could pay to do exactly that, and anything else they wanted.

Melina sat on the floor in the corner, her knees pressed to her chest as she rocked back and forth. Considering the pictures we'd seen, I'd expected her to look far worse, though I could see she'd suffered a lot since coming here. I noted the cuts that would most likely scar. The ones on her wrists looked self-inflicted. I'd heard she'd tried to kill herself after her first night. Seeing the proof made my heart ache for her. A bruise marred her cheek and more covered her arms. Under the layers of pain painted on her skin, I could see how beautiful she was. Not Hollywood gorgeous, but an understated sort of beauty that would make a man take a second or even a third look.

The assholes who'd put her here hadn't even allowed her to wear any sort of clothing. Even the women upstairs had put on lingerie. A way to entice potential customers, most likely. So why hadn't she been afforded the same courtesy? Glancing around the room, the conclusion I drew wasn't pretty. The women upstairs didn't have visible marks. So it seemed they sent the rough customers to Melina. If I'd gotten here any later, would I have only found a blood-spattered room?

As much as I wanted to grab her up and hold her close, I knew it would only freak her out. The Bratva had given her no reason to trust men, and I was a stranger. I should have asked for something to prove I was here to help her. I removed my cut and pulled off my shirt, knowing I'd need to cover her, and I damn sure wasn't going to use the nasty sheets on the bed. I put my cut back on and took my time approaching her. So far, she hadn't noticed my presence, or didn't seem to. I wondered if she'd retreated into her mind in order to keep herself safe.

She reminded me of an injured animal. If I moved too fast, I'd likely scare her, which could end up harming the both of us. Crouching beside her, I lightly ran my fingertips over her forearm. She flinched and curled into herself even more. That's what I'd thought. I didn't know what she'd been like before all this, but the Bratva had broken her.

I hoped she'd heal with time.

"Melina. They call me Stripes." I pointed to my name on my cut. "Like a Siberian tiger. I'm with the Devil's Boneyard MC, and I'm here to save you."

Her gaze flickered to mine for a brief moment before she looked away again. At least she was in there and coherent. She'd heard me, even if she didn't want to speak with me. It was a start.

Shit. I was Russian, like her, and just like the assholes who'd put her in here. What if she thought I was secretly part of the Bratva? I might not have cared if the bitches upstairs thought that, but I needed her to know I wasn't like those monsters.

"Your daughter, Oksana, is safe. *Ponjatno*? She's married to my friend, Grimm. She's the reason we're here to rescue you." I cleared my throat. "I'm Russian. Not Bratva. I live somewhere far from here."

The rocking stopped, and it almost looked like she'd stopped breathing as well. I saw the tension in her muscles and wished like hell I could ease her fears, but we were running out of time. Sooner or later, someone would come check on these ladies.

"Melina, I'm going to put my shirt on you. I'll pick you up and carry you out of here. I expect nothing from you. Won't hurt you." I paused, hoping she believed me. "I have some friends upstairs. They'll help us leave safely."

I eased my shirt over her head and tugged her arms through the sleeves, then picked her up. She didn't relax, but she did put her arms around my neck. The fact she trusted me this much made my heart hurt. Even if I hadn't known her before today, she seemed like a sweet woman. Since Wire and Lavender had married us, I knew I'd have a lifetime to get to know her. Assuming she didn't flip the fuck out when she discovered she had another husband. Poor woman had just lost the asshole she'd been married to before this, and I doubted she was eager for a new husband.

I carried her upstairs and gave a nod to Gator and Specter. Before I reached the door, the dead silence made me pause. Nothing seemed out of place, yet I felt something had changed while I'd been downstairs. I scanned the room and realized the women were gone, except the madam.

"Something I need to know?" I asked.

Specter shrugged. "They seemed uncomfortable. Sent them to their rooms. Doubt any will call for help."

I snorted and shook my head. I looked over my shoulder at the madam. "If any of you wish to leave here, contact the Hades Abyss MC in Missouri. They'll help you. You don't have to live like this anymore."

I walked out the door and down the street, stopping when I realized I had no idea what Specter had driven here. He passed me and opened the door to a Rezvani Hercules. Military edition, most likely, which meant it was bulletproof. I eased Melina onto the seat and buckled her in before lightly pushing her hair off her face.

"This is Specter's vehicle. He'll follow us to my compound. I'll be in front. You can see me the entire time, all right? You get scared, need a break, Specter will flash his lights and I'll pull over."

She didn't say anything. Only held my stare. It would have to be enough for now. I shut the door and shook Specter's hand.

"She'll be safe," he promised.

I nodded at the vehicle. "Not a bad way to spend about three hundred grand."

He flashed a smile. "It's going to be a gift for you and Melina. A wedding present. Thought you might feel better driving her around in something that was bullet and bomb proof."

Was he shitting me? Nope. The look in his eyes said he was dead serious. Crazy fucker. I didn't even want to know the cost of insurance on something like this, but I'd accept his gift. For Melina. Even if I had to work twice as hard for the upkeep.

"She doesn't know yet," I said. "About being married to me. I know I have to tell her, but not now. Not yet. She still hasn't spoken. Seems freaked out enough already."

He nodded. "All right. I won't say a word. Let's

get out of here before our luck runs out."

I walked a few feet away to my bike and pulled a spare shirt from my saddlebag. I removed my cut long enough to tug the shirt over my head, then slipped the leather over my shoulders again. Gator started his bike and pulled off, with me right behind him. I kept an eye on my side-view mirrors, ensuring Specter stayed close. I didn't like not being with Melina right now, but it couldn't be helped. The bike had been the fastest way to get here, and since I'd heard the assassin was coming to lend a hand, I'd figured he'd have a way to transport my new wife. Of course, if he hadn't shown up I'd have had no choice but to put her on the back of my bike. Something told me it would have been traumatizing for her to ride so close to me for that long.

Hell. *Married.* My granddaughter was going to lose her shit. I hadn't told her about any of this yet. While she and Doolittle lived with the Devil's Fury, we kept in touch almost daily, and I saw them every chance I had. I'd have to make sure she didn't drop by for a surprise visit anytime soon. Not until I had Melina in a better place, mentally and emotionally.

Something told me I was in for one hell of a ride. Shit. I really should have prepared Minnie. Or at least made sure Doolittle knew what the fuck was going on. I had no idea if anyone had talked to the Devil's Fury about this mess or not.

I was getting too old for this shit.

* * *

Melina

I tugged at the hem of the T-shirt Stripes had given me. The man sitting beside me hadn't said a word the entire time we'd been in the truck. While the silence should have been awkward, I kept my gaze on the motorcycles in front of us. I didn't know if I could trust any of these men, but whatever they had planned for me couldn't be worse than what I'd suffered already.

Stripes and Specter both seemed to be older. The third man looked to be slightly younger than the other two. Of course, I could be wrong. Not that it mattered. Young men. Old men. They were all the same. Each and every man liked keeping their women firmly under their feet. I was certain these three would be the same. Were they planning to share me? Stripes said he was taking me somewhere safe, but I knew better. There was no such place. Not for someone like me.

It had been far too easy. The Bratva would have never let them take me, not unless they felt I'd continue to be punished. Was this nothing more than a ruse? A way to make me drop my guard?

What he'd said about Oksana... I hoped it was true. Had she really been spared and gotten married? Stripes said she was with someone he knew. Did that mean I'd get to see her soon? Did I want to see her? Would she look at me with disgust? Being with Ruslan was bad enough, but the men who'd used me left me feeling dirty. No amount of scrubbing would remove the filth. I'd forever feel their touch. Remember the pain. Would my daughter look at me and only see a whore? She'd been spared such a fate, for which I was grateful.

What about Yulia? Was she at the academy Feliks had mentioned, or had she been taken elsewhere too? I couldn't stand the thought of her discovering the shame I'd suffered. My sweet, innocent girl didn't need this darkness in her life. I had so many questions, and yet, I didn't dare ask them. I'd learned the hard way what happened when you spoke without permission.

Specter glanced over at me now and then. I didn't know what he wanted. He unnerved me the most. He had the eyes of a killer. While Stripes didn't look like a fluffy teddy bear, he at least didn't terrify me as much as this man did. Which one was in charge? Stripes or Specter?

I saw a sign showing we were heading into another state. No one had mentioned where we were going. As badly as I wanted to know, I wasn't going to ask. I'd wait and see. I didn't know how much time had passed. My bladder felt so full I worried I'd have an accident in the vehicle. Pressing my lips together, I squirmed in my seat. Should I say something? Which would be worse? Speaking without permission, or ruining his seats?

"I need a bathroom," I whispered.

The man didn't say a word or even look my way. Did my request make him angry? He flashed his lights at the men in front of us and we all pulled off a few exits later. He followed them to the parking lot of a twenty-four-hour store, and we all parked close together. Stripes came over and opened my door.

"Give me a moment, Melina." He skimmed my body. "What size do you wear? You need some clothes before you can go in and use the restroom."

"Medium," I said.

He arched an eyebrow like he didn't believe me. My cheeks burned. Well, I'd been that size once. In the last few weeks, I hadn't eaten much, so there was a chance I was smaller now. I knew my clothes from before had started to get loose before Feliks sentenced me to hell.

"Small," I corrected.

Stripes reached out as if to touch me, then pulled his hand back. "I'll be quick. It will be nothing fancy but will work for now."

He shut the door and hurried across the parking lot. I saw him go into the store and waited. It didn't take long for him to return, but I worried I wouldn't be able to hold it much longer. He handed me a sack with a package of panties and a knit dress, as well as a pair of flip-flops. The shoes were a size too big, but I didn't dare complain.

Specter got out of the vehicle, and both men turned their backs to me. I quickly changed and tapped on the window. Stripes helped me out and didn't let go of my hand. Instead, he kept hold of me as we walked into the store together. I didn't know if he worried I'd run away, or if it was something else. His hold wasn't tight or painful. If anything... it was almost comforting.

The thought almost drew me up short. *Comforting?* I couldn't remember ever thinking that about a man before.

He led me to the bathroom and nodded for me to go in. I relieved my bladder and washed my hands, then splashed water on my face. A woman entered the bathroom and froze when she saw me, her eyes going wide.

"Did that man out there do that to you?" she asked. "We can call the police."

I shook my head. "It wasn't him. He wouldn't do something like this."

I'd defended him without thought. It left me feeling confused. If I'd agreed with her, I might have gotten away. Then again, would the police actually help me? I'd seen several enter the brothel. We might not be in the same state anymore, but that didn't mean they'd take the word of a whore.

The woman didn't look convinced, but she didn't

argue with me. Instead, she ducked into a stall and I left. Stripes took my hand again. I'd thought we would leave, but he took me farther into the store.

"We'll get a few things while we're here. You must be hungry. Thirsty. We'll get food for you, and more clothes. We can buy more later. Do not worry about the cost." Stripes stopped in the women's department and released me.

I eyed him, then the surrounding clothes. What was going on? Why was he taking me shopping? Should I tell him about the woman in the bathroom? I didn't think she'd cause any problems, but what if she really did call the police? The more I thought about it the more I realized they wouldn't save me. If anything, once they heard my story, they'd likely arrest me for helping my husband and for prostitution. It wouldn't matter, neither had been my choice.

"Melina, what's wrong?" Stripes asked, moving in closer.

"There was a woman in the bathroom… she said something about calling the police."

"*Gavno,*" he muttered. "Probably thinks I beat the hell out of you."

"I told her you didn't," I said.

"Won't matter. Come. We'll have to hurry. I can't exactly tell anyone where I got you. Not with all the dead bodies we left behind. Grab two changes of clothes, and we'll get some food up front."

I picked out a black shirt and a pair of jeans, then grabbed a gray sweater. He hadn't bought me a bra, and I knew I'd need one. I quickly found one in my size and added it to the items in my arms. Stripes handed me a package of socks and we went to the shoe department. He pointed to some low-heeled black boots, and I selected my size, then we rushed to the front.

"Sorry the clothes I picked left you cold," he said. "It was the first thing I saw. If you're chilly, just tell Specter. He can turn the heat up."

It wasn't that cold outside. Not yet. But he was right about me being cold. It had seeped into my bones when all this started, before Feliks had even called me to his office. I hadn't been able to get warm since then. Fear. Anxiety. It was likely both causing the chill inside me.

By the time we checked out and went back to the waiting men, I heard sirens in the distance. Something told me they were coming here, so I quickened my steps. Stripes helped me back into the vehicle and put the sacks in the back seat.

"I got her something to eat and a drink," Stripes said. "But I think the police are coming. Someone didn't like the marks on her." He turned back to Melina. "We'll talk more later. We're taking you somewhere you'll be protected. To the club where I live. I give you my word, you'll be safe."

Specter nodded and backed out of the space the moment Stripes shut the door. We were all back on the road within a minute or two, and I saw the police pull into the store parking lot behind us. Thankfully, no one had noticed what we were driving, or hadn't relayed that information yet. Either way, I wouldn't have to answer a lot of uncomfortable questions.

I might not know these men, but I'd take my chances with them. It had to be better than prison. At least they'd fed me and bought me clothes. Part of me still worried the Bratva was behind this and I wasn't truly saved. Even with the uncertainty, I didn't have a choice but to go with them. For now, they were taking care of me. Better than anyone had in a long time.

I reached into the back seat and got the sack of food, as well as the sweater I'd bought. Once I'd pulled on the garment, I opened the sandwich Stripes had picked out and took a bite. Ham and cheese might not have been my favorite, but after not eating much for weeks, it tasted like the best thing ever.

I finished it off and sipped at my drink. Specter still remained quiet, and I watched the mile marker signs pass as we got farther and farther away from the Bratva.

Maybe they really were trying to save me... which meant my daughter truly was safe somewhere. I breathed a little easier. As long as Oksana had someone to care for her, I could endure anything. Now I just needed to know Yulia hadn't been harmed. If my babies were all right, nothing else mattered.

Chapter Two

Melina

Married. I was married. To this man. This Russian man, a biker, a man I'd never even met before today.

I was no stranger to arranged marriages. My marriage to Ruslan had been more of a contract, like a piece of property exchanging hands. Stripes said another biker had done this, online, so I'd be safe. So no one could make me go back.

I didn't know what to make of Stripes. The thought of being married to him terrified me. While he seemed nice enough for the moment, what would happen when we got to his house? Would he change? Become a monster like all the other men I'd ever known? Only time would tell, but it didn't stop my stomach from twisting into knots.

Holding his hand gave me an odd sense of comfort, which only scared me more. Why was I having such a reaction to a man I'd never met before? I felt certain I'd only end up getting hurt worse when he eventually turned on me. At least with Ruslan, I'd never been attracted to him, much less loved him. The man leading me into the restaurant was another matter.

Watching him smile at the hostess gave me butterflies. Not only did I find him incredibly handsome, but it seemed other women did too. The woman, who looked slightly older than me, batted her eyes and giggled at him like a young schoolgirl. Some small part of me wanted to tighten my hold on his hand and tell the woman he belonged to me. But I didn't dare.

I lowered my gaze and waited patiently. Stripes lightly touched my chin, and I jolted, looking up. His brow furrowed, and he leaned in closer, lowering his voice so only I could hear him.

"What's wrong, *lapochka*?"

That, for starters. He'd already given me a term of endearment, even though we were strangers. It didn't matter we were married. Russian men seldom used pet names until they'd known the woman for a while. And yet, here he was, letting everyone know I was special. Worse. He actually made me *feel* special. I wanted to beg him not to give me false hope.

He pulled me against his body and put an arm around my lower back. The hug was gentle, and yet, I shuddered and some of my tension melted. How did he do that? No one had ever set me at ease like this. Especially a man.

It felt like a piece of my armor came off with every gentle touch and kind word. Soon, I'd be completely vulnerable to him.

"I do not like that you look down. You should hold your head high," he murmured. "You're beautiful, Melina. I know your life has been hard, and you've suffered greatly. But that's in the past, yes? You're my wife. Melina Petrov. You're the first, and only, woman I've ever married. Remember that."

"I don't understand the rules," I whispered back. "I'm scared I'll mess up because I don't know what's expected of me."

He held me tighter. "Ah, *lapochka*. You're breaking my heart."

The hostess interrupted us. "Your table is ready."

Stripes released me but took my hand as he followed the woman to our table. She set down two menus and some silverware, then hurried off. Her behavior seemed a bit rude, having not spoken to us again. Most asked for a drink order, or at least told us who would be serving us.

It seemed my husband didn't notice. He opened one of the menus and passed it to me before picking up his own.

"Order whatever you want." He eyed me over the menu. "Even dessert if you have a sweet tooth."

Our server came over and froze the moment he saw me. He pressed a hand to his chest, one tipped with blue nails, and his eyes went wide. "Oh, honey. Are you all right?"

"She is now," Stripes said.

The man placed a hand on his hip. "Well, I hope you gave him what for. Whoever did that to her needs a good beating."

Stripes' lips twitched as if he fought back a laugh. "I'll track down every last man who hurt her. No worries there. The important thing is that she's safe now."

I eyed our server. "You didn't think he could have done this to me?"

The man shook his head. "No, honey. Not with the way he's keeping an eye on you. I saw him up front too, being all sweet. You've got a good one. Better hold on with both hands. Legs too."

Stripes snorted, then coughed to cover up a laugh. I wasn't sure what to make of the man. I looked for a nametag and found it pinned to the top right of his shirt. *Brandon.*

"He didn't give off scary vibes?" I asked, pointing to Stripes.

"Nope." Brandon smiled widely. "Grew up near some bikers. They were good people. Didn't care if I went out to play in a sparkly tutu or preferred dolls to cars. They treated me the same as any other kid in the neighborhood."

I looked at Stripes in a new light. He hadn't cringed when he saw Brandon or sneered at him. Ruslan would have done both. He didn't like men who preferred to date the same sex. In fact, he'd hated them. But the guy sitting across from me, the one I seemed to be married to, didn't treat our server any differently than anyone else. Just like the bikers Brandon said he'd lived near when he was younger.

I let down my guard a little more and dared to hope he really was different from the other men I'd known. I couldn't trust my instincts. Not any longer. But just maybe I could believe in Stripes when other people did. Even strangers had seemed on edge around Ruslan... as if they could sense the evil inside him.

"Now, what can I get the two of you to drink?" Brandon asked.

We placed our drink order, and Stripes requested an appetizer, then we were left alone again. By the time we ordered our main dishes, I'd relaxed in the booth. No monsters were going to jump out and grab me. Stripes wasn't going to belittle me in public, or openly leer at other women. It was probably the first time I'd enjoyed dinner out somewhere in my entire life.

After our meal was over, I noticed he left the server a thirty percent tip. Something else Ruslan would have never done. The man was too cheap by far. It didn't matter how large the bill would be, he'd never leave more than five dollars. I'd always felt embarrassed by his behavior, not that I'd dared to say a word about it. I'd meekly gone along, hoping to go unnoticed.

"Why did you leave so much money for him?" I asked after we were back in the truck.

"Because he set you at ease and seemed

genuinely concerned for you." Stripes reached out and took my hand. I tensed for a moment before breathing out and relaxing once more. "I'd have paid much more if he'd gotten you to laugh."

His words left me feeling warm inside, and I couldn't stop myself from giving him a slight smile. I still didn't know if he'd spoken the truth about Oksana and Yulia. It was possible he'd lied to try to gain my trust. And yet, I didn't think it was the case. Something about Stripes screamed *protector*. I'd needed one of those long ago. Now there wasn't much left of me to save. Most days, I felt hollow inside. And when I didn't, I hurt deep down to my soul. I alternated between wanting to cry or scream until my throat was raw. I hadn't dared to do either. Crying would only tell them I was weak. Screaming would have earned me a harsh punishment.

"We're going to stop at a strip mall I saw on the way to dinner. You need more clothes, bathroom items, and shoes. They had stores there for all of that and more." He released my hand, only to reach up and lightly touch my cheek. "You get whatever you want, Melina. *Pontajno*? It will not anger me if you spend money. If it looks like too much, I'll let you know. But until I say stop, you buy as much as you want."

"All right." I bit my lip. No one had ever offered me such a thing before. As much as I feared all this would go away sometime soon, I decided to enjoy it while it lasted. I'd prefer one day of happiness to none. Although, part of me was starting to hope everything he said was true. Being married to a stranger didn't bother me. The thought of having a happy marriage, then losing it? Now that scared me to death. I wasn't sure I'd survive him putting all my pieces back together only to shatter them later.

He drove to the strip mall, and we went into a clothing store first. Stripes didn't just let me grab things and run to the register. He herded me toward a dressing room once I'd picked out several outfits. And while I was inside, he handed me even more. The stubborn man refused to let me leave without at least a week's worth of clothes. The only thing I couldn't get were bras and panties, as well as pajamas.

"There's an intimates store one block up," the clerk said as she rang up the purchases. I noticed she did her best not to look at me directly, and I wondered if it was due to all the bruising and marks on me. It probably made people uncomfortable. "They have really nice items but aren't overpriced."

"We'll check it out when we're finished here," Stripes said. He paid and then took the bags from the clerk. I followed him to the truck, and he stored everything in the back floorboard. He locked up the vehicle, then led me to the shoe store.

I'd heard of shopping until you dropped, but I hadn't experienced it until now. It took two hours to buy everything I needed, and some things Stripes insisted I have. On the way back to the hotel, he pulled into the parking lot of an electronics store and led me inside.

"I don't need anything in here," I protested. He'd already spent way too much. The man didn't seem to understand the word *moderation.* And every disapproving look I received from the other shoppers only made him spend more.

"Yes, you do. For one, you need a phone. I'll have you added to my plan. And one of those portable DVD players and some movies. You can watch something on the way home tomorrow."

"That seems excessive," I said. "It's not like I'm

going to use it again after tomorrow."

He put his arm around my waist, and for the first time, I didn't flinch. It seemed I was getting more comfortable with him. "Melina, I told you about my granddaughter. She's married, and she's given me three great-grandchildren. We can use the device when the children are in the car." He hugged me to his side. "Now, stop stalling. You haven't spent enough to put a dent in my account yet."

I let him lead me into the store, feeling as if someone had yanked the ground out from under me. *Three* great-grandchildren? The man didn't look old enough for that! Wait. Since we were married... did that mean I had a granddaughter close to the age of my daughter, and also had three great-grands? The world spun for a moment as I sucked in a breath. I wasn't ready for this. Not even a little.

* * *

Stripes

We had an eighteen-hour trip ahead of us, and I knew we'd have to stay overnight somewhere. When we stopped for gas, and Melina used the restroom again, I mentioned a hotel to Specter and Gator. It seemed the assassin had thought ahead and already booked two rooms. Gator wasn't thrilled about sharing with Specter, but I had a feeling the bastard did it on purpose. I didn't have a choice but to stay with Melina since there wouldn't be another bed for me. Fucker. Hadn't he even considered how she might feel about the arrangement?

At least she had a change of clothes, but I hadn't considered anything beyond that. As we pulled into the hotel parking lot, I thought about everything else she'd need. I eyed the building and realized the man hadn't skimped on the cost. Gator and I would stick out horribly, and so would Melina, with all her cuts and bruises.

Specter got out of the truck and smoothed his clothes. "I'll go in and get our room keys. Probably best if I explain about Melina as well. Don't need anyone getting the wrong idea and calling the cops. Again."

I nodded and opened her door, wanting to check on her. She tensed a moment, then slowly relaxed when she realized I wasn't going to grab her. It would take time for her to learn to trust me. We'd get there, eventually.

"We're going to stay here tonight, then get back on the road in the morning." I folded my arms, then dropped them when I noticed her lips tighten. If I could beat the hell out of everyone who'd hurt her, I'd gladly do it. Hell, I'd like to bury every last fucker who dared to touch her. "We'll eat, then I'll answer your questions. You'd like that, yes?"

"*Da.*" She studied me, taking her time. I wondered what she thought. I'd been told I looked menacing. It served me well most of the time. But not in this instance.

"There's much for us to discuss." I wanted to reach out and run my fingers through her hair. Hold her close. Promise her everything would be fine. Instead, I held still and gave her the space I figured she needed.

Specter came back outside and handed me a room key. "We can park nearby and go through the main entrance. Our rooms are on the fifth floor."

Melina reached up to touch her jaw. I reached out and gently gripped her hand, giving it a slight squeeze. Her eyes widened, and I felt her pulse race. "He already spoke to the hotel staff. They will say nothing. All right?"

She nodded. I scanned the parking lot and pointed to three spots close together. Gator gave me a thumbs-up and I got back on my bike. After we parked, I helped carry Melina's bag up to the room, and grabbed a few things from my saddlebags. She needed more than what I'd bought so far. I'd have to find a store nearby and take her shopping again. I wondered if she wanted makeup to cover the bruises. It didn't matter to me. I just wanted her to be comfortable, whatever it took.

Our rooms weren't next to each other. Specter and Gator moved farther down the hall, and I led Melina into the room we'd be sharing. I let the door shut behind us and sat our things on the bed. I tried hard not to start cussing. Why the fuck had Specter gotten us a room with one Goddamn bed? He had to know it would freak Melina out.

"I'm sorry. Specter is such a *hui*," I muttered, glancing her way. "I did not ask for this."

"For what?" she asked.

I waved a hand at the bed. "This. No reason for one bed. Could have gotten two. Have a seat. Looks like we need to have a talk now instead of later."

She moved over to the bed and sank onto the side of it. I remained standing and leaned against the wall, facing her. Specter might scare the shit out of most men, but if I had the chance, I'd wring his fucking neck for putting me in this situation. Since his sister was married to my club's President, I figured I *might* get away with it. Hell, if Dakota found out what he'd done, she might beat me to it.

"First, I'll not touch you. Even with only one bed, I expect nothing from you. What happened... wasn't your fault. Not of your choosing, yes? You were a victim, Melina. I might be Russian, but I'm nothing like those assholes who hurt you. In fact, I'd like to crush them all." Her lips twitched a little, and I wondered if she'd almost smiled. Maybe it was the image of them being crunched into tiny bits that did it. Hell if it didn't make me want to smile too. "Your daughters are safe. I don't know what they've suffered. I don't think it was pleasant. But they're okay now. Yulia is with a club called the Reckless Kings. One of their Prospects will help her heal, yes? Ease her pain. Oksana is married. Grimm is also Russian. Not Bratva, but his family was. He's not like them."

"My girls are safe?" she asked.

"*Da*. They are staying elsewhere." I ran a hand down my beard and wondered how much I should tell her. More than that, I considered the questions she may have about her girls. Ones I didn't have the answers to. It would be best if they didn't see her in this condition. Not only the physical marks, but the internal ones too. Her eyes… At times, they were vacant. It might scare them. "I know about your husband. How you ended up a whore. I do not know everything, but I understand you've suffered. I'll listen, should you wish to talk, yes? But I will not push."

"Why?" She licked her lips. "Why would you be so nice to me? You have to want something. Some form of payment. No one does anything for free."

"My club, and several others, have hackers. Um, men who are good on computers. By now, they know everything of your past but will say nothing. Some like to meddle. Wire and his woman. They get into everything. All records. Nothing is too hard for them."

"I don't understand. Meddle how?"

"Your name is no longer Melina Romanov, in case you've forgotten." I cleared my throat. Whenever I found myself in stressful situations, my accent became thicker. Like now. "It's Melina Petrov. Wife of Mikhail Petrov. Otherwise known as... Stripes."

Her gaze dropped to my cut, or more specifically the patches on the front. She paled a little as she stared at the one with my road name. Yeah, she understood. At least partially.

"After what you've been through, I'm sure my accent is off-putting. I'm Russian but not Bratva. I said it before, but you maybe did not hear me. You were... shocked, I think. I'll not hurt you the way they did. I will demand nothing from you, Melina. Not unless it pertains to your safety. I will not endanger you or your children. Understood?"

She nodded, still staring at my patches. Fuck. This wasn't going the way I'd wanted. Hell, I hadn't planned to say anything yet. It seemed too soon.

"Do you have children?" she asked.

"*Nyet*. Not anymore. I had a daughter." My throat tightened at the memory. It had been roughly a year since I'd learned of what my daughter suffered. "Lost her a long time ago, but she gave me a beautiful granddaughter. Her name is Minnie, and she lives with the Devil's Fury in Georgia. I've asked her not to visit anytime soon so you'll have time to adjust to your new life."

"Granddaughter?" Her gaze lifted to mine. "How old are you?"

"Sixty-five," I said, knowing damn well that made me far older than she was. According to Oksana, her mother was only thirty-eight. She'd still been a kid herself when she had Oksana, and then Yulia a few years later. "I know. Big difference in our ages. I'm probably not who you'd have chosen for a husband."

"Age doesn't matter," she said. "Age. Skin color.

None of it. Men are the same regardless."

I winced. "*Nyet*. Not all. I'll prove it. Show you can trust me. I'll not break your trust, or harm you. For now, we should eat, and then I need to take you to a store to finish shopping. You didn't have time to get everything you needed earlier."

"My daughters…" She bit her lip.

Whatever she'd been about to say, she stopped. Did she want to see them? Speak to them? I wasn't sure how Oksana or Yulia would feel about our marriage. Nor did I think it would benefit Melina to reach out to them right now. Perhaps if she held onto the thought of speaking with them later, it would help her put one foot in front of the other. She'd already given up once. I didn't want her to do it again.

I could tell she wanted to ask for something. Perhaps her lack of faith in me held her back. Our first big test would happen tonight. I'd keep to my side of the damn bed, or sleep on the fucking floor, if that's what it took. I pulled out my phone and texted Gator, asking about dinner plans. When he sent an image back of fast food, which they already had in their room, I glared at the damn device in my hand.

A knock sounded at the door, and I went to answer, pausing to peer through the peephole first. When I saw Specter on the other side, I opened the door and yanked him inside.

"You're an asshole," I said.

He grinned. "You're welcome. Here, take the key to the truck. You'll need it if you're going to take her to buy more things and get food."

I took it, shoved it in my pocket, then glowered at him. "What makes you think we're shopping?"

He snorted. "Because all you bikers are the same. Can't stand to see a woman in need. Take care of your wife, Stripes. You can give me the key back tomorrow before we leave."

He waved at Melina, then let himself out of the room. There were times I really didn't like that man.

"Come on, *lapochka*. Let's eat and gather the things you'll need." I held out my hand, and she stood, timidly taking it. I curled my fingers around hers and led her downstairs to the truck. It was a small victory, but I'd take it.

Chapter Three

Stripes

I couldn't remember a time I'd had so much trouble getting a woman to spend my money. It made me want to know more about the man she'd been married to, and her father. Had both of them trained her to be like this? Made her feel so unworthy of even the smallest thing? If they weren't dead, I'd crush the fuckers under my boot.

I'd picked out a player for her to use in the truck tomorrow but figuring out what she liked to watch had been really damn hard. She hadn't wanted to pick out a single movie. In the end, I'd had no choice but to message Shade and ask him to figure it the fuck out. More than likely, he'd call Wire, who would just ask Oksana. But I knew we were trying to be careful about communications so the Bratva wouldn't be able to locate Melina and Yulia easily.

It didn't take him long to get back to me, and I bought six movies I'd been told were her favorites. I'd also bought her ear buds to go with the phone I'd purchased and decided to add some music to her phone. Also, with the help of Shade. The way she kept eyeing the two devices, I could tell it pleased her to have them, and yet, she wouldn't touch them or say a word.

"Melina, I know you're scared. Nothing I say will convince you I'm not a bad man. You've got too much *gavno* weighing you down. I want to lighten the load, even if it's just by a little. Use the player and the phone. Watch the movies and listen to the music. It's okay to escape from reality. We all need to from time to time, yes? Even men like me. This does not make you weak, *lapochka*."

She cautiously reached for the phone and opened the music app I'd put on the front screen. When I realized she didn't know how to pair the ear buds to the phone, I helped her out, and within a few minutes, she was leaning against the headboard and listening to the playlist I'd made for her.

I used the time to touch base with my club President and give him an update. Charming answered on the first ring.

"Everything okay?" he asked when the call connected.

"I've got Melina. We're staying at a hotel overnight. Specter got us the rooms, so even if someone at the brothel noticed my cut, they wouldn't be able to trace us here. This does not mean they will not show up at the gate, though."

"Shade and Wire are keeping an eye on things. How's your wife?" he asked.

"Not ready to trust me, or anyone else. As much as I want to set her at ease, I'm not sure she wants to speak to her children. She's not ready to believe they're safe, but I don't think she wants them to see her like this. There's a haunted look to her eyes. It wouldn't be good for them or her."

"Yulia is in rough shape. Not sure about Oksana," Charming said.

"What happened?" I asked.

"The footage we received of her was all wrong, but something bad did happen to her. One of her teachers at the academy raped her. Kye said she's... broken. I'm not sure when she'll be ready to talk to anyone."

I fisted my hand, wanting to beat the hell out of someone. What the fuck was wrong with this world? How could so much evil exist? No, I wasn't a saint. Not by a long shot, but I did more good than harm, and I never fucking hurt the innocent. Never had, never would.

"Who went to get her?" I asked.

"Samson and Nitro picked her up. She's already with the Reckless Kings at Kye's house. I think the fact he has a daughter will help her be a little less frightened."

"I really hate people sometimes," I muttered.

"Which reminds me… Doolittle is trying to re-home some more animals. He's sending one to Kye and Yulia after she's had a few days to realize no one is going to hurt her. It's an older dog that was used for therapy at a hospital. His handler died, and the kids didn't want it anymore."

"Are you trying to tell me that Minnie and Doolittle are bringing me something furry?" I asked. "I told her not to come around yet. My *zaichik*, she does not listen. Melina needs time and space. Not to mention, they don't need to be at our compound with the kids in case the Bratva comes looking for Melina."

I didn't want to add that I worried about Melina's reaction to them and vice versa. The way she looked right now would scare them. And I had a feeling their energy and questions would be too much for her.

"I've reminded them," Charming said. "But if you think a pet might help Melina in some way, let Doolittle know. I think he already has something picked out for her. You know anything he sends will be perfect for your family. He seems to have a knack for pairing people with pets."

"I do not want to make a decision yet. I want time to get to know Melina better. Not to mention I have no idea if she's allergic to any animals. You might want to check Yulia as well. Have someone do an allergy test for dogs and cats."

"Good idea," Charming said. "I'll pass that on to Beast and make sure Doolittle thinks about that. I'll keep everyone away from your house the next few days. After that, I make no promises. My woman is especially eager to meet Melina and make sure she feels welcome."

"Give me a day or two. After that, I will not stop Dakota from visiting. Although, I think Grey would be the best choice as her first introduction to the old ladies. You know she has a soft touch. Everyone loves her. I have not yet discussed the club with Melina. She doesn't know the rules or what to expect. I didn't want to overwhelm her."

"At least tell her the basics. I'll make sure Grey is the first to visit, and she can walk her through everything else. Dakota will be disappointed, but she'll understand. She can be a little much for some people, especially when she's excited."

"Thanks, Pres. I'm going to go. We'll be there tomorrow, hopefully by dinnertime."

I ended the call and turned to find Melina watching me. She'd removed the ear buds from her ears, which meant she'd heard everything. Or at least, part of the conversation.

"What rules?" she asked.

Yep. She'd heard me. I hadn't wanted to do this today, but it seemed I didn't have a choice. I doubted she'd been around bikers before, much less a club like mine. I sat on the foot of the bed, as far from her as I could get. Only for her comfort. I ached to hold her, but knew it was too soon.

"What do you know about motorcycle clubs?" I asked.

"Like the TV show?" she asked.

I tried hard not to laugh. Why did every woman immediately ask that? I had news for her. If she expected Jax Teller to walk through the door, she'd be disappointed. None of us looked like him. I'd always thought he was too pretty to be a biker, but nearly every woman I'd met loved him.

"Not exactly. My club has a compound, which is fenced and gated. Someone stands guard at all hours. We also have a clubhouse, which is where the parties are held. At those parties…" How the fuck did I put this without sending her running for the hills? "My club has a lot of single men. They like to drink and have fun. So… women come to those parties, and they, um…"

She tipped her head to the side and watched me, not saying a word. It was rather unnerving, and I had a feeling I was about to fuck this to hell and back. After what she'd been through, how did I tell her we called those women club whores? No matter how I put it, I couldn't make it sound or look pretty. At the moment, I felt ashamed of myself and my club. We needed to do better. How the hell could we marry or claim women like Melina, and still have club whores at the clubhouse? Shit.

"They aren't forced to be there. They're free to come and go as they please. But the women who show up for the parties, they're there for a reason. They like sleeping with random bikers." There. That sounded… bad, but at least I made it clear they weren't forced. Right?

"I don't understand," she said.

I wanted to bang my head against the wall. Why the hell was this so damn hard? "We refer to those women as club whores, but they aren't actual whores.

They do not suffer the way you did, *lapochka*. They aren't paid for their services. No one forces them to come to our clubhouse."

She paled and looked away. Great. I knew I'd only made things worse. How had Phantom managed this? Or Cinder? Any of them! Most of the men in my club had fallen for women who'd been abused in some way.

"I promise, we aren't assholes," I said. "Well, some of us are."

"Is that where I'll be going? The clubhouse?" she asked, her voice so soft I nearly didn't hear her.

"What? *Nyet*! Of course not, Melina! You're my wife. You'll get a property cut." At her confused look, I realized we had a lot more ground to cover. She really didn't have a clue about motorcycle clubs or bikers. This was going to take a while. "The leather vest I have on is called a cut. You'll get one that says *Property of Stripes*. It doesn't mean I own you. It's a way of showing I'm responsible for you, and lets other bikers know if they dare touch you, I'll be coming for them. Think of it as a layer of protection."

She digested my words for a moment. I could tell she had questions, so I waited patiently.

"Are there other couples?" she asked.

"*Da*. Quite a few. Charming, my club President, is with Dakota. You rode in the truck with her older brother yesterday. Specter. And you'll meet Grey soon. She's really sweet and can be kind of quiet. She's with Samurai. I've asked everyone not to overwhelm you by visiting all at once. We have twelve couples at my club. Thirteen if you include us. There's a lot of children too, so you'll hear them playing and running around during the day."

"So your compound is like... a community? A

neighborhood?" she asked.

"Exactly like that. We're one big, happy family. I think you'll like them."

"And the men, they don't want anything from me?"

I reached across the bed for her hand but froze halfway. Better not to touch her while she seemed so uncertain about her place in my life and the club. Didn't want to push too hard, too fast.

"They only want you to be safe," I said.

"All right." She still seemed a little tense, but at least she was trying to trust me. It was a start. There was still a lot to tell her, but it could wait. It wasn't like she'd be leaving the house anytime soon, anyway. The rules didn't matter right away. If anyone said or did anything to upset her, I'd deal with it. And if she said the wrong thing at the wrong time... Well, I didn't think anyone would care. Not after hearing what she'd been through. If anyone did make a big deal out of anything she said or did, then I'd knock them on their ass.

* * *

Melina

I couldn't remember the last time I'd taken a shower without someone watching me. Not only had the Bratva kept me under surveillance since they'd decided to punish me, but Ruslan hadn't trusted me either. Stripes had given me the sack with my new pajamas and bathroom items, then gone to sit across the room. When I went into the bathroom, I stared at the door, waiting for him to get angry I'd shut it. It remained quiet in the bedroom until I heard the TV turn on. I still watched and waited as I undressed and got into the shower.

The hot water hurt when it hit the cuts on my body. Most had scabbed over, but they hadn't completely healed yet. I welcomed the pain. It helped me remember men weren't to be trusted. Although… I sniffed the shower gel Stripes bought for me and wondered if I wasn't holding on to my anger and fear for no reason. I kept waiting for him to change. No one could possibly be so kind. Could they?

I washed my body and my hair, shaved, and then got out and dried off. Not once had Stripes come into the bathroom, or even knocked on the door. I put on the pajama pants and shirt before going back into the bedroom. Stripes lounged in the chair by the bed, his feet up on the ottoman, and his hands folded behind his head. He'd put on a movie I'd seen several times before. It didn't surprise me he liked action flicks.

I stood beside the bed, wondering if it was all right to pull down the covers. He'd offered to sleep on the floor. He hadn't meant it, had he? The bed was large enough for two people, and yet the thought of sharing it with him made me want to throw up. I took a breath and tried to calm my mind. So far, Stripes hadn't given me a reason to distrust him. So why did I keep doubting his intentions?

In my heart, I knew not all people were evil. But after everything I'd experienced since marrying Ruslan, men still made me nervous.

"It will take time," Stripes said.

I lifted my gaze to his and found him watching me. He hadn't moved. Still remained in his relaxed pose, and yet he'd noticed me, and seemed to know what I was thinking.

"Time?" I asked.

"To trust. Men have hurt you for years. I don't

expect you to heal immediately. But in time, you'll learn not all men are bad." He paused. "I want you to meet Grey. Perhaps you should meet Samurai too."

I didn't understand where he was going with this. Why did I need to meet the two of them? Why would meeting another man set my fears at ease? What was so special about him? Something flashed in his eyes, an understanding, as if he'd heard my question.

"Samurai, he was hurt too. By a woman." Stripes lowered his arms and sat up straighter. "It's not only men who can hurt others. Anyone is capable of darkness, *lapochka*. Even you, yes? The pain you feel... You could turn that on others."

My lips parted, a denial on the tip of my tongue, but I realized he was right. I chose not to be cruel to other people. I'd witnessed plenty of people who couldn't say the same. Whatever had hurt them in the past, they turned it on others. Fearing men because others had hurt me didn't make any sense. Of course, I doubted logic played a big role in my body's responses. The Bratva had trained me to expect pain from men. He was also correct when he said it would take time to heal. Would I eventually learn to trust others?

"Take the bed, Melina. I'll sleep here," he said.

While he'd seemed comfortable enough watching the movie, I doubted he'd sleep well in the chair. For one, he was too large. I stared at the bed again. How brave was I? If I wanted to change, to live a different sort of life, then maybe I needed to face some of my fears. How else would I ever get better?

"We can share the bed," I said. "To sleep. Not for... anything else."

"*Lapochka*..."

I shook my head and pointed to the other side of

the mattress. "You can stay on that side, right? There's nothing to be scared of. You haven't hurt me."

Stripes stood, and my heart hammered in my chest. I curled my fingers, fisting my hands at my sides. I forced myself to remain still and not run. He eased onto the bed, on top of the covers, then pulled back the blankets on my side.

I got into bed, and he covered me. We watched one another, and my heart rate started to slow. He placed his hand on top of the blankets between us, and I reached for it, letting him lace our fingers together. I waited for the intense anxiety to creep in, but it didn't. If anything, my body started to relax even more.

"Tell me about your family," I said.

He smiled, his features softening. "Minnie... she's my *zaichik*. I didn't know about her. Thought my daughter was long gone. Found out she'd moved to this country. Her mother lied to me."

"You weren't married to her?"

"*Nyet*. I would have, had she been willing. Minnie's grandmother was..." He winced. "In the old country, things were hard. Especially for women, yes? I loved her. Nothing else mattered, but she'd stayed alive by selling herself."

So the woman he'd loved had been a prostitute? No wonder he'd let those people marry us regardless of what the Bratva had done to me. It really didn't matter to him. Not in the sense that he thought I was dirty. I hadn't met anyone like Stripes before.

"She sold our daughter," he said, his voice hardening. "I never knew. Thought they'd both died."

"How did you discover Minnie, then?"

"Fate." He smiled once more, his eyes lighting up. "She came to my club. Needed help. I offered her a spare room. Time to gather her thoughts. Make a plan."

"You didn't know the two of you were related?" I asked.

"*Nyet.* A hacker pieced it together. Minnie brings joy to my life. I decided I didn't need a woman as long as I had her."

"And now you're married to me." I tried to tug my hand free, but he wouldn't let me. "You should have left me there."

His eyes darkened, and his jaw tightened. I'd never seen him angry until now. He leaned in closer, and I tensed. "Never. *Never* say such words again. *Ponjatno?*"

"*Da.* I understand." Although, I really didn't. Why did he care? Sure, we were married on paper. It didn't mean he had feelings for me. I was just a stranger he'd hauled out of a brothel. A broken woman who'd lost her will to live.

"Seeing you like that. Small. Hurt. Damaged. It hurt me, here," he said, releasing my hand long enough to thump his chest. Then he took my hand in his once more. "I wanted to hold you. Tell you everything would be all right. But I knew I would scare you more."

My chest felt tight, and it was hard to breathe. Tears pricked my eyes at his words. No one had ever cared. Not like this. The men had delighted in harming me. They liked making me scream. Cry. Beg and plead. I'd learned they lost interest when I became silent. Most of the time. Not always.

"I'm glad my club was chosen to save you," Stripes said. "Being married to me... maybe it's not what you wanted. I will treat you like a queen. *My* queen. No one will hurt you again, *lapochka.*"

"Don't make promises you can't keep."

He held my hand tighter. "I can and will keep that promise."

I shook my head. "Stripes, you can't control other people. Their actions are exactly that. Theirs."

My own words made me freeze. I was right. A man's actions were *his* and only his. I'd painted all men with the same brush, but it was wrong of me. Stripes, Gator, and Specter hadn't done a single thing to hurt me. They'd done their best to set me at ease, to help me, and I'd distrusted them from the start because of my past experiences.

"Sleep, *lapochka*. Tomorrow is a big day."

I closed my eyes, but I knew I wouldn't fall asleep. Not anytime soon. I had too much to think about.

Chapter Four

Stripes

I could tell she wasn't really sleeping. Her chest rose and fell too quickly. Her body hadn't relaxed enough for sleep to have claimed her. Stubborn woman! I wanted to soothe her. Erase all her worries and fears. Others had suffered like her and now lived normal lives. They had families. Husbands who loved them. Children who made them smile.

I was beyond the point of having more kids. The last thing I needed were children running around my house who were younger than my great-grandkids. Would Melina feel the same way? I knew women could still have children at her age, and even older. Did she want that? A bigger family?

There was much I wanted to discuss with her. For now, I needed to get her home. Get her to trust me and my club. After that, the rest would fall into place. I hoped. It had for my brothers. Even Doolittle had won over Minnie, convinced her to move back home with him, and he'd nearly let his club destroy my *zaichik*.

I held her hand, studying her features. The bruises and cuts would fade with time. How long before she healed inside? I'd learned long ago the mind was the most delicate part of our bodies. Even once she looked perfect on the outside, mentally and emotionally my *lapochka* could still be a wreck. It wouldn't be the slightest bit surprising. Not after all she'd been through.

I didn't know everything. Not even close. I wasn't sure I wanted to. If I did, it might tempt me to track every fucker down who'd hurt her. And as satisfying as that would be, right now, Melina needed me by her side. She might not realize it, or want to admit it, but I knew. The marks on her wrist could have only been made one way. She'd already tried to end her life once. Would she try it again? It made me want to stay close, keep an eye on her.

My phone buzzed and I pulled it from my pocket. *Wire*. Great. It meant he likely had news for me about Melina, or her daughters. I didn't want to wake her, so I released her hand and stepped out into the hall, pulling the door shut behind me.

"Hello," I said, as I accepted the call.

"You in a place where you can talk?" he asked.

"I'm in the hallway."

"Not good enough. Go knock on Specter's door and ask one of them to guard Melina while we talk. I have some things you need to hear."

I did as he said, and Gator answered. "Need you to stand outside my room while I take a call from Wire."

He didn't say a word, just pushed by me and went down to my room. I stepped into his and Specter eyed me from the chair. He didn't stand, so I assumed he didn't mind me being there.

"I'm in Specter's room. Gator went down to mine."

"I did more digging on your woman. Before she went to the brothel, some of the Bratva men beat her. Raped her. After her first night in hell, she tried to kill herself."

I grunted. "Saw the marks."

"They have violated her every day and night since she landed in that place. Didn't matter how battered she was. They didn't care." Wire cleared his throat. "There's some video footage, as well as pictures. Worse than what you saw before. Not sure you want to see them. Just... tread carefully, Stripes."

"I'm doing my best. She doesn't speak much. Doesn't trust easily. It will take time."

"I know she's in good hands," Wire said. "As for a way to earn her trust... I'm going to text you a picture of Oksana with Grimm. Lavender snuck a shot of Oksana, smiling at her husband. It might make Melina feel better and will show her you told the truth. Her daughter really is safe."

"And Yulia?" I asked.

"It's not good. She's with the Reckless Kings, and she's not in danger for the moment. That's as much as I can say for now."

"I'll do what I can. Melina may ask about Yulia when I show her Oksana."

"Just tell her that's all you received so far. It might buy you some time." I heard someone talking in the background and figured Lavender was there with him. "My woman is setting up an account in Melina's name. She's funneling some money from one of Ruslan Romanov's accounts into it. The Bratva missed one. For that matter, he had it so well hidden we almost didn't find it either. There's not a fortune in there, but it's got about thirty grand. Enough to make Melina feel secure, especially since she'll be the only one with access to it. Make sure she understands that."

"Tell Lavender thank you."

I ended the call and sighed. I didn't know how to begin helping her heal. Patience, that I had plenty of. Time was another matter. If things were as bad as Wire said, she would possibly try to end her life again. What would happen when she found out about Yulia? Would it be too much for her to handle?

The thought of her no longer being in this world made my heart ache. I might not know her well, but she was my wife. To me, that meant something. It didn't matter if we were strangers. She shared my name, and I felt responsible for her. I hoped, in time, we would grow close. Maybe even learn to love one another. It was a second chance for both of us.

"How well-stocked is your kitchen at home?" Specter asked.

"Why?" What the hell did that have to do with anything?

"You want her to feel at home when you get there, right? Have you paid attention to what she likes to eat and drink?"

"I don't have much to go on, but I see where you're going with this. I'll text a Prospect and have them fill the cupboards and fridge."

Specter nodded. "How homey is your place?"

"It's a house." I frowned. "Minnie added a few touches when she stayed with me."

"Ask one of the old ladies to make sure the place looks inviting. It needs to have a certain warmth to it," Specter said.

I wanted to ask what the hell he knew about it, since last I'd heard, he was single. Of course, that woman had shown up at the compound when he'd come to visit Dakota. Surely if he'd gotten married or had someone serious in his life, Charming and Dakota would have known about it. Then again, with Specter, I wasn't entirely certain that was true.

"I'll handle it," I said.

I left and sent Gator back to his room. When I shut the door behind me, I found Melina had finally fallen asleep. I texted both a Prospect and Grey. Once I knew Melina would walk into a place that felt like a home and not just a house, I went back to the chair and closed my eyes.

Melina might have said I could sleep next to her,

but clearly she hadn't been comfortable. Otherwise, she'd have fallen asleep before now. I'd rather have some aches and pains tomorrow than make her anxious. I couldn't get my mind to shut off long enough to sleep. Instead, I kept wondering how she'd react when we got home. Should I have made sure Minnie's room was ready? I doubted she'd want to share a bedroom even though we were married. It was the only guest room I had right now.

Should I talk to her about seeing a counselor? Would that help, or would I be pushing too much too soon? What about a regular doctor? I needed someone to treat her wounds. Run blood work to make sure those assholes hadn't given her anything. Check for a possible pregnancy. Even though I felt all those things were necessary, I worried it would only send her deeper into the darkness.

If I'd paid more attention to Minnie's grandmother, had realized what sort of woman the harsh world had created, could I have helped her? Or had her pain festered until she'd rotted from the inside out, and I'd not noticed? I'd been young. Self-absorbed. We'd given one another comfort, or so I'd thought, but had I ever really known her? I doubted it. She'd shown me what she thought I wanted or needed to see. Would Melina do the same?

I looked over and watched her sleep. Her relaxed expression made her seem younger than thirty-eight. Her anxiety melted away. I hoped her dreams were pleasant. Did she still have hopes for the future? If so, what were they? Was there something she wished she could have done in her life? A job? A place she wanted to see? Maybe something she wanted to learn?

I ached to ask her these things. Maybe she'd be receptive after I got her home. Right now, I worried the more questions I asked, the more likely she'd be to run from me. And I knew if she were on her own, the Bratva would find her and drag her back. I couldn't protect her if she wasn't by my side.

Her eyes slowly opened, and she stared at me, holding my gaze.

"Sleep, *lapochka*."

"I can't," she whispered. "Talk to me. Distract me."

I wanted to contradict her. She'd been asleep just a moment ago. But if she wanted to insist she couldn't sleep, then...

"Anything in particular you wish to hear?" I asked.

She shook her head, then hesitated. "I want to know more about you."

Me? I couldn't think of much I could tell her that would paint me in a good light. For one, I worked at our club-owned strip club. Not many women would tolerate me having such a job. Certainly not one with Melina's past. She probably would view those women as victims. Some were, but not anymore. I made sure they stayed safe. Only those who wished to work that sort of job were welcome. No one did drugs or sold themselves in the back rooms. I'd helped clean up the establishment and made it a good place to work. Would she see it that way? I wasn't so sure.

"Was that a hard question?" she asked.

"*Da.*" I smiled a little. "I worry you'll not like me when you know more."

"Do you hurt women or children?" she asked.

"Of course not!"

"Do you prostitute them?" she asked.

"*Nyet.*"

"Then I think I can handle the rest. Talk to me,

Stripes."

"Mikhail," I said. "When it's just the two of us, call me Mikhail. It's a privilege for only you to use my name."

"All right. Mikhail. What's so horrible about you?"

"I will tell you, as long as you promise not to run from me. The Bratva could be searching for you. I don't know if they can track you here or not."

She nodded. "You have my word. I won't run."

And so... I took a breath and started to spill my secrets.

* * *

Melina

I could tell Stripes thought himself to be a bad man, or to at least have done terrible things. While it might be true his hands had blood on them, he was nothing like the men I'd known all my life. In comparison, he seemed like an angel. From what I'd gathered from his confession, he'd only taken down men or women who had hurt others. To me, that made him a savior and not the least bit evil. He'd thought his admission would send me running, but it didn't. The only thing he'd said that made me squeamish was the place where he worked.

Even if the women at the strip club were there voluntarily, I wasn't certain how I felt about him working with them. I'd never been jealous. With Ruslan, I'd always felt relieved when he paid attention to other women. So why did the thought of Stripes being surrounded by beautiful naked women bother me?

"I won't be returning to work right away," he said.

"When you go back to work, could I go with you?" His eyebrows rose and I realized my question probably sounded odd, especially with all I'd been through. The thought of being surrounded by loud men wanting to see naked women wasn't on my top ten things to do. However, I needed to see the place where he worked. Maybe it would make me feel better about the situation.

Stripes reached out and lightly touched my jaw. I didn't flinch. If anything, I wanted to lean into his touch. The more I learned about him, the better I felt.

"*Lapochka*, those women are my responsibility, but I do not touch them. Ever. Besides... None are as beautiful as my wife."

My cheeks warmed and I dropped my gaze, but I felt like smiling. I couldn't remember anyone calling me beautiful. Not in a long time. When I'd been younger, I'd heard it frequently. Then I married Ruslan. I had to start covering up the marks he left on my face and body. The heavy makeup was far from flattering.

"I know this wasn't your choice," he said. "But I will treat you like a queen. Perhaps one day, you'll feel something for me. Love can grow between us over time, yes?"

"Love?" I asked. I'd given up long ago on falling in love. Wasn't sure I even believed in it anymore. I'd never met anyone who felt the emotion.

"If not love, then respect and friendship." He gave me a slight smile. "I will not push for more than you wish to give, Melina. Not now. Not later."

"Sometimes, it feels like you're too good to be true. I keep waiting for you to change, to show me you're the same as all the other men I've known." I folded my fingers together in my lap. "But you aren't, are you? You really are different."

"There's an entire club of men you'll meet who are nothing like the ones you've been exposed to so far. They aren't saints. They have their issues, but they'd never hurt you, *lapochka*. I'd trust every one of them with my family, and with you."

"Then I'll do my best not to paint them all with the same brush. I'll give them a chance. Just... maybe I can meet them one or two at a time? I'm not sure I'm ready to be around a lot of them at once. I can't promise how I'd react, and I don't want to embarrass you."

He sighed. "Ah *lapochka*. They will understand. Do not worry overmuch about it, yes?"

I nodded and settled against the pillows once more. Perhaps this time, I'd fall asleep and not open my eyes again until it was time to leave. Fatigue pulled at me, but until now, I'd felt too anxious about the future. Talking more with Stripes had helped a great deal.

I glanced over at him, and realized he had every intention of sleeping in the chair. Patting the bed, I drew his attention, and motioned for him to come lie down. He shook his head, his jaw set. Stubborn man!

Sitting up, I started to toss the covers aside, and it was all the prompting he needed. Stripes stood up, gave a low growl, and stretched out on the bed.

"Happy now?" he asked.

"*Da*."

I heard him snort as I shut my eyes and tried to sleep. The smell of him, and the heat of his body so near to me, made it difficult. I found myself wanting to study him. While we'd gotten to know one another a bit more, I still found him rather curious and a bit fascinating.

"Rest, Melina. Tomorrow is a long drive."

"Any longer than today?" I asked.

"*Da*. Much. We have another ten hours on the road before we reach home. We're not quite halfway."

I hadn't realized he lived so far from the place I'd called home all my life. I'd been born in this country, as had my father. My mother was another matter. She'd come over when she was a teenager and had soon been betrothed to my father. They had an arranged marriage, and he hadn't waited until she'd turned eighteen to marry her. Sick bastard probably liked the fact she was so young. There had been more than twenty years between my parents.

I peered at Stripes. There was a big age gap between us as well, but he'd sounded concerned over it. I didn't think he was the sort to get off on being with a much younger woman. Then again, if I understood about club whores correctly, he'd had access to plenty of women over the years, and I'd imagine most were younger than me. Possibly as young as my Oksana.

My heart ached for my children. They'd suffered needlessly. All because they'd been born girls in a world dominated by men. Since neither remained with the Bratva, I hoped it would mean a brighter future for them. I'd suffer through everything again if it meant they'd manage to escape that horrid life. Although, their freedom hadn't been my doing. If anything, my Oksana was the reason I no longer remained in the hellish brothel.

How could I ever look her in the eye? Would she be ashamed of me now? What of Yulia? Would my youngest understand any of this? I'd sheltered her as much as I could, hoping I'd find a way to give her a different life. Instead, Ruslan had dragged all of us into his mess.

"*Lapochka*, what's worrying you?"

"Nothing. Just thinking."

He turned onto his side, facing me. Gently, he ran a finger down the bridge of my nose. "Whatever it is, it can wait until tomorrow, yes? Nothing will be solved tonight."

He was right. I knew it, but it didn't make it any easier to turn my brain off and fall asleep. Too many what-ifs or should-haves. Thinking of all the things I wished I'd done differently wouldn't change anything now. It was all in the past, and the only thing I could do was hope for a better future.

The dark whispers in my mind wondered if everyone wouldn't be better off without me. As long as I lived, I'd taint the lives of my children. They'd have a whore for a mother. Being married to Stripes didn't change anything except my scenery, and perhaps yielded me more freedom. However, nothing would erase the things I'd suffered. No amount of scrubbing would ever make me clean.

With Stripes' past, I knew he didn't care that his wife had been in a brothel. But it mattered to me. I wanted to hold my head high. Make him proud of me. For that matter, I wanted to feel pride in myself. I didn't know if it would ever be possible.

I turned over and stared at the opposite wall.

Would Stripes have been better off if I'd succeeded before? What if he'd arrived only to be told I'd died? I doubted he'd have been sad. We hadn't known one another. I rubbed a finger across the mark on my wrist. If they hadn't come to check on me, I'd have already left this world.

The dark whispers continued, and tears pricked my eyes.

They'll be better off without you.

You're worthless.
Dirty. Trash. Nothing but a whore.
You have nothing to offer anyone.

The words circled in my mind again and again. When I finally succumbed to sleep, tears streaked my cheeks, and my heart ached.

Chapter Five

Stripes

Listening to her cry last night had nearly broken me. I'd wanted to pull her into my arms and tell her everything would be fine. Instead, I'd forced myself to lie still and give her space. If she'd wanted me to know, she'd have turned to me. We weren't there quite yet. I'd warned the others not to mention her puffy eyes. Anyone who saw Melina would know she'd been crying. The last thing I wanted was for anyone to make her self-conscious. She'd hidden her tears from me for a reason.

My bike ate up the miles and before I realized it, I'd pulled up to the gates of the compound. The Prospect on duty opened them and I pulled through, not stopping until I reached my house. Specter came to a stop in the driveway, handing me the keys to the vehicle, before walking off. I thought he'd most likely go to Charming's house, since his little sister lived there.

"Want help with her new things?" Gator asked. I shook my head, and he gave me a nod, then drove off.

I helped Melina from the truck and led her inside. When we entered the house, I almost didn't recognize the place. Minnie had already added a few touches when she'd stayed with me, and more with every visit, but it seemed the club had gone all out for my new wife. A large rug covered the living room floor, and I noticed the furniture looked brand-new. What else had they replaced while I'd been gone?

"This is your home now, *lapochka*. Change whatever you wish."

She barely glanced at anything. Seeing her so despondent made me feel powerless. The little bit of light I'd seen in her the day before was gone once more. I'd thought we'd made great progress while we'd shopped and had dinner. Now I wondered if I'd only been fooling myself.

I led her into the kitchen and showed her where I'd stored everything. The fridge and pantry were fully stocked, and I noticed a few new items, like mixing bowls and other cookware I hadn't owned previously. The dishes were also ones I hadn't seen before. It felt like my club had tried to erase an ex from my life before bringing home my new wife, except I'd never had a woman here. Well, Minnie... but I didn't think Melina would be jealous over the items my granddaughter selected for the house.

"Are you hungry?" I asked. "I should have asked Specter to stop for dinner along the way, but I'm happy to cook something for us."

"I..." She looked around, and I realized she must be feeling overwhelmed. She'd been through so much and had a lot of big changes in her life recently. I needed to take things slower, give her time to adjust.

At the same time, we had something we needed to discuss. We were married, but I wouldn't force her to share my bed. However, the only other room with a bed was the one Minnie used when she came to visit. I didn't know how comfortable Melina would be using another woman's room, even if Minnie was my granddaughter.

"I think we need to talk," I said, and led her over to the couch. She sat, and I claimed the spot beside her, keeping enough space between us so she'd be less anxious. "We may be married, but you didn't agree to any of this."

Her brow furrowed and her lips pressed tightly together. I couldn't read her expression, but could tell something I'd said either displeased her, or worried her. I wasn't good at things like this and had a feeling I was about to fuck everything up. I started to reach for her hand and stopped myself.

"I guess I'm trying to ask what you want, Melina."

"What I want?" she mumbled, looking away. "No one's ever asked such a thing."

"Never?"

She shook her head. I couldn't understand a father never wanting what was best for his daughter, or a husband who enjoyed hurting his wife. I knew there were men like that in the world. I'd killed quite a few of them. But knowing Melina had been treated so poorly all her life made me want to put my fist through a wall. I didn't know how to undo nearly forty years of trauma. Was it even possible for her to heal? Or would some part of her always be broken?

"Melina, even if you don't wish to share a bed with me, I will never force you. You understand that, yes? We can have a marriage in name only if that's all you ever want."

"I don't know what I want."

I gave in to the urge to hold her hand and laced our fingers together. "Then take your time and figure it out. Tomorrow. Next week. In a few months. Whenever you know, you tell me, yes?"

She nodded. "All right. And until then?"

"You meet the people here. Make this place your home. However, I will ask you to not leave the compound until I know it's safe. The Bratva will likely search for you, and I wish to keep you away from danger. *Ponjatno?*"

"I understand. And... thank you. For everything." She audibly swallowed. "I'm doing my best to trust you've told me the truth, and you won't hurt me. But it's hard. I've never known kindness from anyone before, except my daughters. It's difficult to believe all of this is real."

"There are only two rooms with beds here. One is mine, and the other is the one my granddaughter uses when she visits. I will leave it to you as to which you will sleep in. If you decide to share my room, it will be like last night. We will sleep and nothing more."

"What about…" Her cheeks turned red.

"Whatever it is, you can ask. I won't be angry."

"What about sex? I know men have urges."

"Melina, I'm not as young as I once was. Do I still enjoy being with a woman? Yes. Will I force myself on you, or guilt you into being intimate? *Nyet*. If you do not wish to be with me in that way, then I will do as I have these many months and I will abstain."

Her eyes went wide and her jaw dropped. "You haven't had sex in months?"

I shrugged a shoulder. "It was not necessary, and I find I do not enjoy casual sex as much as I once did. If our relationship were to ever reach that point, then I would cherish those moments with you. Going to the clubhouse and being with a random woman… it no longer holds any appeal for me."

"I think I'd like to share the bedroom with you," she said softly. Her cheeks remained slightly flushed as she looked away.

"Then I will put your things in there, and make sure there's space for your new clothes and shoes. Please, wander the house and become familiar with your new home. And never hesitate to ask me for something." I released her hand and caressed her jaw briefly before standing and moving away. I found her more lovely the longer I watched her, and the more I knew about her, the more certain I became that I'd made the right choice. If she ever came to give herself to me fully, I knew she would be the greatest treasure I'd ever had. "You're not a guest here, Melina. Do whatever you wish with the house. You don't need my permission."

She remained on the couch as I brought in her things. After making sure there was space for her things, I went to the kitchen to figure out what I could make for dinner. Even though she didn't seem to be hungry at the moment, I knew it could easily change. Something told me she wouldn't eat unless I offered her food. Not yet.

I pulled out my phone and sent a quick text to Charming.

We're home. I need a few more days off from the strip club.

It only took him a few seconds to reply. *Done.*

I checked my pantry, cabinets, and fridge before deciding what to make. I didn't know what sort of meals my new wife preferred. While we'd dined out last night, cooking at home would be different. For instance, I could make something that reminded me of Russia. In this region, finding a Russian restaurant would be impossible. So if she liked traditional dishes of my home country, we'd have to make them. One of my favorites, especially when I wanted what my *zaichik* called comfort food, were pirozhkis.

I pulled out the ingredients to make the breaded portion. I mixed the ingredients, then covered the bowl and set it aside so it could rise. While I waited for the dough, I browned the meat, cooking it with minced garlic and a little salt. I also made a pot of rice. It took a while to make them, but they turned out nicely. Once they were done, I plated them and set them in the center of the kitchen table.

I hadn't heard anything from Melina since I'd started dinner and went to check on her. She hadn't moved from the couch, and I realized she'd fallen asleep. Lifting her into my arms, I carried her to the bedroom and eased her down onto the mattress. I took off her shoes and pulled a blanket over her. Watching her sleep for a moment, I hoped she was having good dreams. If anyone deserved them, it was her.

As much as I hated to eat without her, I consumed half the pirozhkis, and left the rest for her. I didn't know what to make of my wife. At times, she seemed so fragile, I worried she'd break. Other moments, I could see the strength inside her. I would prefer her to get counseling for all she'd suffered, but it wasn't up to me. Until she wanted help, it would be pointless. For now, I'd keep an eye on her, and make sure she had everything she needed.

It would have to be enough.

* * *

Melina

I woke feeling disoriented. For a moment, panic filled me until I remembered where I was. Stripes had brought me to his house. I'd fallen asleep in the living room, too overwhelmed to move. He must have carried me to the bedroom. I tossed the covers aside and stood. Through the window, I could see that night had fallen. I heard the living room TV going. Before going to find Stripes, I went into the bathroom to wash my face and smooth my hair.

As I patted down the wayward strands, I froze. When was the last time I'd cared about my appearance? Long before my husband had sold me out to the Bratva. I'd had to dress a certain way all my life, and my mother made sure I knew what would be expected of me as Ruslan's wife. But this was different. I wanted to look nice for Stripes. Not because it was something he'd demanded of me. No, I simply wanted him to find me pretty.

I stared at my reflection. Bruises still marred my skin, as did scabbed-over cuts. I could have put on makeup, curled my hair, and put on the nicest outfit I owned... but none of it would change the fact men had used me. Beaten me. My vision blurred and instead of my face, I saw the leering smiles of the men who'd hurt me. A whimper escaped me, and I curled in on myself. Sinking to the floor, I rocked back and forth.

Dirty.
Shameful.
Whore.
Worthless.
Useless.

The words pounded inside my brain, repeating over and over. My fingers curled against my palms, and I knew if I'd access to a knife, I'd try to end it all again.

He doesn't need you. Doesn't want you. You're nothing but a burden.

The vicious whispers left me trembling and tears streaked my cheeks. I jolted when arms wrapped around me, bringing me back from the abyss. Stripes sank onto the floor and pulled me onto his lap. I didn't fight him. Didn't struggle in the least. No, I pressed my face to his shoulder and sobbed until my throat ached. The sweet man who called me his wife simply held me.

"Let it out, *lapochka*. Cry. Scream. Hit something. Hit *me*. Whatever you need, you shall have."

His words broke me even more, and I worried

I'd never stop crying. How had I ever ended up with someone like him? I'd thought men like Stripes only existed in stories. Yet here he was. My husband. My heart skipped a beat when I realized he was exactly the sort of guy I'd always dreamed of marrying. Strong. Capable. Kind. And yet tough enough to stand up to the Bratva. I wished I'd met him sooner. Before I'd married Ruslan. Maybe I could have run away with him. Lived a happy life.

Except then I wouldn't have my girls. Or at least, they wouldn't be the Oksana and Yulia I knew. Ruslan may have been a monster, but he was their father. The only good things I'd gotten from my marriage to him.

"I want you to consider something, yes?"

I nodded and lifted my head to hold his gaze. I sniffled and sucked in a breath, trying to calm myself.

"When you're ready, I'd like for you to speak with someone. A counselor. I think it will be of much help to you. These tears…" He wiped my cheeks. "They break my heart, *lapochka*. I want you to heal. To be happy."

I didn't like the idea of speaking with a stranger. For one, could they really understand what I'd been through? Would they look at me differently once they knew my story? I didn't think I could handle it.

"Do I have to?" I asked.

"*Nyet*. It is merely a suggestion."

"How could I tell someone what's happened to me? Some stranger who knows nothing about me, or the Bratva… they'd never be able to help me."

"Then you don't have to speak with them," he said, shrugging a shoulder. "If you change your mind, let me know. For now, would you like to shower and change before eating your dinner? I made pirozkhi."

My stomach rumbled and my mouth watered. I

hadn't realized he could cook. Well, I should have known he had some sort of skills since he said he'd lived alone, and he'd offered to make something when we got here. It hadn't occurred to me he wouldn't just make something from a box or a frozen meal. Then again, he hadn't said they were any good, only that he'd made some. Either way, I'd eat it and be grateful.

"Come, *lapochka*. I'll start the shower while you get your pajamas. You wash, then you eat, yes?"

I nodded. "Okay. Thank you... Mikhail."

I'd nearly called him Stripes and remembered at the last moment he'd told me to use his real name when it was just us. I felt honored. He helped me stand, then started the shower. I went into the bedroom and realized he'd placed all my things near the dresser. I found my new pajamas and panties, grabbing one of each, then returning to the bathroom.

Stripes ran a hand down my hair and leaned in. I tensed only for a moment. He paused, then slowly moved in closer and pressed a kiss to my forehead. Closing my eyes, I held back tears at his tenderness. The way he'd held me, comforted me... It made me want to crawl back into his arms and ask him to never let go. It was the only time I didn't doubt myself. The dark voices in my head quieted, and I had hope for a brief time.

"I'll leave the bedroom door open in case you need to call out to me," he said. "But I will not enter while you're getting ready. I'll wait for you in the kitchen."

He watched me another moment before walking out, and he pulled the bathroom door shut behind him. I heard his footsteps retreat through the bedroom and then down the hall. Stripping out of my clothes, I stepped under the spray and washed myself quickly. I didn't dare linger for fear the whispers would start again. As my fingers brushed over the cuts on my inner wrists, I wondered why I'd been spared.

I finished my shower and dressed, then went to the kitchen to find Stripes. He'd reheated the pirozkhi and provided a glass of ice water. I sat and started to eat, my mouth watering once more as the taste of the meat pie exploded on my tongue. It was good. Really good. I smiled and took another bite.

"If you'd like, I can make borscht or ukha sometime," he said.

"I don't mind cooking. I'm not great at it, but we won't starve."

He reached over and ran his finger over my hand. "Rest, Melina. If you wish to cook, then cook. If not, then I'll feed us. Simple, yes?"

"You don't mind?"

"Of course not."

"What about the cleaning? Dishes? What exactly will my responsibilities be here?"

He tipped his head to the side and ran a hand over his beard. "Whatever you wish. There is no schedule. No list of chores. We are two adults. No reason we cannot both cook or clean. Why should you do it alone?"

I stared at him, thinking I'd misheard. Did he really not expect anything from me? There wouldn't be a list of demands? Nothing I had to do or face the consequences? Even when I'd lived in my parents' home, I'd still been required to do certain things around the house.

"You finish your meal, and we'll watch a movie. Tomorrow, we can talk more. You think on what you'd like to ask. I'll answer. And I'll not get angry, *lapochka*. We are husband and wife. Equal partners, yes? There is nothing you cannot say to me."

I'd no sooner taken my last bite than he stood and took my plate. He carried it to the sink, rinsed it, then placed it in the dishwasher. The longer I was around Stripes, the more confused I became. The big, burly Russian looked intimidating, but I'd learned he was a teddy bear. Or so it seemed.

If this was a dream, I hoped I never woke up.

And if it wasn't...

I watched him, admiring his profile. Could I heal enough to have a normal relationship again? No, not again. For the first time. What I'd had with Ruslan was nothing like a marriage. Not the type I read about or saw on TV at any rate. Ruslan owned me. Forced me to bow to his will. No matter what the task, I'd had to comply or face the consequences. I'd been a slave, much like every other Bratva wife I'd ever known.

What would it be like to be loved by someone like Stripes? To laugh together. Make happy memories. To share the daily tasks and have conversations with one another. All of those were things I yearned for -- or had at one point. Maybe I could dare to reach for that sort of life. This time it might very well be within my grasp.

Please. Please don't break my heart. If I ever give it to you, you'd have the power to destroy me. And I knew it was true. If Stripes ever turned on me, it would be far worse than anything I'd suffered so far. Because for the first time in my life, I actually wanted something... and thought I might get to have it.

Chapter Six

Stripes

I'd left Melina in the living room while I showered. Except I'd told her I wanted to rinse off and change. In reality, I needed to take care of a problem before she realized what was going on. I stared down at my hard cock and winced. All this time, and it picked *now* to take interest in a woman. Sure, she was my wife, but Melina was far from ready for anything like this. She might never want to be intimate with me. And honestly, if what she needed was a friend and nothing more, then that's what I'd be for her.

It didn't take long for the water to warm and I removed my clothes before getting into the shower. The hot water hit my neck and shoulders, and I bowed my head, breathing deeply. The steamy air filled my lungs, but it did nothing to ease my tension. I soaped my hand and gripped my cock, tugging it with long, slow strokes. Closing my eyes, I pressed my forehead to the tiled wall and pictured Melina in here with me.

If she knew I was having these sorts of thoughts, she'd probably run as fast and as far as she could. I wouldn't blame her. While I'd never hurt her, or force her to have sex with me, the simple fact I wanted to be balls-deep inside her would likely terrify her. But I couldn't help it. My wife was beautiful and sexy. Yes, she had bruises and cuts. Her husband and the Bratva had badly abused her. And yet, she still shone bright as a star in the midnight sky.

I stroked my cock faster. "Melina. My *lapochka*."

My balls drew up and two more tugs had me coming all over the wall. I groaned and opened my eyes, frowning at my still-hard dick. I hadn't had this issue in a lot of years. More than a decade, at least. For a while, I'd wondered if I needed those little blue pills. It seemed that wasn't the case. I only needed my wife. The one woman I would possibly never be able to fuck.

This was complete bullshit. I couldn't walk back in there with my dick hard as a fucking post! It's why I'd come in here to shower to begin with. If she'd noticed, she'd have been scared of me. I didn't think I could handle her watching me like I was a monster, waiting for me to strike at any moment.

"Now what?" I muttered.

The shower door opened, and I jolted, my eyes going wide when I saw Melina. Naked. The curtain of her hair hid her face, and she refused to look up. She stepped into the shower, and I held out a hand, hoping to stop her.

"Melina, what are you doing?"

"You own me. You're in need. This is my job, isn't it?"

I fisted my hands at my sides and backed away from her. "*Nyet*. We're married. Being together like this, being intimate, isn't about a job. It's not a chore you must do."

I saw a tremor rake her body and cursed myself for an idiot. How the fuck was I getting out of this without causing her further trauma? I couldn't reach for my towel. Didn't want to push her out of the shower. For that matter, I was scared to touch her at all, since I wasn't wearing clothes. What made her do this? I'd been clear, hadn't I? About my expectations of her?

"Melina, why did you come in here? I've told you I expect nothing from you, yes? So why did you feel you needed to do this? Help me understand, *lapochka*."

"You're hurting, and it's my fault," she

mumbled. I nearly didn't hear her over the water.

"Hurting?" She nodded and waved a hand toward my cock. The motion made her hair slide back enough for me to see her face, and I noticed her cheeks were tinged pink. I cleared my throat and used my hand to try to cover myself. "It's nothing. You need not worry about the state of my, um…"

She quickly peeked up at me, and fuck if my dick didn't twitch before getting even harder. Shit. This wasn't good. I needed to get her out of here. Quickly.

"I don't mind," she said. "I trust you not to hurt me the way the others did."

Well, if anything could kill my hard-on, that was it. Her words had my cock shrinking immediately. Better than being doused in ice-cold water. I tried to skirt around her, then reached outside of the shower for my towel. I covered myself before pushing past her and getting one for her as well. I wrapped it around her and stepped back.

She didn't bother catching the towel, and it fell to the floor. I looked up at the ceiling, not having a clue how to fix this mess. The little I'd seen of her had been enough to know she'd suffered more than I'd realized. I'd tried to take stock of her wounds when I'd retrieved her from the brothel, but I'd been in a hurry. Now that I had more time, I wanted to thoroughly inspect each one.

"You said you've been with women before. Why are you making a big deal out of this?" she asked. "I'm offering you the use of my body. How is it not the same as any other woman you've been with?"

"Because they were willing, Melina. Despite your words, I know this isn't what you want. Do you desire me? Are you wet and ready?" I hated to be so blunt but trying to be nice wasn't getting us anywhere.

"I can… I can try," she said softy.

"*Lapochka*, when you truly want me, when you crave my touch, want my kiss, and feel as if you'll die if we can't be together in that way, *then* I will gladly have sex with you. Until then… it's not happening." I cleared my throat. "Please put on clothes, Melina."

I felt her hand skim over my chest, and I tried not to flinch. My cock started to rise again, and I took a hasty step backward. She followed, refusing to back down. I hadn't thought this would be something I'd have to deal with. The way she acted, I'd never considered she'd try to please me. If anything, I'd assumed she'd keep her distance.

I grabbed her hand. Not hard, but with enough pressure to stop her from touching me again. "Melina, stop."

"Why?"

"If we do this, I'll feel as if I've forced myself on you. I'm not the type of man who rapes women."

She tensed, and I studied her face. She'd gone pale, but it seemed I'd finally reached her. When she tugged on her hand, I released her. My beautiful wife didn't move away, but at least she wasn't advancing on me anymore.

"I'm not a monster, Melina. Please, don't make me into one. Never do something like this again. Not unless you truly wish to be with me, yes?"

"All right. I'm sorry." I heard the tension in her voice and noticed her eyes were getting glassy with unshed tears. I felt like an asshole. The last thing I'd wanted to do was make her cry.

"My beautiful Melina." I lightly brushed her cheek with my fingertips. "If the time comes when you want a true marriage between us, I will feel honored. Until then, I will be your friend. Your protector. Or whatever else you need from me."

She gathered her clothes and left the bathroom, shutting the door behind her. I leaned against the counter and pinched the bridge of my nose. So far, our first night wasn't going as well as I'd hoped. I knew we had a long, rocky road ahead of us. It hadn't occurred to me her trauma could cause her to react this way. I should have been better prepared. Next time, I would be.

* * *

Melina

After I dressed, I sat on the edge of the bed, wondering what had just happened. I'd stayed in the living room at first, wanting to give him space. But the doubts started to creep in again. What if he got tired of having a wife who wouldn't see to his needs? What if he decided to go to another woman and kicked me out later? *What if... what if... what if...* So I'd gotten up, swallowed my fear, and decided to go offer myself to him.

And it had backfired.

Or maybe it hadn't. I wasn't sure how I felt right now. He'd brushed me off. In fact, he'd almost appeared frantic to get away from me. The way his towel tented said he wanted me, and yet he'd refused to accept what I offered. A slight smile curved my lips, and I shook my head. I'd already thought multiple times that Stripes was different from anyone I'd met before, and he'd proven it yet again. What man could walk away from his naked wife throwing herself at him?

He'd been right, though. I wasn't into it. I hadn't come in because I'd wanted to have sex with him. I'd just been scared of what would happen if I didn't. At first, I'd thought I'd offer him a massage after his shower. I'd often done that for Ruslan. Not by choice, but by command. Still… I wouldn't have minded rubbing Stripes' back or shoulders to ease his tension. Then I'd heard the sound of him jerking off, and he'd said my name, and my plan had changed.

I should have stuck with the original idea of a massage. Although there was a good chance he'd have turned me down, anyway. Stripes knocked on the door, and I stood to open it. The way he looked at me made me want to disappear. I'd disappointed him, and I honestly felt ashamed of myself. I'd let my old fears take over, and I'd automatically treated him as if he were Ruslan. I shouldn't have done that. "I'm sorry," I said.

He shook his head. "There's nothing to apologize for. But I still do not understand why you did it. After what those men did to you, how could you have offered yourself to me in such a way?"

"We're married." I crossed my arms, rubbing my biceps. It was a nervous habit I'd had for as long as I could remember. "With Ruslan…"

"I'm nothing like the asshole you were married to before. If you wish to sleep in the other room, I'll understand."

I licked my lips and moved a little closer to him. "Did you think I only said I'd share the bed with you because I felt obligated?"

His brow furrowed. "Share for sleeping or…"

"Sleeping." I took another step toward him until I could feel the heat of his body. My fingers twitched at my side as I fought the urge to run. Some part of me wanted to take off and get as far from him as I could. But I tried to calm my racing heart and reminded myself Stripes was kind and gentle. "We slept in the same bed last night. You didn't hurt me. We're married. There's no reason to use two bedrooms."

"Was there any other reason you came in here during my shower?" he asked.

Did I dare confess I'd been worried he'd find someone else and get rid of me? I didn't want to sound as pathetic as I felt. I didn't delude myself into thinking I'd survive without him. Not only was he going to keep the Bratva away from me, but he'd given me a home, clothes, and anything else I could possibly need. And so far, he hadn't asked me for anything in return. Since he hadn't taken what he clearly wanted earlier, I now knew for certain I had nothing to fear from him. Not when it came to sex, at least. And he hadn't raised his voice or lashed out with his fists.

"Melina." He lifted his hand, moving slowly, as he reached out to cup my cheek. "You can tell me anything, *lapochka*."

I briefly leaned into his hand and closed my eyes. "I was scared."

"Of what?"

"That you'd find someone else. Someone less broken. Then you wouldn't want me around anymore, and I'd have to leave."

Saying the words lifted a weight from my shoulders. When he pulled me against his chest, I went willingly. He held me, running his hand down my hair, and I let him comfort me. Breathing in his scent, I let his strength surround me. For the moment, I felt all right. Somewhat normal. Or at least, what I thought *normal* might be like.

"I will *never* ask you to leave, Melina. You're my wife. It may not mean something to the men you've known, but for me, it does. I will not be divorcing you or throwing you away like unwanted garbage. You're my first and only wife, yes? Special. Mine. And I will do everything in my power to give you a happy life."

"Thank you, Mikhail."

"Come. Are you ready to sleep? Perhaps we should rest. It's been a long day, yes?"

I nodded. I wasn't exactly sleepy, but I did feel a bit drained. I didn't think it would take much for me to fall asleep. With Stripes beside me, I knew I'd be protected. I didn't have to worry about someone harming me after I closed my eyes. No one would try to hurt me. Not anymore.

"I should thank the others," I said. It hadn't been Stripes alone who'd saved me. He'd had two men with him. The one I'd ridden with, and the other one who'd had a motorcycle. What had been their names? Specter and Gator?

"They already know, *lapochka*. Neither expects anything from you. They helped me bring you home because they knew it was the right thing to do. They are good men. A bit rough, but we all are."

"I'm not the first, am I?"

"First?" he asked.

"Woman you've saved. There have been others. The way the three of you got me out of there, I can tell you've done this before."

"*Da.* I've helped others who were in bad situations. I did not bring any home with me. Only Minnie. She needed a place to stay when she had problems with Doolittle and his club. My President said she could come here. I offered her my home while she figured things out. And then…"

"Then?" I lifted my head to look up at him.

"I found out she's my granddaughter. I'd treated her as family from the first. The more I got to know her, the more she felt like a daughter. But one of the hackers did some digging, and discovered Minnie is actually my blood. I'd never been so happy." He smiled. "My little *zaichik*. She fills me with such joy."

"And her mother? Your daughter?" I asked.

He nodded. "*Da*. Her mother was my daughter. Oksana."

I bit my lip to hold in my gasp. Oksana? Had it even occurred to him we'd named our children the same thing? What would it mean if he ever met her? Would he resent my sweet girl for not being the child he no longer had? If he'd told me her name before, I hadn't been present enough to hear him properly. We'd talked a good bit last night, and yet, I only remembered bits and pieces.

"You will meet Minnie soon. I do not think Doolittle will be able to hold her back for long. But I will do what I can to keep her away until you're ready, yes? You are my priority now, Melina. My wife. My *lapochka*." He smiled at me softly. "There is no rush. You will be ready when it's time. Tomorrow. Next month. Next year. It does not matter."

I let his words sink in. He was choosing me over his precious granddaughter? Making me first in his life? Another piece of the wall around my heart crumbled. No one had *ever* put me first. Not until now. Until Stripes.

* * *

Stripes

Waking to a text from Charming wasn't how I'd planned to start my day. I stared at it through blurry eyes. *Church. Now.* Shit. I checked the time and realized he'd sent it nearly twenty minutes ago. I had a feeling I was in for an ass chewing when I got there. Looking at the space beside me, I saw Melina had scooted to the far edge of the bed, but at least she still slept soundly. I got up and took a fast shower, then pulled on my clothes. Even though I needed to leave immediately, I took a moment to write a quick note so Melina wouldn't worry if she woke and realized she was alone.

While I'd talked to Melina a bit about the club, there was still a lot she didn't know. If I told her I was going to Church, I didn't think she'd understand what that meant. So instead, I told her I had a meeting with my club and would be back later. I left it in the center of the table, where I hoped she'd find it easily, then went out to my motorcycle. It surprised me the Pres hadn't blown up my phone, wondering where the fuck I was. Or maybe he'd understood the toll the last two days had taken on me and knew I hadn't seen his message.

I pulled up outside the clubhouse and parked at the end. The moment I stepped through the doors, I saw Hunter behind the bar. He gave me a quick nod and glanced across the room. I followed his gaze and saw three of the club whores sitting at a table along the back wall. Thankfully, they all knew not to bother me. I wasn't up for any drama today.

Heading down the hall, I entered Church and noticed the room was completely silent. A few of my brothers looked my way, but most stared at the table. What the fuck had I missed? Charming didn't say a word, but merely pointed to my seat. I pulled out the chair and sat, then waited for him to either chew me out, or bring me up to speed. Instead, he surprised the fuck out of me.

"How's your wife?" he asked.

"Still broken." I winced. That hadn't been a kind way to put it, but accurate. "It's going to take a long time for her to heal. I don't see this being a quick trip to a happy ending."

"Her daughter is asking to speak with her." Charming leaned back in his seat. "I stalled them for now. Grimm is worried about his wife, but Melina is our priority right now. The Dixie Reapers can take care of Oksana."

That's when it hit me, and it felt like a fucking punch to the gut. Oksana. Melina's daughter, and mine, shared the same name. How fucked up was that? Or was it merely fate? I knew she had two children, but I didn't really think of them as people. As Charming said, the priority for us was Melina. I couldn't think about anyone else right now. Not even my *zaichik*.

"I'm sorry I was late," I said. I wouldn't bother giving any excuses. Then again, if they'd been concerned I hadn't shown up on time, they'd have either called me or sent someone to the house. Since they hadn't done either, I figured Charming wasn't bothered by my tardiness today.

"Did she sleep okay last night?" he asked.

I shrugged a shoulder. "Well enough. She's still…"

Scared? Yes, but it was more than that. She'd suffered years of abuse. In fact, I'd be willing to bet it was all she'd known, even as a child. I knew what it meant to be born into the Bratva. The world was hard and cruel. Even more so for the women.

"Whatever she needs, she'll have it," Charming said. "Now, what we discussed before you arrived, is the latest update. The hackers are still working to figure out as much as they can about the situation. Anything Wire finds, he's sending to us, as well as to the Reckless Kings, since they have Yulia. For now, all we can do is watch and wait."

"I've told Melina to stay inside the compound." Even though I knew my brothers would do whatever they could to keep her safe, I didn't like the idea of going back to work and leaving her behind. But it wouldn't be a good idea to take her with me. At least, not in terms of keeping her hidden from the Bratva. However, her concerns over where I worked made me hesitant to ignore her wishes. "She wants to go with me to my job when I go back to work."

Charming's eyebrows went up. "She knows you work in a strip club, doesn't she?"

"*Da.* I've kept nothing from her. She worries I'll fall in love with someone and throw her away. She has much trauma to overcome. It will not be easy for any of us."

"Grey wants to meet her," Samurai said. "Will she be receptive to speaking with her? Or do we need to hold off?"

I didn't like bringing up his past. He'd shared it with us, reluctantly, and I knew it still pained him a great deal. But for Melina, I would do anything.

"Tomorrow. And I'd like you to come too." I held his gaze and hoped he understood what I meant. His jaw tightened, but he gave a nod. If there was anyone here Melina would trust other than me, I knew it would be Samurai. Simply because of what he'd suffered. It made him different from the rest of us.

"I'll need someone to help with the strip club until Stripes is able to go in to work again. I think it's better for him to stay with Melina until she learns to trust him and the club. I don't want him gone for hours and have her freak out, or feel as if she'd been abandoned," Charming said. He'd softened a lot since meeting Dakota. In a good way.

"I'll do it," Gator offered.

"The women aren't going to hold off forever," Scratch said. "Clarity wants to meet your new wife, and I know the others do too. They understand she's been through a lot, so they're trying to be patient."

I closed my eyes for a moment and thought of how Melina looked when I'd found her at the brothel, and the same haunted expression on her face when she'd come into the bathroom while I'd been showering.

"She has a lot of cuts and bruises. I haven't asked to see them yet." I opened my eyes and looked around the table. "They didn't just dump her in the brothel. They beat her, and whatever else happened left her so broken she tried to take her own life."

"Jesus," Cinder muttered. As the ex-President for the club, he'd seen a lot of shit over the years. In fact, men had raped his wife for years before we rescued her in Colombia. Most of the women here had suffered traumatic events in their lives.

"I'm trying to move slow. She's starting to trust me. I think. But for every step forward, something happens that sends us even further back. She seemed all right last night, so I went to take a shower. Then I discovered I'd been wrong." I ran a hand down my face. As much as I didn't want to share all the personal details, they needed to know exactly how bad the situation was. "She tried to get in the shower with me. Offered herself up, like it's what would be required for her to stay with me."

"Did you turn her down?" Phantom asked.

"Of course I did!"

"Might not have been the best decision," Phantom said. "What if she thinks you were rejecting her?"

"I made it clear I wouldn't take her by force, and that she owed me nothing." I had, hadn't I? Or was Phantom right? Did I need to speak with Melina again, and make sure she knew I found her desirable but wouldn't touch her without permission?

"Looks like Stripes needs to head home soon," Charming said. "For now, we won't be making any runs. We'll only use the legit businesses we own around town to bring in a profit. I won't leave us open to attack or give the Bratva an easy way to get their hands on Stripes' wife."

I eyed Cinder. The more I thought about it, the more I realized Cinder's woman might be a good person to invite over. Maybe even today.

"Hey, Cinder. Would you send Meg by my house around lunch?" I asked. "I still want Grey and Samurai to visit in a day or two, but perhaps what Melina needs is to speak with Meg right now."

"I'll ask her to prepare something to bring with her. A pie or casserole." Cinder smiled. "She'll enjoy stopping by and meeting Melina. Make sure your woman is all right with her coming inside the house. If not, they can use the picnic table in your backyard."

I nodded. "I'll warn her of the visit so she's not surprised."

"I think I've covered everything," Charming said. "As we get updates, I'll either send out a mass text, or I'll call Church if there's anything we need to discuss. Be vigilant. In fact, I want extra eyes on the clubhouse. I won't completely shut it down right now, but I want to make sure those club whores don't go wandering. No men coming in unless they have prior permission."

He slammed his fist onto the table, and we all stood up to leave. I didn't even know if Melina had woken yet, but I found myself eager to return to her. Even though we were strangers, she was still mine. I hadn't thought I'd ever have a woman of my own. Now that I did, I looked forward to the future more so than before. I adored Minnie and my great-grandchildren. But having a wife was different.

I'd make sure Melina knew how special she was. That I would care for her. Cherish her.

But first... I needed to help her heal.

Chapter Seven

Melina

I'd changed my clothes three times. When Stripes said one of the women wanted to meet me, I'd wanted to run and hide. What would she think of me? I worried she'd think I wasn't good enough for Stripes or tell me I needed to leave. For some reason, Stripes seemed to think it would be good for me to speak with her.

"*Lapochka*, you look beautiful. Stop fussing," he said, coming to stand behind me. He placed his hands on my shoulders, gave them a gentle squeeze, then backed off. I wanted to ask him to keep holding me, and I almost did.

"Why is she coming over? You said it would be two other people I met first."

"It's my hope Meg will share her story with you. First, there's something I need to clarify." He came closer again, not stopping until our toes nearly touched. "Last night, I didn't tell you no because I wasn't interested. You're beautiful, and I'm very attracted to you. But I do not want you to come to me because you feel it's necessary. I want you to desire me as much as I do you, yes?"

"I know." I chewed on my lower lip. "I'm sorry about last night. I shouldn't have done that."

"No need to apologize. You're trying to survive, Melina. It's something you've done all your life, yes?"

He wasn't wrong. Ever since I'd been old enough to realize my parents didn't love me, and only wanted to use me to gain more, I'd done what I had to. Marrying Ruslan, for one. Although, it had been the biggest mistake of my life. In the end, he'd been the one thing to ruin me.

"But, Melina, you no longer have to live by those rules. Things have changed. In time, you'll see." He smiled at me softly. "Now, you're perfect as you are. No more changing. Would you prefer to meet with her in the backyard? We have a picnic table."

"Outside?"

He nodded. "We're away from the fence. No one will see you there, except those who live inside the compound. You won't be in danger."

"I think… I'd like being outside."

"Go wait for our guest." He kissed my forehead. "Meg will not hurt you, *lapochka*. She's not scary."

That remained to be seen. I ran a hand over my clothes once more before hurrying from the bedroom. When I stepped into the backyard, I saw the picnic table he'd mentioned, as well as a small fire pit and four chairs around it. He'd also added a sandbox and slide, which I guessed was for his great-grandchildren. What I didn't see were plants or flowers. The place seemed a little… spartan.

I heard the gate open and shut, making me tense.

"Are you Melina?" a woman asked. I turned and froze. She seemed to be somewhat close to my age. The difference between us was the carefree smile on her face, and the relaxed way she approached me. "My name is Meg. I'm with Cinder. He used to be the club's president before he decided to step down."

"Hi." She took a seat across from me and folded her hands on top of the table. "Stripes is bringing out drinks."

"You're probably confused right now. Scared. Not sure who to trust. I get it." She sighed and looked away for a moment. "I came to meet you, and to tell you my story. We aren't very dissimilar. Will you listen?"

"Yes." And I did... I spent the next thirty minutes or more absorbing every word she said. She didn't seem to hold anything back. Everything she'd been through might have been different from my story, and yet, she'd been right. We did share the pain of suffering at the hands of men. "How did you know Cinder wouldn't hurt you?"

"At first, I didn't. I thought all men were the same. I'd been here a short while when I knew I wanted to repay the kindness of the people here. So I started to clean Cinder's home, and I'd make meals for him. He wasn't married, and as the club President, I knew he carried a heavy burden."

"How did you end up together?"

She smiled and stretched her arms over her head before relaxing once more. "It wasn't easy. He hurt me. Not physically, but emotionally. Made me feel as if I weren't wanted anymore. He yelled at me, and being as sensitive as I was, I cried. Then he did something completely unexpected."

"What?" I asked, leaning forward, eager to find out more.

"He threw a birthday party for me. I'd already been falling for him by then. That night, things changed between us. Until I got hurt again and ran away."

"But if you ran..."

"Cinder came for me." Meg smiled again. "Just as Stripes went to rescue you. He cares for you, doesn't he? Makes sure you have something to eat. Clothes to wear. He's gentle and tries not to scare you, right?"

My jaw dropped a little. "How did you know all that?"

"Because it's how these men are made. They're rough on the outside. Hard. And when it comes to battle, they will take no prisoners. However, with women... the *right* woman... they will do anything to make her happy and keep her safe. For Stripes, you're that woman. He's never been married. Never shown interest in keeping a woman around. The moment he heard your story, he not only volunteered to get you out of the brothel, but he didn't fight the hackers when they married the two of you."

I digested her words. She'd told me a lot, and yet I'd already known about Stripes. Hadn't I? He'd been nothing but kind to me all along. If what Meg said was true, I could finally relax. I could drop my guard and let him in. Let all of them in. If the others were anything like Meg, then they'd accept me, right?

"Stripes said there was a couple I should meet. Grey and Samurai."

Meg nodded. "They'll be perfect. Grey's story isn't quite like either of ours, but... well, it's hers to tell. Same for Samurai. They're survivors. And so are you, Melina. You may not see it yet. In time you will."

"What's it like living here?" I asked.

"Chaotic. In a good way, though. Lots of kids and families here. There weren't before. More and more of the guys are settling down. We have family events. Potluck lunches or dinners. Picnics. Holiday gatherings. Birthday parties. A lot of the kids carpool to school. The clubhouse is noisy at night when the single men throw parties. Occasionally, the married guys go there for a drink, but they don't touch the women. Charming will beat the hell out of anyone who cheats."

"The ones who hurt you... what happened to them?" I asked.

"Believe it or not, a woman led the rescue. Jordan went after Havoc. He'd disappeared, and once Jordan tortured his location out of someone, she came charging in, causing so much trouble the authorities there asked her to please leave the country." Meg laughed. "It was awesome. I mean, at the time I was freaking out. Now, I can look back on that day and find the humor in the situation."

"Havoc and Jordan? Are they here too?"

"They are, and I'm sure you'll meet them sooner or later. Havoc is the club's Sergeant-at-Arms. He protects everyone, and his wife is just as much of a badass as he is. And their daughter? Holy hell! I feel sorry for whatever boy falls for her. Lanie is more than a firecracker. She's an entire box of dynamite, just waiting to go off."

They sounded interesting. Terrifying, but interesting. I doubted I'd met anyone like them before. Then again, Stripes and Meg were different from the type of people I was used to as well. In a good way.

"Make sure Stripes gives you my number. If you think of any questions, or just want to talk, then give me a call. I'm happy to come over if you're up for company. If not, that's all right too."

"Thank you, Meg. I feel a bit better about being here."

"Anytime, Melina." She smiled again. "You'll make a lot of friends here, if you give them a chance to get to know you. All the women are really friendly and supportive."

While I appreciated her words, and I had enjoyed our conversation, I didn't think I was ready to mingle with everyone. There were still too many dark thoughts in my head. Scary memories. And doubts. A lot of doubts.

I'd follow Stripes' lead for now. When he thought I was ready, I'd trust him. I knew I had a lot of healing to do. Even if I wasn't sure it would ever be possible to overcome my past… for Stripes, I'd try.

* * *

Stripes
Two Months Later

I stared at my phone, reading Charming's message for the tenth time. I'd been off work for so long, and I knew I was letting the club down. At the same time, Melina wasn't healing as fast as I'd hoped. She still struggled on a daily basis, and never ventured out of the house except for the rare visit to the backyard if one of the ladies came over. I worried about her. Hell, I was starting to worry about me too.

Stop worrying about the club. We understand.

How the fuck had the others gotten through this? I knew Meg had been here a long time before she'd hooked up with Cinder, but the others were different. None of them lasted long before going all in with the men who'd claimed them. It wasn't the lack of sex that bothered me. Well, it did if I were being honest, but not because I was tired of yanking one out. The fact Melina didn't seem to be progressing much was concerning. She still wouldn't speak with a counselor, and I wasn't sure what to do for her.

My phone rang, and I saw it was Grimm calling. I knew Oksana wanted to speak with her mother, but I couldn't do that. Not yet. I hadn't told anyone what happened a few weeks back. Melina had scared the fuck out of me. I'd stepped outside to speak with someone, and when I'd come back inside a half hour later, I'd found her in the bathroom with a kitchen knife and blood dripping from her wrist.

I refused the call and sent Wire a text.

Tell Grimm I can't let anyone talk to Melina yet.

She's struggling.

He replied almost instantly. *Will do. Let me know if you need anything.*

I appreciated the thought, but unless he could convince Melina to see a therapist, I wasn't sure what he could do for her. In two months, we'd barely gotten closer. She'd sometimes let me hold her hand. I'd given her the occasional kiss on the forehead or cheek. But in terms of healing emotionally and mentally, I didn't think we were getting anywhere. I wanted to know more about all she'd suffered, and she did share bits and pieces, but I started to wonder if I'd ever get the full story from her.

"Was that the man who's with Oksana?" she asked softly.

I nearly jumped, not having heard her come into the room. "He tried calling again. I didn't have anything new to say, so I declined the call."

Tears filled her eyes and spilled down her cheeks. I shoved my phone into my pocket and pulled her into my arms. At times like this, she let me hold her. It was the only comfort I could give, and it broke my heart every time she fell apart.

"Why am I so broken?" she asked, her voice catching.

"*Lapochka*, I think you need to speak with someone other than me. A professional. I'm lost right now. As much as I want to help, I don't know how."

"I think the not knowing is what's holding me back."

I wasn't quite sure what she meant. "Not knowing?"

"The Bratva. They haven't come for me. We haven't heard anything from them, have we? I have no idea if they've found me and they're lurking outside somewhere, or if they don't even care that I'm gone. I'm scared. Terrified, really. I don't want to accept this new life, start a real relationship with you, only to have it all taken away and be tossed back into hell. I couldn't take it!"

I ran my hand up and down her back, holding her tighter. "Melina, no matter if they come for you or not, I'm not handing you over to them. You do not have to fear starting a new life here. I will protect you until I draw my last breath. *Lapochka,* you're mine. No one will ever take you from me. I won't let them."

"Mikhail... will you kiss me? A real kiss?"

Her words made me freeze. She wanted what? Was she serious? I studied her expression and realized she meant it. I placed my fingers under her chin and lifted her face. I moved slowly, giving her time to pull away, as I leaned in and pressed my lips to hers. She gasped and tensed for a brief moment. When I flicked my tongue against her bottom lip, she opened and let me in. I deepened the kiss, and Melina melted against me.

This. This was what I'd been hoping for. She gave a soft moan and clung to my leather cut, gripping it in her hands. The way she submitted so sweetly made me want to press her against the wall and take everything I wanted. I couldn't contain my growl as I pulled away. If I didn't put some space between us, I worried I'd lose control.

Her eyes were wide, and she pressed her fingers to her mouth. "I never knew."

"Knew what?" My voice came out raspier than before. Deeper.

"That it could feel like that. I've been kissed before. I never liked it. It was something I endured." A wistful looked crossed her face. "I wish I'd met you sooner, Mikhail. How different would my life have been?"

"I'd have treasured you. Treated you like a queen. I still will. You aren't scared?"

"No. For the first time in my life, I'm not. I trust you, Mikhail, and I..." She pressed her lips together. "I want us to have a real marriage. I don't want to keep feeling like I need to hide. I don't like the whispers in my head, the dark voices that tell me I'm not good enough, that everyone would be better off without me."

I cupped her cheek and pressed my forehead to hers. "*Lapochka*, you're more than good enough. You're so strong. Beautiful. And have a long life ahead of you. I look forward to what the future holds for the two of us."

"Do you think I'll ever stop hearing those voices? Or being so scared all the time?"

"*Da*. Not today. Not tomorrow. But one morning, you'll wake up and realize all of it is in the past, yes? We'll be happy together, Melina. I know this. I will give you everything you desire. You only have to ask."

"I don't need material things," she said. "I think I just need you."

I kissed her again and hoped this was a new start for us. But I'd thought she was doing better before, and discovered it wasn't the case. Would that happen again? I wished I knew when the whispers started, if there was a sign I could watch for, so I could intervene before it was too late. I worried I'd come home and find out she'd succumbed to the darkness. I knew it would devastate me.

"Promise me something, *lapochka*. When the voices or whispers start, when you feel yourself spiraling, talk to me, yes? Let me know you need help.

I'll hold you, and we'll get through it together."

"You're such an amazing man," Melina said. "Your granddaughter is lucky to have you. I don't know why you haven't been married before now, but I'm lucky you're the one who claimed me. So, thank you. For saving me, making me your wife, and everything you've done for me since the day we met. I promise, I'm grateful even when it doesn't seem like I am."

Not once had I ever thought she didn't appreciate the things I gave her or did for her. If anything, it bothered me that I might not be doing enough. I hated not knowing what I could do to help her. Having to watch her suffer in silence ate at me. I hoped moving forward she would confide in me.

* * *

Melina

Hours later, I kept pressing my fingers to my lips. I could still feel Stripes' kiss, and every time I thought about it, my cheeks warmed. I didn't know how I'd ended up with such an incredible man. He'd been strong enough to come save me. Even knowing he would be stealing from the Bratva, he'd still come for me. Yet, he was also kind and gentle.

He'd asked me to spend the afternoon resting and to remain in the bedroom. He'd muttered something about a surprise, and I'd decided to do as he said. I'd read most of the day, and even soaked in the tub for a while. My cuts from the Bratva had healed, even though they'd left scars. The bruises were gone. If only those dark whispers would remain at bay. They'd gotten to me not too long ago. Reminding me I was trash. Useless. A burden to everyone around me. Nothing more than filth.

And I'd listened… then I'd tried to kill myself. Stripes found me in time. I'd been angry at first, feeling as if he'd taken away my chance to escape. Now, I felt differently about it. I was glad to still be here. It hadn't occurred to me at the time I'd be leaving him behind, or how it would hurt him. I'd thought it would be a kindness to him if I weren't around. I now saw how very wrong I'd been.

Whatever he'd planned for tonight, I found myself anticipating it. I didn't understand why I had to stay hidden in the bedroom, but he'd made sure I had something to eat for lunch and brought me drinks when I got thirsty. Since he seemed to want to do something special for me, I decided to look nice for the occasion. I'd put on one of the few dresses I owned, and I'd taken my time fixing my hair. I'd even put on a little makeup.

I didn't like the slimy feel of lipstick, or the way it came off and stuck to glasses, forks, and anything else my lips touched. So instead, I had a lip stain I'd used, then dabbed on a little lip moisturizer. Stripes had found one for me that absorbed quickly but kept my lips from feeling dried out. I loved it!

I stared at the tube and realized he'd done a lot of little things for me to show how much he cared. I'd been too blind to notice. The lip moisturizer was only one of many. I'd once watched a movie where the main character said it was often the little things in life that had the biggest impact. Now that I was taking the time to look around and see everything Stripes had done for me, I knew they were right. Maybe individually they didn't do much, but all together was a different matter.

I fluffed my hair and studied my appearance in the mirror. I'd filled out quite a bit since coming here. Getting regular meals had put some much-needed weight on me. A month ago, Stripes had purchased more clothes in a larger size. I'd needed them, even though I'd felt bad he'd had to spend more money on me. The dark circles under my eyes were a thing of the past. My complexion looked better than it had in more than a decade. My eyes even seemed brighter than they had before.

Stripes knocked on the bedroom door, and I hurried to open it. Smiling up at him, I felt happier than I had in a long time.

"You look beautiful, *lapochka*. Give me fifteen minutes, then I'll take you to the other room. I need to shower and change."

He pressed a kiss to my forehead before brushing past me into the bedroom. He gathered clean clothes from the dresser and went into the bathroom, shutting the door behind him. True to his word, fifteen minutes later, he came out freshly groomed and in a clean shirt and jeans. He'd left his cut on the bathroom counter, and I wondered why he wasn't wearing it. I seldom saw him without it.

"Come. Let's eat dinner, yes?" He reached out and took my hand, leading me to the kitchen. Candlelight flickered along the counters and in the center of the table. He'd turned off the lights, and the amber glow gave the room a romantic feeling. He'd made pirozkhi, like my first night here.

"What is all this, Mikhail? Is it a special night?" I asked.

"*Nyet*. I wanted to do something nice for you. You don't feel comfortable leaving the compound to go on a date, so I decided we'd have a nice dinner at home."

"I love it." I smiled up at him. "Thank you."

"Sit. Dinner is not the only surprise. Eat and

you'll get to the other parts."

He pulled out my chair, and I sat down. Stripes placed a napkin in my lap, gave me a quick kiss once more, before taking the seat across from me. I helped myself to the food in the center of the table. I couldn't believe he'd done all this.

"Are you going back to work soon?" I asked. "When I first came here, you said you'd take a week off. It's been months."

He paused, mid-reach for the basket of pirozkhi. "I will return when it's time. The President has agreed you're my priority. Gator and another brother are handling the strip club."

Right. Because I was broken, he'd had to stay home. I'd caused problems not only for him, but for the club too. I swallowed my bite of food and tried to push back the dark thoughts, trying to force their way to the forefront of my mind. The whispers weren't completely silent yet.

Troublesome.

A burden.

I gave myself a mental slap, banishing the voice once more. I couldn't listen to those words anymore. Not while I had a husband who cared for me, and people who wanted to be my friends. Meg and Grey both came over once a week. I hadn't opened up to them as much as I should have. Part of me had been holding back all this time, still too scared to trust everyone.

My fear had to be causing issues for Stripes. I needed to do better. Supposedly, the Bratva wasn't looking for me. I wasn't sure what to think. It wasn't so much I thought Stripes lied to me about it. But why had the Bratva let me go? Felix had sent me to the brothel to punish me. It didn't mean they valued me enough to spend the time and money to find me, though. Maybe that's why they weren't bothering to come get me. Stripes hadn't told me much, only that the Bratva wasn't an issue anymore.

"*Lapochka*, you're worrying again."

"Sorry. I can't help it, but I'll try to do better."

"I was not scolding you, Melina. Merely making you aware of what you were doing. I think you get lost in your head and forget where you are."

I took another bite, savoring the flavor. Stripes cooked for us most of the time, and I'd enjoyed everything he'd made. The times I cooked, he always praised the dishes I made, but I knew my skills were lacking. With Ruslan, I'd had a maid and a cook. Although there had been times he'd made me cook for our family. Usually, he used it as a punishment and a way to belittle me.

"Do you ever regret it?" I asked.

"Regret what?"

"Marrying me. Saving me. Even if you'd gotten me out of there, you could have handed me off to someone else."

He stood and came around the table, kneeling beside me. "*Lapochka*, as I've told you many times, I would do everything the same. Except, I'd have never left you alone that day last month."

I pressed my lips together. I knew which day he meant. The one where he'd caught me trying to kill myself. I still remembered the look on his face. The panic, fear, then resolution. He hadn't left my side for long since then. Not until today. And even though I'd been confined to the bedroom, he'd made sure to check on me frequently.

"I wanted to wait. But I think you need to hear this now and not later." He pulled something from his pocket, keeping his fist tight around it so I couldn't see what it was. "Melina, we were married as a way to protect you. I agreed because I'd never had a wife and did not think I'd ever find one. We're both Russian, and I wanted to help. It seemed like a good decision."

I reached out and ran my fingers over his beard. He'd done all that for a woman he hadn't even known. Of course, he'd mentioned it before. More than once. Perhaps it hadn't sunk in until now, everything he'd given up for me. The chance to find love, being the foremost.

"You do not see your strength, nor your beauty, but I see both. Melina, I do not regret what I've done. I never will, *lapochka*. You're my wife. Your face is the first thing I see in the morning, and the last I look at before I go to sleep at night. I want that to be true until the day I stop breathing." He opened his fist, and I saw a jewelry box. He opened the lid, and I gasped at the ring I saw inside. The band sparkled with tiny diamond chips, and a large ruby set in the center in a marquis cut.

"It's beautiful, Mikhail." He removed it from the box and slid it onto my finger. I marveled at the way it shone in the candlelight. "Why are you giving me this?"

"Because I want you to see it and remember who you are. You aren't the wife of Ruslan. You're not a whore in a brothel. You're my wife. The old lady of a patched member of the Devil's Boneyard MC. You are strong. You are fierce. And you are *mine*, yes?"

"*Da*. I belong to you. My sweet, kind husband. The man who has given me a reason to keep living." I leaned forward and pressed my lips to his. It was the first time I'd ever kissed a man willingly. It was something I wanted to do many more times.

He smiled. "We'll finish our meal, then you get your final surprise. You are precious to me, Melina. Never forget it."

I wouldn't. Not anymore. I was tired of hiding. Of running. Of being terrified I'd lose everything, even myself. He believed in me, and I would make sure I didn't let him down. Stripes said I was his... but didn't that also make him mine?

Chapter Eight

Stripes

Seeing my ring on Melina's finger made my chest ache. I should have given her one sooner. Maybe if I had, she wouldn't have had so many doubts. I'd told myself I was giving her space, giving her time to adjust and heal... Now I wasn't certain I'd done the right thing the last two months. The way she'd lit up, the soft way she'd kissed me, made me wonder if she'd have done those things sooner if I'd done something like this before now.

I didn't know if she'd like final gift. There was still much about the club she didn't understand. Grey had filled her in on a lot of things, and so had Meg. She'd seen their property cuts, and asked questions once she'd become more familiar with them. I didn't know if she realized the significance of a property cut. Since she hadn't left the house or backyard, she hadn't been able to truly submerge herself in the lives we led here.

Even though I'd told her the Bratva would no longer be an issue, she still feared going outside. I wasn't sure how to make her feel more secure at the compound. At this rate she'd never venture into town.

After dinner, I'd placed the leftovers in the fridge and the dishes in the sink. I'd take care of everything later. Tonight was all about Melina. I wanted to spend as much time with her as possible.

I held her hand as we sat together on the couch and watched a movie. I'd let Melina pick whatever she wanted, and she'd selected a romantic comedy. I loved watching her laugh. Seeing her smile. The joy in her eyes filled me with warmth, and I knew I wanted to see her like this every day.

"Have you had a good time tonight?" I asked.

"I have." She smiled up at me. "I think this will be one of my favorite memories. It's the first truly happy day I've had. I've enjoyed my time with you before. Tonight was different."

"A new beginning for us, yes?"

She nodded. "I'd like that."

"We've kissed twice now." I cleared my throat, suddenly feeling nervous. I couldn't remember experiencing anything like it since I'd been a teenager. "Would it be presumptuous to assume I could kiss you again?"

"Mikhail, we're married. We just said we were going to start fresh. You're welcome to kiss me whenever you'd like. I won't run away."

"You shouldn't offer such things. I may kiss you all the time." I grinned at her and loved the way her cheeks flushed. The slight smile curving her lips said my words hadn't displeased her.

"I don't think I'd mind." Her words were so soft I nearly couldn't hear her. I put my arm around her shoulders and tugged her closer. In the past, she'd have tensed or pulled away. This time, she leaned into me.

"So you like these movies?" I asked, waving a hand at the TV.

"Sometimes. When I was younger, I really enjoyed them. Then I married Ruslan and watching movies like this only made me more miserable. Instead of living a fairytale like these women, I'd been lowered into the depths of hell."

"But you wish to watch them again?"

"I do. Being with you has shown me that maybe these movies aren't so ridiculous after all. After marrying Ruslan, I'd thought they made all this up. I didn't think anyone had relationships like these. You're proving these stories aren't as farfetched as I'd thought."

"I'm not like these men, *lapochka*. They're soft. Weak. Is that the sort of man you wish for?" I asked.

"You're neither of those things. However, you're kind and sweet. I don't think you're weak. It took a great deal of strength and courage to come save me. I've told you this before. You may not be *soft* like the man on TV, but you still have some of his qualities. The good ones."

"Melina, were you serious when you said I could kiss you whenever I wished?" I asked.

"Of course. Why?"

I leaned in and pressed my lips to hers. She reached up and grabbed hold of my shirt, and I pulled her even closer. The sweet sounds she made as I deepened the kiss made me crave her even more. Before I'd realized what I'd done, I'd lifted her onto my lap. The bulge in my jeans couldn't be hidden, but it didn't seem to scare her. She wiggled a little, making me groan.

"*Lapochka*, we should stop. If we don't, I may not be able to hold back. I will never do anything you don't want but walking away will be difficult."

"Is everything as good as kissing?" she asked, tracing my lip with her fingers. "I never liked any of it before. I endured Ruslan's attentions because I had no other choice."

"I would love nothing more than to show you how wonderful sex can be. Are you sure you're ready for something like that?" I asked. I'd convinced her to let a doctor come to the house to see her. He'd checked her wounds over a month ago and drawn blood. One of the tests he'd run had been for any sexually transmitted diseases. He'd also run a pregnancy test, since Melina was still young enough to have children.

The thought gave me pause. I'd need to use a condom, even if I didn't want to. Now that I had a fully grown granddaughter and little great-grandchildren, I didn't want to start a new family. I was too old to deal with a baby in the house. What would Melina want?

"Maybe? I won't know unless I try. Would you be angry if we started something, and I asked you to stop?"

"*Nyet*. I will do whatever you wish, *lapochka*."

"Then can we try? Just… go slow."

"I can do that. I had one more surprise for you, but it can wait. Come, my sweet wife." I lifted her into my arms and stood, carrying her to the bedroom. My heart hammered in my chest. It felt a lot like my first time with a woman. Except for once, it actually mattered. I wanted to please Melina and show her things could be wonderful between a man and a woman. She'd only known pain, and I wished to change that.

I eased her onto the mattress and reached into the drawer to pull out a strip of condoms. I showed them to her and watched her expression shutter. It seemed I'd made a wrong move already, and I knew I'd need to soothe her before we went any further. Being married, we needed to have a certain level of trust between us. I wasn't sure what thoughts were going through her mind, but clearly something about the condoms bothered her.

"*Lapochka*, I know you're young enough to still have children, but I'm past the age of wanting a baby in the house. Since I didn't know if you'd ever let me touch you this way, we never discussed having a family." She paled and looked away. My brow furrowed as I stared at the condoms, then at her. Did she think I didn't want a baby with her because of her past? It wasn't the case. Not even a little. "Melina, my decision has nothing to do with you. I know it makes me selfish."

She turned her face toward me again and I realized she was close to tears. Panic filled me and I reached for her, tugging her into my arms. What the hell had I done? We'd been on the verge of sharing an incredible moment and now I'd hurt my sweet wife.

"It's not you," she said. "I… I can't have children, Mikhail. When Yulia was born, Ruslan instructed the doctor to give me a hysterectomy. I didn't get a say in the matter."

I tightened my hold on her and wished once more I could bring back Ruslan if only to murder him with my bare hands! The selfish bastard hadn't deserved a treasure like Melina.

"*Lapochka*, I'm sorry the decision wasn't yours to make. The only reason I wanted to use condoms was to avoid pregnancy. If it's not an issue, we don't need them, yes? We don't have to do more than this for tonight. Whenever you're ready, you let me know."

I felt her tears soak my shirt as I ran my hand over her hair. The night might not have ended the way I'd planned, but I'd learned another important thing about my little wife. Except the more I discovered, the more I wanted to bathe in the blood of the Bratva. Hearing all she'd suffered made me hate them even more. One day, I'd make them pay.

* * *

Melina

I'd ruined the night. No matter what Stripes said, I knew I'd wrecked our perfect evening. The thought of having his baby was bittersweet. Even though he said he didn't want children, I'd have loved to raise one with him. Unlike Ruslan, he'd be a wonderful father. There was so much I wished I could have done differently with my girls. It was too late now. I couldn't undo the past.

Stripes' heart thumped under my ear, and I shifted my head to watch him sleep. We'd changed clothes and crawled into bed. He'd immediately tugged me against his side and gone to sleep while I rested my head on his chest. Even though he hadn't seemed angry about what happened, I felt like I'd disappointed him. He'd been so wonderful. I still hadn't received my third surprise, and now I worried I wouldn't get it. Not because I was selfish and wanted all the things, but it was something he'd clearly chosen for me. It made me curious as to what he'd picked out.

The ring on my finger was beautiful, and I knew I'd cherish it. Not because it sparkled or looked costly. No, I loved it because Stripes picked it out for me. I didn't know why he'd chosen this particular one, and it didn't matter. He could have selected a plain band, and I'd have still loved it, simply because he'd given it to me. With Stripes, there wasn't an ulterior motive to the things he did.

I ran my fingers over his beard and watched him sleep. Sitting up, I wondered if I was brave enough to make the first move. Sure, I'd kissed him earlier, but this was different. He'd said he'd show me how good sex could be. Then I'd fallen apart because I had to tell him I couldn't have children. I worried if we didn't become more intimate tonight, I might lose my courage and the opportunity would pass me by.

I slid my hand from his chest down his abdomen. Even though he was older, I could still feel the firm muscles under my palm. He didn't have an eight pack, or whatever it was called, when men had well-defined abdominal muscles. Still, I could tell he stayed in shape.

"*Lapochka*, what are you doing?"

"Oh." My gaze flew to his face, and I froze when I realized he was watching me. "I, um…"

"Couldn't sleep?" I shook my head. Stripes pulled me back down, so I was lying beside him. He went up on his elbow and peered down at me. "I'm sorry I ruined the mood earlier, *lapochka*."

"It wasn't your fault. I was the one who started crying. I didn't mean to become so emotional. As you said, you didn't want more children, anyway."

"What they did to you was wrong, Melina. No one should have taken away your choice to have another baby. If you'd truly wanted one, I'd have talked to you about it. I feel like I'm too old to raise an infant. There's a big age difference between us."

He wasn't saying anything I didn't already know. He made a good point. At his age, he was probably thinking more about retirement than about starting over.

"Mikhail, make love to me," I whispered. "We can't start a family together, but it doesn't mean we can't share many other things with one another. I want you to be the first and only man to prove to me there's pleasure to be found in the bedroom."

"Are you sure, Melina?"

I nodded and reached for the hem of my pajama top. I sat up and pulled it over my head, tossing it aside, then wriggled out of my sleep pants and panties. I felt a little self-conscious over the scars on my body, but the heat in his eyes quickly melted any fears I had.

Stripes went up on his knees and pulled off his

T-shirt, but he left his sweatpants on. He came down over me, pinning me to the bed. My heart fluttered, and I reached up, gripping his biceps. I ran my fingers over the muscles and couldn't help but compare him to the other men who'd purchased time with me. None of them came close to being even a little like Stripes. Stripes looked like he belonged in Hollywood or on romance book covers.

"What's that look for?" he asked, a slight smile on his lips.

"Just admiring you."

"You get uncomfortable or scared at any time, you change your mind and want to stop, you tell me, yes? You are in charge, *lapochka*."

"All right." He kissed me, then trailed his lips down my jaw, over the column of my neck, and eventually closed his lips over my nipple. I gasped and dug my fingers into his hair. "Oh! Oh, don't stop. Please…"

He flicked his tongue against the hardened peak, and I had to bite my lip so I wouldn't beg him again. I'd never felt anything so wonderful before. He took his time, driving me crazy. When he switched sides, my back bowed, and I gripped his hips with my thighs.

He rubbed his beard against my belly as he worked his way down my body. His shoulders spread my thighs wide, and my cheeks heated. I felt him part the lips of my pussy, and the first stroke of his tongue had me squealing. He circled my clit several times before rapidly flicking it. My thighs pressed against him tighter, and I worried I might break him. A feeling kept building inside me. One I hadn't felt before. One more stroke of his tongue and I came, screaming out his name as my fingers clawed at the bedding.

I no sooner caught my breath than he started

again. His tongue flicked the sensitive nub, and I wasn't sure if I wanted to plead with him to give me more or ask him to back off. The sensation was almost too intense, and I felt like I might shatter at any moment. He eased a finger inside me, pumping it in and out. The friction combined with his assault on my clit was enough to make me come so hard I thought I saw stars.

If anyone had told me the things I'd seen on TV or read about in romances were actually true, I wouldn't have believed them. Until Stripes, I'd never had proof sex could be this good. Now that I'd tasted it, I wanted more. I wasn't sure I'd ever get enough.

Mikhail came up over me again, staring down into my face. He smoothed my hair back. "Still want to continue?"

I nodded, trying to catch my breath.

He got out of bed long enough to strip out of his pants, then joined me again. His cock was already hard, and my fingers twitched as I fought the urge to touch him. It wasn't that I thought he'd stop me. I just didn't think I was ready yet. I needed to let Stripes take the lead tonight, if for no other reason than to prove to myself I could handle it.

"How do you want me?" he asked, reaching down and stroking his cock.

I stared, trying to process his words as I watched him. Licking my lips, I motioned for him to come closer. I'd never enjoyed giving blow jobs, but for some reason, I really wanted to taste Stripes. When he was within reach, I leaned forward and took him into my mouth. He groaned and gripped my hair, giving it a hard tug.

I licked, sucked, and teased him. The ache between my legs built again, and it amazed me that giving him pleasure had turned me on. Stripes gave my hair another pull, and I released his cock. He flipped me onto my back and settled over me, his cock pressing into me.

"Such a tease," he said, his voice a deep growl. "I need you, *lapochka*."

I stared into his eyes, needing the reassurance he was the one stroking in and out of me. I grabbed his shoulders and held on as his thrusts grew faster and deeper. My toes curled, and I moaned as he hit just the right spot, and within seconds, I was coming. He devoured my lips with his and didn't stop driving his cock into me until I felt the heat of his release spilling inside me.

"My beautiful, Melina. Did I hurt you?"

"It was perfect." I pressed my lips to his again and wondered when we could do this again. Even though I was emotionally drained, I'd enjoyed every moment.

Sex was no longer scary, or something I had to endure. No, with Stripes, I had a feeling I'd want to do this often. He made me feel special. Wanted. Maybe one day, he'd even come to love me.

His cock twitched inside me, and my eyes went wide. "Again? Now?"

He grinned. "It seems you bring out the beast in me, *lapochka*. I can't get enough of you."

I clung to him as he sent me soaring again. It seemed I'd finally found my happiness... it was right here in Stripes' arms.

* * *

Stripes

Thanks to Melina's breakthrough, and the new direction of our relationship, I didn't feel as anxious about leaving her alone. I could tell she still struggled at certain times, but in the past two weeks she'd smiled more and no longer tensed or flinched when I reached out to touch her or hold her hand. Which meant today was the first test to see how much she'd progressed.

I slipped on my cut and pulled her into my arms. The smile on her face seemed wistful, and I knew she didn't like the idea of me going back to work. I'd said before I'd take her with me. However, I didn't want to chance her having any setbacks. The Bratva might not pose a threat any longer, but it didn't mean she could be in that sort of environment. The strip club was nothing like the brothel, but I worried it would bring up bad memories.

"I'll be home in a few hours, *lapochka*. It's not a full day of work, but there are things only I can take care of." Like signing the paychecks. So far, someone had brought them to the house, and I'd handled it at home, but I really did need to check on things.

"I can call, though, right?" she asked.

"*Da.* You need anything, or just want to hear my voice, you call. I'll answer no matter what I'm doing."

"Okay." She went up on her tiptoes and pressed her lips to mine. "Be careful and come home soon."

"If you get lonely, ask Meg to come stay with you. The two of you get along well."

"I will. Hurry and go so you can get home faster."

I kissed her once more, then went out to my bike. I hadn't been on a ride in a while. Driving through the compound hadn't counted. I'd left long enough to get gas a few times. Until recently, I hadn't wanted to leave Melina alone long enough to do more than that. I started up my bike and backed down the driveway. I saw her watching from the window and waved at her before heading to the front gate. It didn't take more than fifteen minutes to reach the strip club, and I'd have loved to take a longer ride. But duty called.

The girls all squealed and called out to me as I made my way to the back office. I knew Gator and a few other brothers had kept an eye on them. Mostly Gator, though. Still, this place was my responsibility, and it was nice to be back. The girls trusted me, the bouncers fucking feared me, and I liked feeling useful to the club.

At one point, I'd thought about asking Charming to find me a different job. With everything my granddaughter Minnie had been through, it hadn't felt right working here. However, the girls weren't forced to work at this place, and they needed protection. Minnie hadn't been bothered, so the only way I'd leave is if it truly troubled my wife. I wanted to keep her happy.

A knock sounded on the office door right as I was sitting down. "Come in."

One of the girls, Misty, gave me a bright smile. I kept my gaze on her face, ignoring her bare breasts. This part Melina wouldn't like. It didn't matter that I didn't feel the least bit attracted to these women. My wife was still fragile, and I knew there were still times she doubted her beauty and worth. If she saw Misty in here right now, without her clothes on, Melina would start comparing herself to the stripper.

"Stripes, can I talk to you for a minute?"

"What is it, Misty?"

"Um, did Gator happen to say anything about the shady men who started coming by recently?"

"*Nyet*. What men?" I leaned forward in my chair. What the fuck had been going on while I'd been at home? And why hadn't Gator done something about it already?

"These guys started showing up about two weeks ago. They give me the creeps. Same for the other girls. Anyway, one of them tried to drag Rey off the stage. They waited for her outside when she got off work, and nearly kidnapped her. So... we're a little scared right now."

"What the fuck?" I ran a hand down my face. "If you see them, come get me, yes? I'll handle it."

"Thanks, Stripes!" She smiled brightly. "And congratulations on your marriage! Gator said that's why you hadn't been here."

"*Da*. I got married and have been spending time with my new wife."

"She's super lucky to have a guy like you." Misty waved at me and left the office with a bounce in her step.

Why hadn't Gator handled those men? Or anyone else, for that matter. Who were they? If I'd been here and seen that shit happen, they'd have been banned from this establishment. Looked like I'd have to sign the checks and spend the rest of my shift out on the floor. So much for catching up on paperwork.

Before I left my office, I sent a text to Gator. *Is there a reason you didn't handle the problem at the club? The girls are scared.*

He replied instantly. *It wasn't my place. I kept an eye on them. Didn't feel right doing anything else. That's your club.*

Why did I feel like he'd just not wanted to take responsibility for those men? No matter how prettily he said it, that's what I got from his statement. By the time I made it to the main floor, music pulsed throughout the room, and Rey was up on stage. The waitresses kept the drinks flowing, and the patrons seemed to be behaving themselves. Except for one table. I caught Misty's eye across the room, and she tipped her head toward them. Looked like our troublemakers had arrived.

One of them tried to grab the ass of a woman walking by, and I knew I'd need to intervene. We had a no-touching policy. Even when the girls gave a lap dance, the men weren't permitted to put their hands on them.

I walked up behind the man with the grabby hands and squeezed his shoulder. He tried to slouch in the chair to get away from my grip, but I didn't let up.

"Gentlemen, perhaps you are unaware, but the club has a no-touching policy when it comes to the ladies. Please keep your hands to yourself, yes?"

"Do you know who we are?" one of the younger men asked, starting to stand up.

I kicked the leg of his chair, sending it out from under him, and he crashed to the floor. When the others made a move, I pulled my gun and trained it on the closest one, while keeping my hold of the one in front of me.

"I do not care who you are. Only that you follow the rules." I smiled at each of them and enjoyed the way the younger ones flinched. The man I still held down, however, seemed to be the leader. They kept glancing his way and seemed nervous. "If you cannot keep your hands to yourselves, I'll be forced to ask you to leave."

"We go where we please," their leader said. "Since you don't seem to know who you're speaking to, my name is Reyes, and I'm the leader of the Dark Scorpions."

Of course. Naturally, the most recent gang in the area would decide to come in here and cause problems.

Probably thought they could run us out of here and take over the club. Or pilfer the girls until we didn't have any talent left.

"I think it is you who does not understand. This strip club is the property of the Devil's Boneyard, and so are the girls who work here. Break the rules again, and I'll take it to mean you want a war between my club and your gang."

"Whatever."

The man stood and tried to shrug me off. I squeezed tighter for a moment before releasing him. They all left, but I didn't miss the glare Reyes gave me on his way out the door. That one would cause problems. I waved over one of the bouncers.

"If they linger outside, call the police. And do not let those men into this club again."

"You got it, Stripes."

I watched the floor another half hour, and when I was satisfied no one would cause trouble, I went back to the office to deal with the paperwork. Melina didn't call, which surprised me. I hoped it meant Meg had come over and they were having a nice time. I managed to pay most of the bills, sorted the rest of the items on my desk, and then decided I'd had enough for the day.

I shouldn't have been so cocky. Even if the bouncers hadn't said anything about Reyes and his men still lurking, it didn't mean they weren't there. And that mistake would cost me.

I heard two pops and felt a burning pain that nearly took me to my knees. I glanced down and saw the red blooming across my shirt. *Motherfucker shot me!* The bouncer shouted, and I heard his steps racing toward me. I went down to my knees, and everything started to spin.

"Hold on, Stripes!"

"Melina… Need Melina." I couldn't do this to her. I'd promised I'd be home, and that's where I needed to go.

"Is that your wife?" he asked.

"*Da*. Promised I'd come home soon."

"All right. I'm sure your club would prefer to patch you up and deal with those assholes anyway. Someone will have to come back for your bike, but I'm going to take you home. Don't pass out."

I fought to keep my eyes open. Two men helped me into a vehicle, but I was too far gone from the pain to pay any attention to who was helping me. Even though he'd said not to pass out, that's exactly what I did the moment the car door shut.

Chapter Nine

Melina

I heard a car pull into the driveway and went to peek out the window. I didn't recognize the vehicle, nor the large man who got out. But when he opened the passenger door, and I saw Stripes, I ran from the house without thinking. The blood soaking my husband's shirt had panic filling me.

"What happened?" I asked.

"Some men were waiting outside the strip club. Shot him. He said to bring him home. Are you Melina?"

I startled, not prepared to hear my name. Had Stripes talked about me while he'd been at work? "Yes. I'm his wife."

Two of the Devil's Boneyard brothers were riding past and stopped. I recognized Samurai, and the other man looked similar to him. Perhaps the one they called Phantom? I still hadn't met most of the club. I hadn't felt ready, but it seemed I wouldn't have a choice now.

"What's going on, Melina?" Samurai asked. "Holy shit!"

He froze when he saw the blood. Without another word, the three men lifted Stripes from the car and carried him into the house. They took him straight back to the bedroom and eased him down onto the bed. Samurai removed my husband's cut and passed it to me. I noticed the bullet went through the leather, and I knew Stripes would be angry about it. I wondered if it could be repaired.

A groan drew my gaze to the bed. Stripes' head tossed and turned and sweat coated his brow. Samurai ripped Stripes' shirt down the middle and winced when he saw the two wounds. One had gone through his shoulder, and the other was in his chest. My heart nearly stopped when I saw how close I'd been to losing him.

"He needs a doctor," I said. Why hadn't one been called already? How had this man pulled through the gates without anyone alerting the President, or at least someone, that Stripes had been injured?

"We'll get him one. Wait here with him, Melina. If he said he wanted to come home, it meant he wanted to be with you," Samurai said. I stared at him, not knowing how he'd heard what the man said. He hadn't arrived yet. He smiled slightly. "The only reason one of the strip club employees wouldn't have taken him to the clinic or hospital is if he asked to come home. It wasn't magic. Just deductive reasoning."

"Thank you, Samurai. And... Phantom?" I asked, looking up at the other man.

"Phantom is my cousin by blood, but he's part of the Devil's Boneyard, so in that sense we're brothers. He's also the club Treasurer, which makes him an officer."

"I'll bring a doctor," Phantom said. "I think Samurai should stay here in case you need anything."

Phantom grabbed the arm of the man who'd brought Stripes home and led him from the house. I realized I hadn't even learned the man's name. I hoped I'd get a chance to thank him some other time. I didn't want to contemplate what might have happened if he hadn't found Stripes and brought him home.

"I'll send someone to get his bike and bring it home," Samurai said. He pulled out his phone and tapped on the screen. I figured he was sending someone a text message, and I turned to focus on Stripes again. The wounds still bled, and I worried about him. Hurrying into the bathroom, I got two clean hand towels and rushed back to Stripes' side.

I pressed them to his wounds, hoping to slow the bleeding. My heart hammered against my ribs. What would happen if he didn't make it through this? No, I didn't want to think about it. He had to live! Things were just starting to become good in my life, and the entire reason was lying here bleeding all over the bed. Without Stripes, I'd be dead by now.

"The VP already knew Stripes had been shot. He put some things into motion, so everything should work out fine. But the club wants to come check on Stripes." Samurai held my gaze. "I can hold them off if you want. It's your call, Melina. You're his wife, and this is your home."

"They all want to come?" I asked, panic welling inside me again.

"What if we just let Charming come see him? He's the club President."

"All right." I swallowed hard. I hadn't met Charming yet. Stripes spoke of him from time to time. He sounded like a nice man. What if he blamed me for what happened to Stripes? That man from the strip club hadn't said any of this was related to the motorcycle club, or to the Bratva, but what if it was? Stripes had sounded certain the Bratva wouldn't come for me. Had he only been trying to soothe my fears? Or did this really not have anything to do with them?

"It's going to be okay, Melina. We'll help in whatever way we can. That's what it means to be part of this club. We're a family."

Family. I knew he meant for the word to bring me comfort, but it didn't. I'd had one of those. Two daughters. A ruthless husband who'd hurt me every chance he had. And my girls... I wasn't ready to see them. To speak to them. I couldn't handle the thought they might see me as tainted. Broken. I also worried they blamed me for everything they'd suffered at the hands of their father. I should have taken them and run a long time ago. I'd been too scared.

I continued pressing the towels to Stripes' wounds and waited for help to arrive. The club President showed up first, and I heard him speaking in a low voice to Samurai. I didn't know what they were discussing. None of it mattered, unless they'd found a way to heal Stripes and keep him alive.

Stripes took a shuddering breath. When he exhaled, he stopped breathing. I cried out, tears streaking my cheeks. "No. No, no, no. Please, Mikhail. Breathe! I need you to breathe!"

I sobbed as Samurai moved me out of the way. I watched as he did CPR, and I pressed a hand to my mouth. My vision blurred, and I sank to my knees, crying so hard it felt like I would break apart at any moment.

"Fuck! Come on, you stubborn bastard," Samurai said.

I closed my eyes and did something I hadn't done in forever. I prayed.

Please. Don't take Stripes away. The world still needs him. If you have to take someone, let it be me. Please. Please. I beg you!

"Where the hell is the damn doctor?" Charming asked.

"Damnit, Stripes! Don't do this shit." Samurai kept up with the chest compressions, and after a moment, he gave a triumphant cry. "Got him!"

I ran to the bed and pressed my forehead to Stripes'. "Don't leave me, Mikhail. I need you to keep breathing. Fight!"

A man rushed into the room with a medical bag in his hand. "I need some space."

Samurai pulled me away from Stripes. The blood on his hands smeared down my arms, but I didn't care. I watched from across the room as the doctor worked on him. The bullet in his shoulder had passed through. The one in his chest had remained inside his body. The doctor dug it out before stitching him up.

"He should have gone to the damn hospital," the doctor muttered. "Stubborn fool."

"Will he be all right?" I asked. "He's going to make it, isn't he?"

"As long as he rests and doesn't tear open his wounds, he should be okay. You need to watch for signs of a fever or infection. He doesn't like prescription painkillers, so the best you can do is get him to take some Motrin." The doctor came closer, and I shrank back against Samurai. "Taking care of him won't be easy. You'll need to help him to the bathroom. If he wants to shower, he needs to cover the sutures with waterproof bandages. Or he can sit in the tub and wash everywhere but that shoulder and his chest."

"I'll take good care of him," I promised.

"I'll help her," Samurai offered. "We all will."

"Fine. I'll stop by in a few days and check on him. If anything happens between now and then, you know where to find me."

The doctor left, and I hurried over to Stripes' side once more. I carefully crawled onto the bed beside him. Placing my hand on his cheek, I leaned down and pressed my lips to his. "You were supposed to come home safe. You broke your promise."

"Sorry." I gasped and stared at him. Stripes slowly opened his eyes. "*Lapochka*."

I bit my lip so I wouldn't start crying again. "I'll take the best care of you."

"I know." He smiled a little before falling asleep.

Samurai walked over to the door and paused. "I'm going to let Grey know what's going on, then I'll come back. I know you don't feel like eating, but you'll need to keep up your strength. I'll fix something for you. Focus on Stripes for now."

"Thank you. For everything."

Samurai winked and walked away, leaving me with Stripes. I lay beside him, being careful not to bump him. The last thing I wanted to do was to cause him any pain.

* * *

Stripes

I didn't know how long I'd been out of it. Judging by the smell of my body, it had been a few days. Melina slept beside me, but with some space between us. I didn't like her being so far away, even if I understood it. She probably worried she'd hurt me. Silly woman!

Booted steps came toward the bedroom, and I eyed the doorway. Samurai smiled when he saw I was awake.

"I started to think she'd have to wake you with a kiss."

"Fucker. This isn't a fairytale. You've watched one too many cartoons with your children."

"In all seriousness, we've been worried. You woke for a brief moment the night you got shot, and then nothing. I've had to force-feed Melina. She didn't want to eat. Hasn't slept much. Hell, she barely leaves your side."

"How long?" I asked, my throat feeling dry and

scratchy.

"Five days. You had a fever. Doc had to come back and give you antibiotics because one of the wounds became infected."

"And the guy who shot me?" I asked.

Samurai shook his head. "In the wind. We found several Dark Scorpions, but we couldn't make any of them talk. The one who waited for you outside the strip club was their leader. We've been watching and waiting. No sign of him. Charming has Shade working on it, and I think he's asked for help from Wire and Wizard. We'll find that asshole sooner or later, unless someone else gets to him first. I'd imagine you're not the first person he's pissed off."

It wasn't what I wanted to hear, but I couldn't do a damn thing about it right now. And if the fucker really had left town, I might never get a chance to settle the score. I'd damn sure watch the Dark Scorpions, though, and they wouldn't be allowed in the strip club. Not now, not ever.

"I need a shower," I mumbled.

"Not sure you can stand to take one. Give me a bit. I'll find one of those shower stools. A Prospect can pick one up and bring it here." He pulled his phone out. "We have to cover your wounds with waterproof bandages too. You can't get the stitches wet."

"How's Melina?"

"Honestly? Not good. It about destroyed her when she thought you might die. I know the two of you were already married when you met for the first time, but it's clear she cares for you. I'd even go so far as to say she probably loves you."

I turned my face toward her. As much as I wanted to reach out and touch her, I didn't dare move my arm. I knew it would hurt like a bitch. When it came time to clean myself up, I'd have no choice but to move it. Until then, I'd rest it a bit more.

"I'll bring you some water and get someone to find that shower stool. You need to use the bathroom?" Samurai asked.

"Yeah."

"Come on. I'll help you with that first."

I bit back the curses that sprang to my lips as he helped me from the bed. I staggered my way into the bathroom, and he thankfully left while I pissed. After I flushed the toilet, Samurai came back and assisted me back into bed. Melina didn't wake up, and I worried about her. I could see the dark circles under her eyes, and it looked like she'd lost some weight. Her face appeared gaunt.

I reached for her hand, ignoring the pain in my shoulder. I couldn't wait another moment to touch her. It had to have scared her when I came home unconscious. Not to mention Samurai being here. While she knew him, I hadn't thought she was ready to interact with the club yet. Men made her nervous, and I understood why.

"You died," Samurai said. "Only for a minute or two, but your heart stopped. Melina fell apart."

"What?" I turned my face his way. "I fucking died?"

He nodded. "I did CPR and brought you back. Doc arrived right after and patched you up."

I didn't know what the hell to say to that. I'd died? I'd often heard people talk about what happened when they had an experience like that. Except I didn't remember anything. "Thank you."

"We're family, Stripes. It wasn't like I was going to sit back and do nothing." He looked over at Melina. "That one right there... I think if you hadn't pulled through, she'd have died right alongside you."

"You cannot let that happen. If something ever happens to me…"

Samurai snorted. "Brother, something *did* happen. You. Fucking. Died. You stopped breathing. Your heart wasn't beating. I don't know how those men got the drop on you. Whatever is going on inside your head, figure your shit out. You have a woman counting on you."

"I know."

"She's tough, I'll give her that. Once she pulled herself together, she did everything she could for you. You've got a good one."

I smiled. "I do. She's stronger than she thinks."

"Your water is on the bedside table. Can you reach it?"

"*Da.*" Even if it I couldn't, I'd figure it out. I refused to have Samurai baby me.

"Then I'm going to make a few calls in the other room, and I'll let everyone know you're awake. We've all been worried about you, Stripes."

"It's good to be awake." If only the club had managed to catch the man who shot me. Then things would be close to perfect. I'd love to make him pay.

"Charming will stop by soon. I'm sure he'll give you the official update on the man who shot you, and the Dark Scorpions. It wasn't really my place to say anything."

I wrinkled my nose, thinking about how I smelled. "Ask him to wait a few hours. I want to get cleaned up, and I want time with Melina."

"You got it." Samurai walked out. I appreciated everything he'd done for me while I'd been healing, but I was thankful he'd given me some space.

I tightened my hold on Melina's hand and she

opened her eyes, moaning and rubbing at her face. She froze and glanced down at our joined hands before lifting her gaze to mine.

"Mikhail…" Her eyes grew glassy with unshed tears, and I motioned for her to come closer. She shook her head. "I don't want to hurt you."

"You won't, *lapochka*. Come. I need to hold you." She carefully pressed against my side, and I put my arm around her. My wounds pulled, but I'd deal with the pain and discomfort. "I'm sorry for scaring you, Melina. Samurai said I died for a short time."

"You did. Please don't ever do that again!"

"I'll be more careful in the future. After all, I have something precious here at home. My sweet little wife." I kissed her temple. "I will not leave you alone, *lapochka*. It's why I tried so hard to come home."

"Not that I want there to be a next time. However, if there is, please go to the hospital and have someone call me instead. I think my heart nearly stopped along with yours."

I murmured *I'm sorry* again and again. Whatever it took, I'd make it up to her. I was proud of the fact she'd handled men being in our home. She hadn't fallen apart. Or if she had, it hadn't been bad enough for anyone to mention it. Samurai said my short death devastated her. There had been no word about her reaction to people coming into the house.

Samurai came in a little while later with a shower stool. I felt like a decrepit old man, but I'd been in bed for so long I worried my legs wouldn't hold me long enough to get clean. He carried it into the bathroom, and I sat up. Melina helped cover my wounds with waterproof bandages. With Samurai's assistance, I made it into the bathroom. Melina followed and closed the door after Samurai left, then I began the slow process of removing my jeans and underwear. I couldn't believe they'd left me in the same clothes all this time.

Then again, Melina wouldn't have been able to change me by herself, and the others probably hadn't wanted to do anything to make her uncomfortable. I appreciated the fact they worried not only about me, but my wife as well. I had no doubt they'd taken her issues into consideration.

I held onto Melina as I got into the shower and sat on the stool. She started the water, angling the shower head so the cold spray wouldn't hit me. Once it was the right temperature, she removed the shower head and soaked my hair before spraying down my body.

"I can wash myself," I said.

"I think I need to do this." She kissed my cheek. "I was so scared, Mikhail. I still can't believe you're awake and talking to me. Please, let me help you bathe. I need to feel useful right now."

"Of course, *lapochka*. Do whatever you wish."

Despite the fact I'd just woken after nearly a week, her soft touch against my skin was enough to make my cock hard. She noticed and a blush stained her cheeks. She lathered my hair and beard, washed my skin, then rinsed me off. With a quick glance at the bathroom door, she soaped her hands again before kneeling in front of me.

I couldn't stop myself from watching as she wrapped her hand around my cock and gave it a stroke. Something told me if I came right now, I'd be asleep again in no time. As much as I wanted to stay awake, I couldn't bring myself to stop her right now. The heated look in her eyes and the playful smile on her lips made me wish the moment could last forever.

It only took a few more tugs on my cock before I was coming. I groaned and gripped the side of the stool so I'd remain upright.

"Melina, you didn't have to do that, but thank you." She pressed her lips to mine, and I kissed her soft and slow. When she pulled back, I realized I'd overdone it. I felt dizzy and like I might go to sleep soon.

"I'll get you some clean clothes," she said. I hadn't even realized until this moment that she hadn't undressed all the way. Her bra and panties remained on, and she yanked a T-shirt over her head before going into the bedroom. She returned with pajamas for herself, as well as underwear and sweatpants for me.

It humbled me to have her dress me, like I was little more than a child. And yet she did it without complaint. By the time I got back into the bed, I was barely awake. I heard Charming's voice, but the President would have to wait. I gripped Melina's hand as she lay beside me and let sleep claim me once more.

Chapter Ten

Melina
One Month Later

So many people had been in and out of the house while Stripes healed. When he'd started back to work two weeks ago, I'd been scared to death he wouldn't make it home. I still felt anxious every time he left the house.

Meg called out my name as she entered the house. "Where are you?"

"Bedroom! I'm folding laundry."

She stopped in the doorway and leaned against the doorframe. "You should be resting. Tonight is going to be stressful for you. We all know that, but it's time, Melina."

"I've met almost everyone, haven't I?"

"This is different. It's the club's way of welcoming you. Besides, Stripes said he had a surprise he's never been able to give you. He wants to make a big production of it, I guess, so he's doing it during the party."

"What am I supposed to wear to this thing?" I asked.

"Anything you want. Most of us go in jeans. Some wear casual dresses. It just depends on what makes you comfortable." Meg came farther into the room and lowered her voice. "I'm not supposed to know this, but I heard Cinder talking on the phone. The Bratva is backing down. Has Stripes said anything to you?"

"What?" I froze in the middle of folding one of Stripes' shirts. What did that mean? *Backing down.* He'd already told me they wouldn't be an issue, but he hadn't given me details. Had it not been a certain thing until just now?

She nodded. "Yeah. Apparently, they made a deal with the Dixie Reapers. I guess your daughter is there? Anyway, they aren't going to come after you, Melina. You're free! You can leave the compound. Get a job. Go shopping. Whatever you want! Isn't it amazing?"

It was… unsettling, that's what it was. Why would they do that? What had Oksana given them in exchange? My stomach churned. Those people were supposed to protect her, right? Stripes mentioned she was married to one of them. They wouldn't have handed her over to the Bratva, would they? No. Stripes would have told me if something like that happened, wouldn't he? So why had the Bratva backed off?

"Shit. You're getting paler by the minute. Melina, what's wrong?" Meg asked.

"Oksana… what did she promise them?" I asked. "Did she trade herself for us?"

"Oh, honey. No! Nothing like that. I can guarantee that Grimm wouldn't let those bastards have her. I don't know all the details. Maybe Stripes will tell you later. Now come on. You need to put all this away and take a nap. You look ready to drop."

She wasn't wrong. I felt lightheaded all of a sudden. Meg helped me move the rest of the clothes off the bed and I stretched out. She pulled the covers over me and then left so I could rest. I wasn't sure if I could sleep, though.

Why would the Bratva just give up? And what did she mean the Dixie Reapers had made a deal? What did it entail? Would Oksana or I have to do something for them? Or worse, did it involve this club as well? I worried what would happen if we had to get involved with the Bratva. They couldn't be trusted. No one knew that better than me.

I turned onto my side and stared at the bedroom door. How much longer until he came home? He'd been gone several hours. He'd promised not to be away all day. I didn't like the idea of him being around all those naked women. It didn't matter that he said he wasn't interested in them. How could he possibly ignore the naked breasts in his face? Mine weren't overly large, and at my age, they'd started to sag. Were those women prettier than me?

I stood and went into the bathroom, stripping off my clothes along the way. I stared at my reflection in the mirror. I'd filled out quite a bit since coming here. Even though I'd lost weight when Stripes came home wounded, I'd put the pounds back on in the last few weeks. My hips flared out, and my waist dipped in. I cupped my breasts, lifting them. The moment I released them, they dropped back to where they'd been. I remembered them being perkier.

"What are you doing, *lapochka*?"

I squealed and spun to face Stripes. "When did you get home?"

"Now. Again I ask, what are you doing?"

"I was just…" How did I explain I felt inferior to the women who surrounded him at his job? I didn't want to sound jealous. I was, but still…"Sometimes, I don't recognize my own body. It's not the same shape as it once was. I have stretch marks from being pregnant. My breasts sag. Not to mention all the scars from the Bratva."

"Melina, what brought this on? It seems rather sudden." He came closer and placed his hands on my hips. Turning me to face the mirror, he stared at our reflection over my head. "Do you wish to know what I see?"

"Tell me," I said softly.

"My wife. She's beautiful. I like the silky feel of her skin. The way her hair always smells. She fits against me perfectly." He leaned down to kiss my shoulder. "Does my job bother you, *lapochka*?"

"I'm not asking you to quit your job."

"That's not what I asked."

I sighed and leaned back against him. "Does it bother me? Yes. It's not that I think you're going to touch them or cheat on me. I just know they have to be prettier than I am. How can you look at them all the time, then come home to… this?"

I waved my hand down my body and heard Stripes' low growl. He pushed me forward, bending me over the counter. I gasped and gripped the edge to hold myself steady.

"I haven't been hard all fucking day. Not until I came home and found my wife staring at herself in the mirror. Naked." I heard the rasp of his zipper, then felt his cock press against me. "And now, my cock is hard as a rock. What should we do about it, Melina?"

I wiggled my ass against him. "You know what to do with it."

He nipped at my shoulder, then my neck. "Tell me. I need the words, Melina."

"Fuck me, Mikhail. Please. I need you inside me."

He kicked my legs wider apart, and I felt his fingers slide along my pussy. I closed my eyes briefly. The first swipe across my clit had me moaning and wanting to beg for more.

"That's it. Come for me, *lapochka*."

He stroked the hard little bud until my knees nearly buckled. I couldn't even catch my breath before he worked his cock inside me, stretching me. I tightened my hold on the counter as he filled me. With one hand on my hip, and the other splayed in front of me, he rocked his hips against mine. Every thrust sent me up onto my toes, and hit all the right spots.

"Yes, Mikhail! More!"

"You make me feel decades younger, Melina. I can't get enough of you." He kissed my neck before burying his face against my skin. He made me come twice more before I felt the heat of his release inside me. He didn't pull out right away. If anything, he tried to push deeper into me.

"My legs are cramping."

He chuckled. "All right. Let's lie down for a bit. We don't have to get ready just yet, but soon, yes?"

"Whatever you want, Mikhail. As long as we're together, I don't care where we are or what we do."

He wrapped an arm around my waist. "I love you, Melina. I think I started falling for you the first day we met, and my love has only grown deeper for you since then."

I closed my eyes and let his words wash over me. "I love you too. So much."

"Come. Maybe I can make you scream my name once more."

He lifted me into his arms and carried me to the bed. I really did love him. Adored him, in fact. He was my fairytale hero. My prince charming. And now that I had him, and knew he loved me, I was never letting him go.

* * *

Stripes

The clubhouse was noisy. Music played in the background, but it was the conversations flowing around me, and the laughter of the children that made it so loud. Still, I preferred family nights over the parties. It had been that way for a while now.

Charming stood on a table and clapped his hands to get everyone's attention. Melina leaned against me, a smile on her face. I could tell she was enjoying herself, even if she did look a bit tired.

"Everyone, I have some good news to share. As you all know, the issue with the Bratva has been resolved, thanks to the Dixie Reapers. However, they have a proposition for us, one the Bratva instigated. I can assure you it's something you'd be proud to be part of. I think we can call this one a win, since no one got hurt, or died. The Bratva could have caused a lot of problems not only for us, but the other clubs too. I think this is going to be a good thing. We'll discuss it in Church tomorrow. For now, everyone have fun!"

Charming got down off the table. The Prospect behind the bar passed me the box I'd stashed back there. I handed it to Melina and watched as she opened it.

"It's a property cut," I explained. "I've had it for a while. The timing was never right, so I'm giving it to you now."

She lifted it from the box and handed it to me. I helped her slip it on and knew I'd be fucking her again later while she wore it. Christ! It was like I was twenty again. Only Melina made me feel this way.

"Now you're a proper old lady," Meg said from a table nearby.

"Go, *lapochka*. Visit with your friends while you can. When we get home, I have plans for you."

She kissed me and hurried off to sit with Meg, Grey, and Clarity. I joined Cinder, Charming, and Havoc at the bar. The Prospect handed me a beer, and I popped the top before taking a long swallow. Smiling,

I watched the teens in the corner playing on their phones, trying to act cool. The younger ones either ran around the room or played board games at the tables.

"The two of you going to add to the population around here?" Havoc asked.

"*Nyet*. Melina cannot have more children," I said.

"That there is the keyword. More." Havoc grinned. "You've both had families before all this. Doesn't mean you can't build one together."

Grimm had called not too long ago and pointed out I had two daughters now. Yulia and Oksana. In fact, Oksana had already called me Dad. It had made me feel all warm inside. I didn't know when I'd get a chance to meet Yulia. Shade had informed me she was every bit as damaged as Melina had been. Maybe more so. It was taking her a long while to heal. I'd tried to keep tabs on the girls through the club's hacker, in the hopes I'd be able to pass along any good news to my wife.

Even though I'd told Oksana her mother wasn't ready to see her, I wondered if that was still true. She'd settled in nicely here. When my brothers came around, she no longer flinched or looked ready to bolt. Up until I'd been shot, she'd still startled like a deer. During my recovery, she'd gotten even stronger than before.

"What are you getting at, Havoc?" Charming asked.

"Does Melina want more children?" he asked.

"She..." Now that I thought about it, she hadn't denied she wanted them. I'd told her I didn't want a baby in the house, and she'd gone along with it. Then she'd informed me she couldn't have children, anyway. But had she wanted to start a family with me? "Fuck."

"Yeah, that's what I thought." Havoc smirked.

"I can see why she'd want more children," Charming said. "Her life was hell with the Bratva. That shithead husband of hers probably dictated every little part of their lives. So, meeting a guy like you, being married to you, it probably made her wonder what it would be like to have a family together."

"I'm too old to raise a baby," I said.

"Then don't." Charming shrugged. "There are children in need of homes. No one said you had to only raise your biological family. Make one. With Melina."

I looked over at my wife. She laughed at something Clarity said. What would she think of this discussion? Would it intrigue her? Or did she care about starting over? Her girls were grown now. Or rather, Oksana was. Yulia had a few years before she became an adult, but it wasn't like either of them were in diapers anymore.

"I wasn't going to say anything yet, but the meeting tomorrow is about helping the Bratva remove women from bad situations. A few of them want to make changes within the organization, but they can't just bulldoze through there. They need to move slow. Until then, they'll sneak out women who need a fresh start. Like Melina, Oksana, and Yulia." Charming rapped his knuckles on the bar top. "Part of that will also be finding homes for kids who got caught up in whatever bad shit their parents did."

"Are you saying there's a child now who needs a home?" I asked.

"*Da*." Charming smiled. "Remember my friend?"

"The one who helped us before?"

"That one. He's on his way with two kids. A girl and a boy. He said one is eight and the other is twelve. I'm not sure which is which. If you want to adopt one of them, let me know. The club will let you have first pick."

"First pick of what?" Melina asked. I put my arm around her waist and kissed her on the forehead.

"The President said two children are coming here. They need new families. He wondered if we wanted to adopt one of them."

Her eyes went wide, and I saw the excitement sparking in them for a brief moment, before she shuttered her expression. Ah. So she wanted more children, but because I'd made a big deal out of not having babies, she didn't want me to know. I really was an ass sometimes.

"*Lapochka*, do you want to adopt one of them?" I asked.

Charming glanced at his phone. "You can actually meet them right now. Want to head outside with me?"

We followed him out of the clubhouse. Two children stood on the steps. The smaller one was a girl. She had dark hair and blue eyes. The boy was already closing in on six feet, and I knew he'd be even taller before he was fully grown. His dark eyes didn't miss anything as they scanned the surrounding area.

Charming went to speak with his friend, while I kneeled in front of the little girl.

"My name is Stripes," I said. "What's yours?"

"Ekaterina," she mumbled.

"I'm Anatoly," the boy said. "The man who drove us here said we would be meeting our new parents. Are you going to be our father?"

His words hit me straight in the gut. Both of them? It made sense if they'd known each other before today. They wanted to remain together. I looked up at Melina and saw the way she eyed the children. She wanted them. I didn't even have to ask her.

"*Da*. I'm your new father, Stripes, and this is your mother, Melina. We were not prepared for your arrival, but we'll figure things out." I stood and lifted the little girl into my arms. She clung to me and buried her face against my shoulder. "Come. We'll show you to your new home."

Melina followed me. I left the bike outside the clubhouse, and we walked back to the house. When we got there, I showed the children the only other bedroom with furniture. It might have been Minnie's room up to this point, but starting tomorrow, that would no longer be the case. I only hoped my granddaughter understood and didn't feel as if I were replacing her mother -- or her. I had enough room in my heart for all of them.

"I'll sleep on the couch tonight," Anatoly said. "Ekaterina can have the bed."

The little girl reached for him. "Toly, I don't want to sleep alone."

"There's no reason the two of you cannot share for this one night. Tomorrow, we'll get a bedroom set up for each of you, yes?"

We let the kids go into the room and shut the door. As much as I wanted to talk with them more, I had a feeling they'd had a hard day. Melina took my hand and led me to our room.

"Are you sure about this, Mikhail? You didn't want to raise a family. You said you were too old."

"I said I did not want a baby. Neither of those children are babies. It's fine, Melina. I know you wanted to give them a home. Besides, who better to raise two Russian children than us?"

She smiled up at me. "Thank you. Tomorrow will be busy. There's so much they'll need."

"We'll take them shopping. And at some point, we need to tell the rest of our family. I do not know how Minnie will take the news. She hasn't even met you yet, and already we've expanded and brought in more children."

She reached up to cup my cheek. "Because she's your blood, I'd imagine she's every bit as kind as you. She'll be grateful we took in the children."

I had a feeling she was right. I'd find out tomorrow when I spoke with Minnie. For now, I'd settle for holding my wife and cuddling in bed. The plans I'd had were no longer an option. While I knew parents had sex with their kids in the house all the time, it didn't seem right to do so on their first night in a new house. In the event either of them needed us, I wanted to be ready to run to their room at a moment's notice.

"Come, my wife. We'll sleep for now. We'll need to be well-rested for tomorrow, yes?"

"I love you, Mikhail. Thank you for believing in me. For giving me the time I needed to heal, and for creating a family with me."

"Always, *lapochka*."

* * *

Melina

I couldn't believe Stripes had given in so easily. Anatoly seemed reluctant to trust us, but I didn't blame him in the least. I had no doubt he'd been hurt by the Bratva, possibly in ways we'd never know. All I could do was show him that I wouldn't harm him, and only wanted to shower the two of them with affection. This was my chance for a fresh start!

I loved my girls, and one day soon, I'd be ready to see them. Yet, I couldn't deny all the mistakes I'd made. The times I should have protected them better from Ruslan. Or the fact I should have taken them and run a long time ago. Instead, I'd stayed, and we'd all paid the price. While I hadn't heard any details about Oksana or Yulia, I knew the Bratva well. Whatever Feliks had said could have been nothing more than lies. What had those monsters done to my babies?

While I didn't know everything that had happened with the Bratva, I did know I was safe, and so were my daughters. We could all have a fresh start in life. It only saddened me that we couldn't be together. However, Oksana was married to someone in another club, and Stripes said yet another one was taking care of Yulia. They'd spread us out for fear the Bratva would find us easier if we were together. I could understand their reasoning.

Neither Anatoly nor Ekaterina had clothes, other than what they'd arrived in. Clarity had helped procure a few things for them. Today, we would go on our first family outing and buy everything they needed. Stripes had already asked some of his brothers to clear out the two spare rooms and put everything into storage.

Grey and Meg were waiting for us outside, and I waved at them. The two ladies kept their distance, since both children eyed everyone as if they might be the enemy. In time, they'd learn this was their new family, just as I had. Grey motioned to me, and I went to see what she wanted.

"While the four of you are gone, we're going to paint one of the rooms a light gray for Anatoly and a pale yellow for Ekaterina. It should be dry by the time you get back, and we'll open some windows to air out the fumes," Grey said. "Several of the old ladies and teens offered to pitch in, so it won't take long. Jordan and Havoc had some paint at their place, so we're just going to use that."

"Thank you. I'm sure they'll both like their new rooms." I hugged Grey and Meg, then climbed into the truck.

"We don't need anything," Anatoly said.

"You do." I turned to looked at him. "This is your home now. You'll need clothes, bathroom items, shoes, new furniture for your rooms, and whatever else you can think of. Books. Toys. Don't hesitate to ask for something if you want it. It doesn't mean you'll always get everything you want, but today is special. It's our first day as a family."

Ekaterina smiled at me, and I noticed two of her bottom teeth were missing. I doubted the Tooth Fairy had paid her a visit, but I'd change that with the next loose tooth. There was so much to look forward to! The Easter bunny and Santa, birthdays, helping with homework... I wondered if perhaps I was more excited about it than the children were.

I looked in the side-view mirror as we pulled out of the compound and noticed a truck following us. They stayed right behind us the entire way to the outdoor mall, and even parked next to us. Samurai and Phantom got out.

"What's going on?" I asked Stripes.

"They offered to take the furniture back and start setting up the rooms."

I got out and hugged Samurai and whispered a thank you to both of them. I helped Ekaterina from the truck, and she held tightly to my hand. Anatoly walked between me and Stripes, and I noticed he constantly scanned his surroundings. I'd seen Stripes do the same thing, but it broke my heart to observe a child doing it. What the hell had he been through?

"Furniture first," Stripes said. "Then we shop for everything else, yes?"

We decided to shop for Ekaterina first. A salesperson pointed the way to the children's bedroom sets, then left us in peace. With every set we checked out, the more reserved my new daughter seemed to become.

"Rina, what's wrong?" I asked.

She gasped and her eyes went wide. "Rina?"

I nodded. "It's a nickname. Unless you don't like it. Do you prefer being called Ekaterina?"

"I like Rina," she said softly, a bashful look crossing her face. "Toly, will you call me Rina too?"

"If that's what you want," he said.

"Rina, do you not like any of the furniture here? We can pick another store."

"It's all so pretty. Can I really pick something?"

Stripes kneeled down in front of her. "You're my daughter now, yes? I wish you to have the best. Whatever you like, you may have. Bed. Dresser. Everything. Do not worry about the cost."

"Toly too?" she asked.

Stripes smiled. "*Da.* Toly too."

"I like that one," she said, pointing to an all-white set with gold trim.

"Then we'll buy it." Stripes leaned in to kiss her cheek, and Ekaterina giggled. He stood and lifted her into his arms, carrying her off to find the saleswoman.

"Toly, want to go pick out something for your room?" I asked. He gave me a curt nod and walked off. I followed, wondering what he'd choose. When he circled the area twice, and stopped in front of the cheapest, plainest bedroom set in the store, I knew I needed to say something. "Did you pick this because it's a style and color you like? Or did you think you needed to get something inexpensive?"

He held my gaze and didn't say a word for the longest time. I saw Stripes and Ekaterina heading our way and waved them off. Something told me, if my husband came over right now, Toly would never talk to me. I needed to break through his hard outer shell and get him to open up a little.

"Toly, do you think this is only a temporary place for you?" He eyed me and gave a quick nod. I felt tears gathering in my eyes, because I understood his pain. When Stripes brought me home, I'd worried he'd get tired of me and send me away. This poor boy didn't know how to dream for a better future anymore. "It's not. I swear, you will never have to look for another home again. Not until you're old enough to move into your own place. Even then, we aren't going to throw you out. I know words don't mean anything. You've probably been lied to countless times."

I didn't know how else to reach him, so I showed him my wrists. The way he studied them, and the slight shift in his gaze, told me that he knew exactly what the marks were. Now I just needed to explain how Stripes had saved me from a fate worse than death.

"These marks are from a dark time in my life. Stripes rescued me, then he brought me to his home. I was so scared, constantly worried things would change, or that I'd find out he was lying to me. You know what happened?" I asked.

"What?"

"I fell in love with him." I smiled. "Everything he told me was true, and I discovered he was an amazing man. The best I'd ever met. So when I say you're now our son, and Ekaterina is our daughter, it means this is forever. You can go to school, make friends, and live the life of a normal twelve-year-old boy. The only expectations will be things like keeping your room clean or helping with chores around the house. Making good grades. Nothing sinister."

"Why do you want us?" he asked.

"My children are grown. You have two older sisters. One is married, and the other is in high school. They don't live with us, and I'm not sure when I'll get to see them again. Their father was a monster. We all barely escaped with our lives. You and Rina are a gift! I made mistakes with my older daughters. I didn't protect them because I was terrified of my husband. Things will be different this time. You'll have a wonderful father, and I'll get the chance to be the type of mother I wanted to be before."

"So, this is not just for us, but for you as well?"

"*Da.* For me and for Stripes. You see, he had a daughter too. He didn't get to raise her, and now she's passed away. He has a granddaughter about the age of my oldest girl. This is his chance to have a family of his own and get to do all that dad sort of stuff, like teaching you to drive a car, or fix a motorcycle. The two of you are precious to us, Toly. So please... pick something you really love, something you'll want to use for years to come. Because it's our hope you'll want to remain with us until you become an adult and want your own house."

"All right." He reached for my hand, and I threaded my fingers with his. It was a start. I only hoped the rest of the day would go smoothly.

* * *

Stripes

We'd been shopping for hours. The children had furniture, which Samurai and Phantom had taken back to the compound. They had clothes and shoes. We'd taken a break to eat lunch at a pizza buffet, since that's what the kids wanted, and now I found myself in the toy aisles at the nearest store.

Ekaterina held my hand as she stared at the shelves with a look of complete awe on her face. If it were up to me, I'd just put one of everything into the cart, but I had a feeling Melina would tell me no. Although, she'd gone to the Lego aisle with Toly, and they hadn't returned in the last twenty minutes.

"Rina, right now, you don't have any toys. There are children around your age where we live. I'm sure you'll make friends quickly, and you'll want them to come over and play, yes?" She nodded and stared up at me. "Then we need to buy some things. Has nothing caught your eye? There's not a single toy you like?"

"I like them all," she whispered.

I bit my lip so I wouldn't laugh. Of course. Before I could help her pick anything out, Melina came around the corner with a shopping cart. I arched my eyebrow as I stared. They'd filled it with Legos, video games, and a gaming system. It seemed my *lapochka* had tossed out the idea of *moderation*.

"Are we just buying everything, then?" I asked.

Her cheeks flushed. "We may have gotten slightly carried away, but he didn't really like anything other than the Legos, and I know Clarity is always talking about how much her boys like to play video games. We did get the cheaper system out of what they had available, and only a few games."

I walked over and peered into the cart. It looked like she'd already paid for the system and games. I opened the sack to see how many were inside. Three. I snorted and shook my head. I knew they were expensive, since I'd bought them for the club children on special occasions like birthdays.

"He needs a few more," I said. "I'll go with him. You help Rina select some toys. Might as well fill that cart too."

"Daddy, stay!" Ekaterina said.

It felt like I'd been punched in the chest. How long had it been since I'd stopped dreaming of ever hearing a child call me that? I kneeled in front of her and took her hand.

"You want all of us to shop together?" She nodded. I stood, keeping hold of her hand. "All right. Toly, we'll shop for your sister, then go find more games for you, yes?"

The boy smiled and started taking items off the shelves to show Ekaterina. The two of them picked out a few dolls with extra outfits, as well as a tea set. I eyed a house on the top shelf. It looked like it had animals that lived in it instead of dolls. I pulled it down and added it to the cart. Melina saw and immediately started adding furniture, the animals, and anything else that would go with it.

It didn't take long to fill the cart, and we went over to the gaming section so Toly could buy three more games. We checked out at the front and loaded everything into the bed of the truck. I knew Melina wanted to get them more things, like books, and take them to the grocery store to pick out snacks they wanted to try or already knew they enjoyed. But this vehicle wasn't made for that sort of shopping when there were four people inside it already.

We had plenty of time. For now, we'd help the children set up their rooms, and enjoy a family dinner. If it hadn't been for Charming's text earlier, I'd have bought the children bedding and curtains as well, but he said the old ladies had it covered. I didn't know what we'd be walking into, but I hoped the kids liked their new rooms.

I pulled into our driveway and noticed the place seemed empty. Whatever the club had done, they'd left when they realized we were heading home. Perhaps I shouldn't have told anyone. The children might wish to thank them for their hard work. I knew I did, and Melina would too.

"Everyone go inside. I'll call a Prospect to come unload the truck. Let's see your new rooms." I smiled as I led Ekaterina into the house. Toly stuck by Melina's side. The first room had pale butter-colored walls, and Ekaterina's furniture looked perfect against the color. Someone had hung gauze white curtains over the window. The bedding looked to be fit for a princess, as did the soft rug on the floor. I noticed a small table with two chairs. Ones I hadn't purchased. It seemed the club had really stepped up. In addition to the bed, the set had come with a dresser, nightstand, and bookshelf. We may not have made it to the bookstore today, but the ladies had provided a few story collections.

"It's beautiful," Ekaterina said.

"Like you." I winked at her. She giggled and ran off, throwing herself onto the bed.

I pulled out my phone and messaged all the Prospects, asking them to come unload the toys and put anything together that required assembly. It didn't take them long to arrive.

"Toly, are you ready to see your room?" I asked.

We checked on the bedroom that had belonged to Minnie before, and the transformation astounded me. Instead of the plain gray the ladies had mentioned for the paint, someone had added darker blue stripes on all but one wall. In addition to the full-size bed, dresser, and nightstand, Toly also had a bookshelf and a desk with a rolling chair. On top of the desk sat a computer box, with a sticker on top that read *welcome to the family*.

"I didn't pick all of this," Toly said.

"This is the club's way of welcoming you. The computer is most likely from Shade. He's our resident hacker."

"I keep thinking I'll wake up and find out I'm only dreaming, that I'm still stuck in the cage."

Cage? I wanted to ask more about his situation but didn't. Not for the moment. When he was ready, he'd let me know. Until then, I'd give him all the support I could, and make sure he knew we cared about him. Just as I'd done with Melina, I would do anything in my power to help him heal.

Once their toys were put away, and we'd ordered dinner, we sat in the living room and watched movies together. My heart felt full, and I realized that while I'd had Minnie and her children, this was far different. My family was now complete. I only hoped Oksana and Yulia would welcome the children. I hadn't met either of them yet and worried they might not like the fact their mother was starting a new life.

Soon enough, I'd find out. I knew I needed to call Grimm and Beast. They both needed to be aware our daughters were now welcome whenever they wished. Same for my *zaichik*. I wasn't sure how Doolittle had held her back so far, but she'd be here within a day or two once I placed the call.

Best to get the family reunion over with... and sort out any potential issues now rather than later.

Epilogue

Melina
Two Weeks Later

Charming had been nice enough to clear out the clubhouse for us, and I was going to see Oksana for the first time in months. Stripes' granddaughter Minnie was coming too with her family. I wasn't the only one feeling nervous. Little Ekaterina had changed her clothes at least three times, and Anatoly couldn't seem to sit still. I knew they were worried the others wouldn't accept them.

Honestly, I was a bit concerned too. What if Minnie hated me? What if Oksana couldn't forgive me for my part in all this? I'd been too scared to do something. Instead, I'd let her and Yulia grow up in a house with Ruslan, and he'd done his best to destroy them just like he had me.

"*Lapochka*, everyone is waiting for us. Are you ready?" Stripes asked. He placed a hand on my waist and kissed the top of my head. I leaned into him, wishing we could stay like this a while longer.

"I guess I am."

The four of us got into the truck and drove over to the clubhouse. We walked through the doors, and I stared at my daughter. The man beside her seemed closer to my age than hers, but the tender way he looked at her told me enough. He loved her. I couldn't ask for anything more. As long as she was happy, that's all that mattered.

"*Zaichik*," Stripes said, holding his arms open. The other woman in the room rushed over and threw herself into his embrace.

"*Dedushka*! I've missed you."

"I missed you too. How have you been?"

"Good." She smiled up at him. "The kids are excited to see you."

"Minnie, I need to introduce you to some people. My wife, Melina, and... my children." Stripes tensed, as if waiting for her to throw a fit.

"Children. The ones you said you were adopting?" she asked.

"*Da*. The adoption is done. Anatoly and Ekaterina." Stripes cleared his throat. "Melina and I talked and decided we would wait and tell everyone at the same time."

Minnie went to the kids and held out her hand. Anatoly shook it, but Ekaterina seemed unsure. After a moment, she tentatively gave Minnie a hug. It warmed my heart to see her accept the children. She hadn't spoken to me yet, or even made eye contact. It didn't matter. As long as she was nice to the kids, I could handle her disliking me. After all, she probably felt like I was trying to replace her grandmother. Or perhaps her mother, since I would be closer in age to her. Even though Stripes was her grandfather, he was the closest thing she had to a dad. I'd heard her stepfather was also gone.

"What do I call you?" Minnie asked.

"Whatever you'd like. You can just call me Melina if that's what you're comfortable with."

Minnie nodded. "All right. It's nice to meet you, Melina. I hope you and *dedushka* will be happy together. I know the kids want to meet you. After you've spoken with your daughter, come say hi."

She wandered back to her family, and I forced myself to walk over to Oksana. She hadn't approached me, and I wasn't sure how welcoming she'd be. However, she'd shown up, and that had to mean something. She wouldn't have come all this way if she hated me, would she?

"Hi, Mom," Oksana said.

"You look beautiful. Are you happy?" I asked.

"Very. Grimm is such a good man. And… we're expecting a baby!" Oksana clasped her hands in front of her. "I'm sorry we didn't tell you sooner. Stripes wasn't sure how you'd react, and I thought it might be better to talk about it in person."

"Really?" I wanted to hug her, but she hadn't made a move yet. As much as I wanted to treat her the way I always had, something held me back. Even if she did seem to be in good health, and her smile was brighter than before, there was also a darkness in her eyes. One that hadn't been there previously. What had the Bratva done to her?

"Did you know Minnie named one of her kids Oksana?" she asked. "That's going to get confusing during holidays."

"It was her mother's name," I said. "I didn't realize she'd named her little girl that, though. Stripes did tell me about Minnie's mother."

"So you have two new kids, huh?" Oksana peered around me to look at Anatoly and Ekaterina. "They look terrified."

"I'm sure they are. It's only been two weeks since we adopted them. I still don't know everything they've been through, but the Bratva had them. I doubt their lives were easy."

"Did anyone tell you about the money?" Oksana asked.

"Money?"

"The Bratva gave you money. It's in an account under your name, and you can use it for whatever you want. Save it for the kids. Take an extravagant vacation every few months. It's *a lot* of money."

"No, nobody mentioned it. I'm sure Stripes had his reasons. He'll tell me when he thinks the time is right. I'll try to appear surprised." I smiled. "I think you'll like him, Oksana. He's so good to me. I never knew men like him existed."

"I'm glad, Mom. And I know Yulia will be too."

The smile slipped from my face. No one would tell me anything about her. I'd heard they were sending her to a school. How had she ended up with another motorcycle club? And why?

"Oksana, what happened to your sister?"

"Mom, I don't think that's something you're ready to hear."

I collapsed onto a chair. I knew it. They'd hurt my little baby. No matter how much time passed, would Yulia ever want to see me again? I wouldn't blame her if she didn't.

Stripes kneeled at my side and placed his hand on my thigh. "*Lapochka*, what's wrong?"

"She asked about Yulia. I wouldn't tell her, so I think she drew her own conclusions." Oksana sighed. "You can't keep everything from her forever."

"I'm aware," Stripes mumbled. "When she's ready, I'll tell her. Until then, please refrain from upsetting your mother. I nearly lost her once already. I can't go through it again."

Oksana flinched, and I knew then, no one had told her I'd tried to kill myself. It seemed her husband was just like Stripes -- keeping things from her for her own good.

"We have the clubhouse for a few hours. Come. We'll set up a game on two different tables. It's a good way for everyone to get better acquainted." Stripes took my hand and stood. He led me to a table and pulled out a chair for me. When I saw the stack of board games nearby, I wondered which of them had prepared all this. It was a good idea, though.

And that's how we spent the next few hours... playing games and getting to know another. By the time we went home, I felt a little lighter. I still worried about Yulia, but it was nice to see how happy Oksana was, and I'd enjoyed meeting Minnie and her family.

"We should have everyone over for Christmas," I said, once we'd gotten back home.

"I think we'll need a bigger house for that, *lapochka*. But we'll figure something out."

I still didn't know what the future held, but I felt certain it will be full of good things. We had been blessed with an amazing family, and with each other. As long as Stripes remained by my side, I knew everything would okay.

* * *

Stripes
Three Weeks Later

Anatoly and Ekaterina were officially enrolled in school and seemed to be doing well. I was back at work on a regular schedule, and Melina seemed to be thriving. I often came home to her singing in the kitchen as she cooked, or I couldn't find her at all because she'd run off to someone else's house. She'd become close with Meg, Clarity, and Grey. While she would speak with the other old ladies, she hadn't bonded with them. I had a feeling she would in time. My *lapochka* was slow to build relationships, and everyone understood. No one faulted her for it.

Today, the smell of cookies teased my nose when I walked through the door. Neither Anatoly nor Ekaterina were anywhere to be seen, and I couldn't find Melina. I shrugged off my cut on my way to the bedroom and stripped once I got there. A shower was in order, and some comfortable clothes. It had been one hell of a day at work. A rowdy group of young men had gotten drunk off their asses and caused some trouble. At least I wasn't coming home injured.

The sound of water made me pause. I tipped my head and listened. It wasn't running water. More like a slight drip. After I finished undressing, I went into the bathroom, and smiled at the sight in front of me. My sweet Melina must have decided to soak in the tub, and then fallen asleep. I'd chastise her later, but for now, I was enjoying the view.

I moved closer and dipped my hand into the water, wincing at how cold it felt. Instead of waking her, or adding warm water, I started the shower. I waited until steam billowed out, then I lifted Melina into my arms and stepped into the shower with her. She moaned when the hot water hit her, and her eyes slowly opened.

"Sleeping in the tub is dangerous, yes? You could have drowned, *lapochka*."

"Sorry. I guess I was more tired than I realized. I made the kids a snack before they came home from school, but they were barely here before they both ran off. I think Anatoly is over at Renegade's house so he can visit with Holt. Our precious daughter and Cleo went over to Irish's house to play with Simone. I doubt we'll see either before dinner."

"You've been tired a lot lately. I'm worried you're getting sick."

She reached up and cupped my cheek. "I'm fine. Just overdid it. I worked in the backyard this morning."

She'd insisted on creating the perfect place for our family. So far, she'd requested a gazebo, which I'd start building in the spring, as well as a large playset for Ekaterina and our grandchildren. In addition, she'd been setting up flower beds. Even if it was about to be too cold to bother planting anything, she'd said she'd rather have everything ready when the time was right.

I sat on the portable shower stool and held her on my lap. She smiled up at me. I should have gotten rid of this thing once I'd healed from my gunshot wounds, but at times like this, I rather liked having it. I listened to her ramble about her day while I held her, and I realized my life couldn't possibly get more perfect than it already was.

"You're my sun, my moon, my stars… You're my entire world, *lapochka*. I wake up looking forward to each day with you by my side. I love you, Melina."

She pressed her lips to mine. "I love you too, Mikhail. More than you'll ever know. You didn't just save my life when you brought me out of that brothel. You continue to save me every single day. The way you look at me. Your touch. Your kiss. Everything about you gives me a reason to keep living."

"Good. I cannot survive without you, Melina. If you were to die tomorrow, I'd lie down beside you and not get back up."

She yanked on my beard, and I growled at her, but her next words stopped me.

"No, you wouldn't. Anatoly and Ekaterina need you, Mikhail, and I know you'll do whatever it takes to give them a good life. So promise me here and now… If something ever happens to me, you'll do your best to raise them with love, make them laugh, and create a lot of happy memories."

"I promise," I said grudgingly. I knew she was right. Didn't mean I had to like it. The thought of surviving without her made it feel as if I'd be swallowed whole by the darkness. And that's when I understood a little of what she'd been going through. The battle she'd faced to stay alive, and it made me love her even more.

"This weekend we'll go to the zoo, yes? Start making those happy memories." I kissed her temple and breathed in her scent. She amazed me a little more every day. Whatever it took, I'd make her the happiest woman in the world, because she meant everything to me. I loved her, more than my next breath. I'd give up everything if it meant she could find peace. But since she didn't want that, I'd remain by her side... because there wasn't anywhere else I'd rather be.

Ram (Devil's Fury MC 12)
A Dixie Reapers Bad Boy Romance
Harley Wylde

Talia -- Every man in my life, including my father, has betrayed me. My past has made me cynical, twisted my mind, and left bruises that will never fade. Then I'm kidnapped and this big biker jumps in to save the day. I watch as he kills four men, and the blood on his hands should terrify me. Seeing how kind he is when rescuing everyone, how he takes charge and won't leave anyone behind, makes me wonder if not all men are useless. He says I can trust him, and he wants me to stick around. I've always run before, but something about this man makes me want to give him a chance. I only hope I won't regret it.

Ram -- I left my club and never planned to go back. They thought I was dead, and I wanted to keep it that way. But things don't always go according to plan. I roll up to the gates with six women in tow. One of them, Talia, I'd love to claim as my own. She's prickly and defensive, but I find her utterly adorable. I want to keep her, but she pushes me away. When one of the other victims asks to stay with me, I know it's my one chance to convince Talia to give me a shot. Now I've gone from a vigilante with no home to a family man. No matter how many men I have to kill, I will do whatever it takes to keep them safe. Never again will someone hurt those who are precious to me.

Prologue

Ram
One Week Earlier

The predator had become my prey and the bastard didn't even know it. The justice system had failed once again, setting loose a rapist and murderer, who had already claimed his next victim within an hour of being released. He'd been free for a little over two weeks. After losing his trail the first day, it had taken me a while to find him again. If the law-abiding officials couldn't do anything about filth like Martin Vega, then I would take matters into my own hands. He wouldn't be the first man I'd killed, nor would he be the last. Spilling blood wouldn't make me lose any sleep, not if it meant innocent people would be safe.

How many fucking hideouts did this bastard have? I'd already checked a handful of places known to be associated with either Vega or his buddies. Every one had been a bust. The only business left I could even consider as a potential place where I might find him was the strip joint in front of me. Watching mostly naked women dance on stage wasn't really my thing. Legit clubs didn't let you touch the girls. Of course, this club let the girls make extra cash on the side, which meant a man like Vega might be tempted to blow off steam here.

It wasn't my first time coming to this place. I didn't have the option of free club pussy anymore, and while I could head to a bar and have a one-night stand with someone, these girls were professionals. I didn't have to worry about them getting clingy, or wanting to sleep beside me all night.

I paid the fee and walked in, scanning the room through the haze of smoke. The girls on stage were shaking their tits and using every trick they had to drive the audience wild. The more the men wanted them, the more money they'd make. A waitress walked by, brushing against me. I felt her hard nipple graze my arm and didn't miss the sexy wink she tossed my way. Unfortunately, she wasn't why I was here.

After prowling the room, trying to appear as if I were searching for something in particular, a girl finally approached me. She slid her hand up my chest and gave me a smile. Too bad it didn't reach her eyes. Her tits were bare, and her G-string didn't leave much to the imagination. It was clear she was here because she needed the money, and not because she enjoyed the attention.

"Hey, handsome. Looking for something a little more hands-on?" she asked.

"Lead the way."

She grabbed my hand and guided me down the hall to the room I'd only been to once before. I'd met a woman here twice since I'd been in the area, and while we hadn't had full-on sex, I'd gotten off. She'd seemed into it, but I couldn't find her tonight.

The woman leading me pushed open a curtain, and we stepped into the heart of this place. Up front, it looked like a legit strip joint. In back, women made money on their knees, getting fucked in front of everyone, or however else they wanted. Two feet in front of us, a man had his pants around his ankles as he pounded into a woman from behind. She'd gripped the back of a chair, and her tits bounced with every thrust. He smacked her ass and fucked her harder, not even caring if she got off. She moaned and begged for more, but even I could tell she was faking it.

Another man sprawled in a booth to my left. A stripper was on her knees in front of him, with his dick in her mouth. She bobbed up and down, licking and sucking on him. A second woman sat beside him with her legs splayed. He had his fingers inside her, pumping them in and out.

The scent of sex filled the air. The young woman who'd brought me in here led me farther into the room. We stopped in front of a tall throne-like chair. The man sitting on it perused the room. He hadn't been here the last two times I'd visited. When he focused on me, I knew he had to be the man in charge of this place. His expression remained dead, lifeless eyes staring at me. If this man ever had a soul, he'd clearly given it to the devil long ago.

"You a cop?" he asked.

My eyebrows rose nearly to my hairline. "I look like one?"

"Wouldn't be the first time they sent in someone undercover. You'll have to pardon me for being cautious. This is a rather lucrative business after all. Can't have men like that coming in and shutting us down."

"Just here looking for someone," I said.

"Who?"

"Spent some time with Candy before, but I don't see her. This place has a good variety of women. I'm sure someone else can get me off tonight." I needed to be cautious. While I wasn't a cop, if he didn't believe me, he could still try to have me hauled out of here and killed. Guys like him would do anything to protect their businesses.

"See anyone you like?" he asked.

"Honestly? No. They all seem to be a bit..." I looked around the room again. "This is a job for them. Not one single stripper looks like she's having fun."

Candy had enjoyed our time together. I'd seen it

in her eyes, and while I hadn't fucked her, I'd let her suck me off, and I'd used my fingers to make her come. Hell, I couldn't remember the last time my dick had been in a woman's pussy. Far too long. My balls ached at the thought of fucking someone.

"Ah. So, you want a woman who enjoys sex? Most who come here don't really care. You want Bunny. She's my best, and I promise she's clean. However, she doesn't come cheap."

I took out my wallet and pulled out five hundred dollars. Last time, I'd paid Candy one hundred, so I'd come prepared. "That's all I've got on me. I don't usually carry a lot of cash."

"Her price is much higher. But I'll make a deal with you."

I didn't like where this was going. What sort of deal would a sleaze like him make? But if I didn't agree, I had a feeling he'd cause trouble for me.

"What are your terms?" I asked.

The man snapped his fingers, and a woman hurried over to him, immediately kneeling at his feet. "This is Rose. She's still relatively new and can be a little shy. Let her watch while you fuck Bunny so she can learn a few things."

Well, that wasn't as bad as I'd feared. Assuming this Bunny woman really did enjoy fucking and wasn't being coerced, then I didn't have an issue with it. Candy didn't need to be saved from this place. Maybe Bunny didn't either.

"Fine. As long as Bunny agrees."

The man pointed to a door across the room. "She's in there. Take this one with you."

Giving that asshole five hundred of my money really pissed me off, especially when I considered the possibility some of the money might make it into

Vega's hands. If that monster wasn't hiding here somewhere, then I didn't know where he'd gone. From what I could tell, he hadn't left town. I'd find him, sooner or later, even if it meant chasing him across the state.

I entered the room, and the blonde on the bed looked at me over her shoulder. Her feet were crossed at the ankles as she lay on her stomach. I saw the phone in her hand and wondered what she'd been doing before I came in.

"Looks like I get to have some fun now," Bunny said. "Who did you bring with you?"

I stepped aside so she could see the other woman. She gave a brisk nod and then held her hand out to me. I walked over, wondering what she'd do next. The warmth in her eyes, and the way her nipples hardened were enough to tell me she really did enjoy having sex, even if it was with a stranger. Better than feeling like I was forcing myself on someone. It was why I'd chosen Candy before.

"Is she participating?" Bunny asked.

"Your boss said he wanted her to watch and learn a few things."

"Oh, now that *does* sound fun. Come around here, Rose. Sit on the edge of the bed so you'll have a good view." The woman followed Bunny's instructions. Where Bunny wasn't wearing anything, Rose had on a sheer wrap around her waist. Bunny noticed the direction of my gaze and reached over to lift the gauzy material, showing me Rose didn't have anything on underneath it. "Do you like watching women fuck each other? Rose here prefers girls."

"Not really my thing," I said. And if Rose liked women, why the hell was she going to learn how to please a man? Was that asshole forcing her to do this? I couldn't ask, not with Bunny in the room. She might very well go running to her boss and tell him I'd tried to save Rose.

"Pity. I could have gotten her off while you fucked me." Bunny shrugged. "What sort of things do you enjoy in the bedroom? And what do I call you? Sir? Master? Or do you prefer a more dominant woman?"

"Call me R." I wasn't about to tell her my name, not even my road name. But the first initial shouldn't be an issue. It's what I'd used with Candy.

"You going to fuck me with your clothes on, R?" she asked.

"What if I am? Got a problem with it?"

She crawled toward me on her hands and knees, giving my shirt a tug. "No, but it seems a pity to hide what's underneath. How much am I allowed to see?"

I unfastened my belt and jeans, then shoved them and my underwear down under my ass. I had ink that could easily identify me, which meant my shirt was staying on. "Only this much."

She pursed her lips and frowned as she stared at my semi-hard cock. It wasn't that I didn't find her attractive, or Rose, but I refused to let my dick get fully hard unless I knew a woman really wanted me to fuck her. I had a feeling this woman was like the club whores I'd been with in the past.

"What do you want me to do?" she asked.

I threaded my fingers through her hair and dragged her face lower. "Suck my cock, Bunny. Let me hear how much you enjoy it."

She gave me a wicked smile before licking her lips. Opening wide, she took me into her mouth, humming as her tongue slid down the shaft of my cock. My balls drew up at the sensation, and I gripped her hair a little tighter. I used it to guide her motions. From the corner of my eye, I saw Rose inch closer. She stared as Bunny swallowed on the head of my cock, then drew back, only to take me deep again.

Rose's nipples went hard and she bit her lip. All right. Maybe she was into both men *and* women. At least I didn't have to worry about her being forced to take a cock. Looked like she'd be up for it. A flush climbed up her chest, and I found myself watching her more than Bunny. Her chest heaved and she squirmed, as if need was building inside her and she wanted to come.

Bunny sucked me harder, and I fought for control. I wasn't ready to come yet. Tonight was more fun than I'd thought it would be, and if I was lucky, when I left the room I might run into Vega. A guy like that wouldn't be able to resist watching the women.

I released Bunny and pushed her onto her back. She grinned up at me, clearly eager for what came next. Rose still stared at my cock. Her hand inched between her legs, and I reached out to stop her.

"Do you want to come?" I asked. She nodded. "Then use me to get off."

Bunny lifted up on her elbows to watch us. "Condoms are on the table."

I reached over to the bowl she indicated with a tip of her head and rolled one down my cock. I sat on the edge of the bed and helped Rose straddle me. She didn't take my cock inside her, instead she rubbed against me. Gripping my shoulders tight, she bucked her hips. My cock slid between the lips of her pussy, the head bumping her clit. It didn't take long for her to come, thrusting her breasts out and tossing her head back.

"That was fucking hot to watch," Bunny said

with a smirk. "Is it my turn?"

"As long as you make me come, we can do this however you want," I said.

"No!" Rose shouted, her cheeks turning pink. "I… I want to be the one to do it."

Bunny scowled at her, but Rose seemed determined. "Fine. You can have his dick, but you better get me off after he's gone. And I don't mean a quick orgasm either. Make it last."

Bunny got up to give us more room. She stood beside the bed, watching our every move. As I lay back and let Rose slide her pussy down onto my cock, Bunny played with her nipples and amused herself.

I shoved the sheer wrap out of my way so I could see my cock splitting Rose open. Using my thumb, I rubbed her clit. That's all it took to get her moving. She rode me with wild abandon, getting off at least twice. Deciding to take matters into my own hands, I pulled her off me, flipped her onto her hands and knees, and fucked her from behind. Long, deep strokes that made the bed slam against the wall. Rose gripped the covers and cried out as she came again. Feeling her pussy ripple around me nearly sent me over the edge. I fucked her hard and fast, taking what I wanted until I filled the condom with my cum.

When I pulled out, my cock was still hard. Bunny removed the condom and wrapped it in a tissue. The hungry way she eyed my cock made me think she still wanted to ride me. Instead, she shooed me off the bed. I pulled up my pants, fastened them, then grabbed the tissue with the condom inside. No way I'd leave it behind.

"Thanks for the good time, girls."

"It was our pleasure." Bunny winked at me. "Come back anytime, R."

I hung out at the strip joint a while longer, hoping to see Vega, but I never did. When I got back to my motel room, I showered and tossed the condom into the trash. I didn't feel satisfied. Easy women like those never did it for me. Sure, I got off, but it was only a physical release. The older I got, the more I wanted a deeper connection to someone. Unfortunately, that wasn't in the cards for me. Not anymore.

"Where the fuck are you, Vega?"

I needed to find him, kill him, and move on to the next guy. Preferably before more innocent lives were destroyed.

Chapter One
Ram

I'd been too late to save the young girl Vega targeted, but I wouldn't fail this time. The woman in his grasp looked to be no more than nineteen years old. The way she slumped told me she'd either been drugged or knocked unconscious. I knew Vega would do unspeakable things to her. As much as I wanted to rip her from his arms right here and now, I knew it was better to wait. He likely had other victims and I hoped he would lead me to them. If at all possible, tonight I would save more than one life.

The ink on my back felt as if it burned, a reminder of the life I'd left behind. I hadn't worn my club colors in more than a decade. After I'd gone nomad, I'd disappeared, making sure my brothers couldn't find me. They didn't know of my failed mission, and I hoped they never did. Because of me, multiple lives had been lost. I knew saving this woman and the others couldn't make up for what I'd done before, but it was the only way I knew of to ease the burden on my guilty conscience.

I clung to the shadows out-of-sight, a knife gripped in my hand. The woman let out a soft moan and I hoped she wouldn't wake any time soon. Vega would do whatever it took to keep her quiet, and I wanted her to suffer as little as possible. There was no telling what he had already done to her.

Following silently, I kept him within sight. Vega made his way through the shady neighborhood, fast approaching the warehouses on the opposite end. I held back as he entered the last structure on the right. The few windows I saw were covered in dust and grime, but I knew I needed to at least try to get a glimpse inside the building. If I had my brothers with me, things would have been different. I didn't know if they'd ever accept me back again, or if they even knew I was still alive. Only Badger had kept in touch. Confronting Vega alone wasn't a good idea. I knew he had multiple men working under him including extra hired muscle. Many would call this a suicide mission. Perhaps they were right, but I didn't care if I died today as long as the innocent women and girls inside the building would be safe.

Through the dirt-encrusted glass, I could see Vega and three other men. The woman he'd carried inside was now slumped in a chair, her wrists tied to the arms. A trickle of blood ran from her temple down the side of her face. I wondered how else he'd hurt her. Scanning the room, I saw a row of cages, each filled with at least one teenage girl or young woman. None looked over the age of twenty and the youngest appeared to be near thirteen. I couldn't stand sick fucks like Vega.

I watched for another twenty minutes, keeping an eye on any changes. So far, it didn't look like Vega had other men with him. Three didn't seem like much for someone like him. Which meant they were either on their way or he felt secure with such a small detail. If I had my sniper rifle, it would have been much easier to take them out. Instead, all I had was my nine millimeter and my knife. There was no way to end their miserable lives without getting closer.

Part of me wanted to feel Vega's blood and watch as the light dimmed from his eyes. The average person might have considered him a monster, but tonight I was the vicious thing lurking in the dark. My heart kept a steady rhythm as I watched and waited. I knew I'd have to move before he harmed the woman any more, yet I couldn't be careless and rush into danger. Doing so would only end all our lives.

I backed away from the window as the phone vibrated in my pocket. Pulling it out I checked the screen. A familiar name flashed on the display. *Badger*. Why the hell would he be calling now?

My curiosity got the better of me and I stepped farther away from the warehouse to answer the call.

"To what do I owe the pleasure?" I asked when the call connected.

"Why do you always have to be a dick when you answer the phone? You could at least *try* not to sound sarcastic."

"Maybe I just seem like one because we haven't spoken in so long. It's not like we talk more than once every two or three years. Is there even anyone else at the club who knows I'm still alive?"

Badger sighed. "I got the feeling you didn't want anyone to know you were alive. Was I wrong? And don't think for one second I'm not aware of what you've been up to. I've left you alone to do your thing, but this is news that couldn't wait any longer."

My gut churned. What the hell could have possibly happened to make him say such a thing? "What's wrong?"

"It's Grizzly. I don't know how else to say it so I'll just spit it out. He's gone. Died a few months ago. I'd have called sooner but shit hit the fan around here."

I pressed a hand to my chest, feeling the loss of my ex-president. I hadn't seen him in over ten years. It never occurred to me the last time I walked out would be the last chance I ever had to speak with him.

"What happened? How did he die?" I asked.

"Too many years of bad decisions caught up to him. His health began to decline a little while back.

Finally, his body just gave out. It hit the entire club hard, especially his daughters."

The way he said the word daughters made me think there was something more to it, but now wasn't the time to ask. I could mourn Grizzly later and ask for more details about the club. Right now, I needed to focus on the women and girls who needed my help. Besides, I'd been gone from the club for so long I didn't even know any of Grizzly's adopted daughters. I'd heard about them from Badger previously, but it wasn't the same as meeting them in person.

"I appreciate the call, but now isn't a good time. Sorry, Badger. I've got to go." I hung up before he could say another word.

Creeping back over to the warehouse, I looked into the window again. While I'd been on the phone, Vega had been having a bit of fun. The poor woman tied to the chair now had multiple wounds. I could see the rise and fall of her chest and said a silent thanks she was still alive. But I worried she wouldn't be for much longer. Whatever it took, I needed to get her and the others out of there as quickly as possible.

One of Vega's men pulled out a pack of cigarettes and headed for the door. I knew this was my chance to take out at least one of them. When he didn't return, Vega would suspect something was up. It was a risk I'd have to take.

I heard the warehouse door open and shut. Gripping my knife tightly, I crept around the corner. I saw the flicker of the flame from his lighter, then the soft glow from the end of a cigarette. While he remained preoccupied, I moved swiftly on silent feet. Before the asshole had a chance to even realize I was there, I placed my hand over his mouth and slit his throat.

The coppery scent of his blood filled the air, and I knew it would attract other predators, both human and animal. The clock was ticking. I leaned against the building, melding with the shadows, and waited for my next victim. It wasn't long before another of Vega's men came outside.

"Joe, where the fuck are you? Vega is starting to get pissed. Stop screwing around and come back inside."

I had bad news for him. Joe wouldn't be going back inside. He had a one-way ticket to hell, and soon this fucker would too. The unnamed man moved closer. I knew the moment he spotted the dead body. He let out a muffled curse, but before he could get his hands on his weapon, I'd tackled him to the ground.

He struggled and tried to fight me off, but he was no match for me. Slamming his head against the pavement, I saw his blood splatter on the ground. The moment he stopped struggling, I stuck my knife into his neck, then stabbed him again between the ribs.

I'd thought these men would be more of a challenge. They were going down far too easy. Something told me the remaining man and Vega would be harder to take out. It didn't mean I was backing down. Even if it meant giving up my own life, I'd make sure those innocent girls and women made it out of here. No one deserved to live a life of torture and prostitution, except for assholes like Vega. If I didn't think it was too dangerous to let him live, I'd find a way to give him a taste of his own medicine.

I knew the moment I entered the building, even if I managed to take out the other man, Vega would still have time to get a shot off. There was no way a man like him was unarmed. First I'd look through the window and check their position again. It wouldn't guarantee they wouldn't move before I went inside, but it would give me an idea of where they stood and how close they were to the woman in the chair.

I muttered a curse under my breath when I saw Vega cutting the woman's clothes. I was out of time and needed to move fast. It didn't matter if I wouldn't have a clear shot at Vega, waiting wasn't an option.

Walking around to the front of the warehouse, I kicked the door open. I immediately shot off two rounds taking down the unnamed man, one in his gut and one to the head. Vega drew his weapon. I took a chance and shot at his hands where they both gripped the gun. He cursed and dropped the weapon, immediately scrambling to pick it back up. It would be so easy to shoot him and take him out right now, but I wanted him to suffer. I needed him to experience even a small amount of the pain he'd inflicted on countless women and girls. There was a burning inside me, an anger so intense I could taste it. Nothing would make me happier right now than to rip him open, spill his guts on the floor, and watch him bleed out.

On the other hand, I knew that wasn't something any of the women and girls needed to see. They'd been traumatized enough, and I didn't need to add to it.

"What do you want?" Vega asked. "I'll give you anything. You want a girl? How about two? Pick any of them you want. They're yours, free of charge."

His words disgusted me. Vermin like him didn't deserve to live. He preyed on those who were weaker, took whatever he wanted. He wasn't a man, merely a waste of space.

"Nothing you say will change your fate. Consider me the Reaper. I'm here to send your soul to hell, assuming you even have one." I walked closer, making sure to kick his weapon far from him. He kneeled on the floor, hands in the air, with a calculating gleam in his eye. Someone like him wouldn't go easy, would never give up. It hadn't occurred to him he wouldn't make it out of here alive. "If you don't believe me, ask the two men who went outside. You don't find it odd they never returned? By now, their blood is cooling on the ground. There's nothing you can say or do to save yourself."

Vega snarled and lunged at me. I hadn't expected him to make such a stupid mistake. With a quick sidestep, I watched him crash face first into the floor. Before he had a chance to recover, I brought my knife down into his back, severing his spine. He screamed and convulsed from the pain. There was no way he'd ever get up again, and before I left, I'd make sure he had breathed his last.

Leaving him, I slowly approached the woman in the chair. She'd regained consciousness and stared at me with a calm acceptance. It was clear she thought I meant to use her the same way Vega had planned. What had she been through to this point that all the fight was gone from her?

"Easy," I said softly. "I'm not going to hurt you. I'll cut you free, then I'll unlock the cages. All of you are safe now."

I could tell she didn't believe me, and I couldn't blame her. If our roles had been reversed, I wouldn't take me at my word either. Actions always spoke louder than words. Once I'd freed her, I helped the other women and girls. They crawled from their cages, with tears streaking their cheeks. A few looked at me with hope, while others appeared more like wild animals escaping a trap. I knew those were the ones who had been here the longest and had suffered the most. Vega may have only been free a little more than two weeks, but it didn't mean his hired men hadn't abducted these women and children while he'd been locked up. What better way to make himself appear innocent than to have the crimes continue while he wasn't a free man?

The woman who had been tied to the chair held out her hand. At first, I didn't realize what she wanted. Once I knew she wanted my knife, I held it out and let her take it. If the weapon made her feel better, I didn't mind her having it. While it was true she could easily stab me, something told me she wouldn't.

I arched my eyebrows as I watched in amazement. Without any hesitation, she walked over to Vega, kneeled down beside his body, and stabbed him repeatedly. It was my first time meeting such a fierce woman, and I had to admit I admired her in that moment. It not only took strength to endure this ordeal, but she had done whatever she must in order to survive and ensure Vega would never come for her again. Instead of relying on someone else, she'd taken matters into her own hands.

That is one hell of a woman.

I didn't know who she was, or where she'd come from, but I knew no matter how long I lived I would never forget her.

The youngest of the captives latched on to me. She stared up at me with wide eyes, and I could see how broken she was. There was a chance she would never fully heal. Her physical wounds might go away, but the mental ones could last forever.

"What's going to happen to us now?" she asked.

"I can help you get back to your family." Before I'd even finished speaking, she was shaking her head. I didn't know if it was the fear they would no longer accept her, or if they'd had a hand in Vega owning her.

Regardless, if she didn't want to return home, I wouldn't make her.

Another woman came closer, this one appeared to be around seventeen or eighteen. She looked tired. Resigned. Something told me she'd been with Vega for quite a while. Maybe before his arrest. It was possible the arresting officers hadn't found all the women. Since I didn't have access to the reports, I couldn't say for certain.

"Some of us have nowhere to go," she said. "Living on the street wouldn't be any better than being locked in those cages. Either way, we'll have to use our bodies to survive. I for one would rather die."

I hadn't anticipated the need to shelter these women. I thought I would free them, and they'd return to their homes, or seek out their loved ones. They weren't the first I'd ever rescued, and I didn't think they'd be the last. In the past, I'd never had to worry about what came next. One of the women usually took charge. They'd thank me, then I'd be on my way. It seemed this time would be different.

"My name is Ram," I said. "If you truly have nowhere to go, I know of a place that might help you. A motorcycle club called the Devil's Fury. They may look scary, but I swear on my life they will never hurt you."

I hadn't planned to return home. Not now, not ever. But this was one of those times life had thrown me a curveball. I couldn't leave these women on their own, especially the teenage girls. They needed protection, and there was only one place I knew to take them. I only hoped my brothers would welcome them, and wouldn't turn their backs on me, even though I'd done exactly that when I walked away over a decade ago.

Chapter Two

Talia

I didn't know how much time had passed since the man had freed us. While he'd gotten rid of the bodies, I'd taken the time to get to know the other women and the younger girls. We'd all been taken from different cities and even different states. None of them had been forthcoming with what they'd been through so far, but I could use my imagination. It was clear Vega had planned to either sell us outright or prostitute us himself. I had a feeling he'd already done that to most of these women and girls. If the man who called himself Ram hadn't freed me tonight, I would have joined them. The thought of owing him a debt didn't sit well with me.

I didn't know why the others trusted him so easily. Sure, he may have killed Vega and the others, but it didn't make him a hero. What if he'd only been taking out the competition? Had it not occurred to them they could be trading one monster for another?

The youngest, a fourteen-year-old named Riley, clung to the man. I wanted to pull her away. I would have if she had been the only one looking at him in amazement. After everything they had been through, how could they be so trusting?

Idiots.

"Is everyone going with me?" Ram asked. "If anyone wants to return to their homes, I will make sure you get there safely."

"I think they've made it obvious they plan to go with you," I said. "You haven't told us where the Devil's Fury is located. How far do we have to go? How are we going to get there? You don't honestly expect us to go into this completely blind, do you?"

He smiled faintly, crossing his arms and rocking back on his heels. Something about the look on his face rubbed me the wrong way. Perhaps life had made me too jaded. I might only be twenty, but I'd already lived through hell. And I didn't mean this particular instance. Life had chewed me up and spit me out multiple times.

"First off, no I don't expect you to completely trust me. In fact, I'd be surprised if you did. Second, the club is located in southern Georgia near the Florida Panhandle. As to how we're getting there I'm not sure. All of you will certainly not fit on my bike."

Great. He'd promised to get everyone to safety and didn't have a clue how to actually do it. Had he even planned to help us to begin with? I still had my doubts as to why he'd taken out Vega and those men. For now, I'd be cautious. At least one of us needed to be.

The woman who'd introduced herself to me earlier as Heather lifted a hand as if asking for permission to speak. Ram gave her a nod, which seemed to be all she'd been waiting for.

"If you don't have a large vehicle for us, I know how to hot-wire a car. What little I saw of this neighborhood when we were brought in was enough to tell me no one would report a stolen car from this area." She paused a moment. "We were brought here in a large van without windows. Dumped in the back like cargo. There was another man, and I think he left, so I doubt the vehicle is still here."

Her words surprised me. She didn't seem like the type to know how to do something like hot-wiring a car. Judging from the expression on Ram's face he hadn't expected that from her either.

"You're right. No one around here would report

a vehicle theft. There are a lot of things everyone needs right now, including clothes and food, but it would be best if we got those items after we left town." He shoved his hands into his pockets. "I may not be rich, but I can afford to buy you the basics. Once we reach the club's compound, my brothers will make sure you have everything you need."

"How can you be so certain they'll help us? What if we get there and they turn us away?" If no one else would voice any concerns, then I would. I refused to run off with a man I'd never met before, careening toward an uncertain future. To some, perhaps going with him was better than staying here. I supposed being on my own and earning a living could be done from anywhere. It was better to go with the group. Worst case, Ram ended up turning on us. If that happened, I didn't think these women and girls would stand a chance. None of them had any fight left in them. I hadn't thought I'd had any left either.

But what if he wasn't a bad guy? What if the Devil's Fury really would help us? It wasn't an opportunity I could pass up. While I'd always prided myself on earning the things I had, I wasn't stupid enough to struggle if I didn't need to.

"I know the club president has a soft spot for women and kids in trouble. As to how I know, that's his story to tell," Ram said.

"Fine," I said. "We'll go with you to Georgia."

Ram smirked. It made my fingers itch to reach out and slap him, but I refrained. Even if he turned out to be the biggest asshole on the planet, as long as he didn't hurt, it still made him better than Vega. As the saying went, better the devil you know than the one you don't, and if this man was truly part of a club called the Devil's Fury... Well, the name really said it all.

Heather left, taking one of the other women along with her. I knew Ram would ride his motorcycle. I might not be overly familiar with bikers, but I did know one would never leave something like that behind. Which meant we needed a vehicle large enough for myself and five others.

"Will it set your mind at ease if I call the president of the club and let him know I'm bringing all of you there?" Ram asked.

"It's a good place to start," I said.

"What exactly happened when I left the building? Did they make you their spokesperson? Or did you just take charge all on your own?" he asked.

"Does it matter?"

He smiled again. "No, I just find this bossy side of you rather cute. I wasn't sure if it was a temporary thing or if this is just who you are."

Was he flirting with me? It didn't seem like the time or place, but the men I'd known all seemed to follow their dick and not use their brain. For some reason, I really hoped this man was different.

"That's something you'll have to keep wondering about. Even though you're helping us, it doesn't mean I want to get to know you better. Then again, you might be one of those men who assumes all women want him."

"Ouch!" He pressed his hand to his chest. "Don't hold back. Tell me how you really feel."

"It's probably better if I don't. I'm not sure your fragile male ego can handle it."

Ram threw back his head and laughed hard. The sight did strange things to me. I felt an odd flutter in my stomach, and my heart sped up. *No. No, no, no.* I couldn't be attracted to him. There was absolutely no way. And yet I recognized all the signs. Maybe it wasn't a crazy biker I needed to worry about. Instead, I should have been concerned with myself. Clearly someone had scrambled my brains. Why else would I react this way at such a bad time, and to such a cocky bastard?

He removed his shirt and handed it to me. "Put this on for now."

My ripped clothes hadn't even been a concern, until he'd made me aware of them. Although, the flimsy things the others wore could hardly be considered clothes. All of us needed something else to wear.

Begrudgingly I accepted the shirt and pulled it over my head. Heather and the other woman returned. She motioned for us to step outside. Parked near the door was a large van. Not new by any means. I only hoped it would be sufficient to get us where we were going.

Everyone got inside with Heather behind the wheel and me in the passenger seat. Ram held my door open, leaning in. The scent of him filled my nose, and if I breathed a little deeper, then no one had to know except me. *Why does he have to smell so good?*

He gave me a wink, agitating me even more, then he focused his gaze on Heather. "Follow behind me. If you need to stop, flash your lights and I'll pull off at the next exit. I know you're all hungry, tired, and probably want to take a shower, but I want to put some miles between us and this place before I find you clothes and food. The compound is about five hours away."

"Did you forget you said you would call your president to let him know we're coming?" I asked.

"Right." He took out his phone and pulled up a

number in his contacts list. He put the phone on speaker -- we could all hear it ringing. A man with a deep, gruff voice answered, and I heard some of the women whimper. "Badger, it's Ram. I need a favor. And before you start cussing me out, you should know you're on speaker with several women present."

"Does the favor have to do with them?" he asked.

"Yeah, it does. Remember earlier when I said I had something to take care of? Well, this is it. I took down Martin Vega and his men. He'd captured six women. Some of them are barely more than girls. They don't have anywhere to go and they need help getting back on their feet. The younger ones either don't have a home to return to or don't want to go back."

The man he'd called Badger sighed. "How long before you get here? And -- just double-checking -- you said six beds, right?"

"Yes, six beds, and it will take us at least five hours. They're going to need clothes and food as well. I'm going to purchase them each a new outfit on the way there, as well as a meal, but they'll probably want to shower and change after we arrive."

"Why didn't Why didn't he ask you who Vega was?" I asked after he ended the call.

"Because Vega's been plastered all over the news. There isn't a single person in this entire country who hasn't heard of Martin Vega. I'm going to assume the charges were not false, which means I know what all of you have suffered. You'll be safe when you get to the compound. No matter how rough some of us look, we'll never hurt you."

I bit my lip to keep from saying anything more. Honestly, though, did he really expect us to just take his word for it? It wasn't like the bad guys always advertised they were bad. No, most pretended to be nice, even caring, and would lure in their victims that way. If anyone else in the van felt apprehensive, I couldn't tell. I had to wonder if I was the only one thinking logically right now. These women might have given up, but it seemed as if some of them still had a small spark of hope. For right now that meant they would take Ram at his word and believe he would protect them. But the moment he slipped up, the very second I thought things would take a sinister turn, I would do everything I could to fight for myself and the others.

I wasn't brave. Truth be told, I was terrified. While the others might tremble and shake in fear, I faced it head-on, pretending to be stronger than I really was. It was a bluff and nothing more. Perhaps I was a bit like my gambler of a father after all, except my stakes were higher because the only thing I had to bet was my life.

Please don't let me down, Ram. Prove me wrong. Be the hero all of us need because one stiff wind and I'll fall down like a house of straw. No matter how much I wanted to keep my distance, or how badly I wanted to distrust him, in the end I knew I needed someone to lean on. I could be cruel and sarcastic if necessary. My survival instincts were strong. Much like the wild animals who puffed up to make themselves appear larger in front of a predator, I was doing much the same thing. I only hoped it wouldn't backfire on me.

"Are you expecting us to pay you back for anything you purchase tonight, Ram? It's not like any of us have a wallet or purse with us. Or do you plan to take payment in another way?" The moment the words left my mouth I immediately wanted to cringe. He hadn't said or done anything to make it seem as if he would harm us. It still didn't mean I was ready to trust him one hundred percent. Maybe more like ten percent.

He slowly reached toward my face, his fingers brushing my chin. As I focused my gaze on his, the concern and pain I saw nearly took my breath away. Ram didn't appear to be the same as the men he'd just killed. However, I didn't easily put my faith in anyone, not even blood relatives. No, especially not my family. If anything, they were the first to teach me about betrayal, and it was a lesson I wouldn't soon forget.

He gently rubbed his thumb across my chin, and it felt like my heart skipped a beat. My reaction to him didn't make any sense to me. Not once had I ever felt attracted to anyone like him. Why this man? What made him more special than anyone else I'd met before?

He leaned in a little closer and my breath caught. Was he going to kiss me? Before I could react or pull away, he whispered to me in a low raspy tone only I could hear.

"While I love your ferocity, and I'm happy to see you would defend yourself when you're in danger, I promise you'll always be safe with me. So, Talia, give me just a little bit of your trust and a chance to prove I can take care of you."

His words left me shaken. I shot a quick glance toward Heather and the others. It was clear they were curious as to what he'd said. The fact I wanted to lean into his touch, and to believe in him, frightened me. Something told me Ram was far more dangerous than anyone I'd ever met. Not to mention, I didn't remember telling him my name. Had he been listening to our conversation while he'd been outside?

"Don't forget what I said, Heather. If you need to

stop, flash your lights. I'll pull over when we're at least forty-five minutes outside of this town." With those parting words he backed away and walked over to a motorcycle I hadn't noticed in the shadows. He started the machine and it gave a deep rumble. A minute or two later, Ram pulled away and Heather fell in behind him. I couldn't decide if I was running toward something better or far riskier than my current situation. Only time would tell.

Chapter Three

Ram

I'd done my best to not stare at Talia too much. The sight of her in my shirt did things to me. I could have easily gone to my bike and pulled one from my saddlebags. Nope. Instead, I'd given her the one I'd been wearing. Even worse, I'd liked knowing my scent was all over her now.

What are you, a randy dog?

Thankfully, I'd managed not to get hard so far. If the women thought for one second I might want to fuck one of them, I imagine chaos would ensue. They needed someone to take care of them right now. Which meant I needed to focus on giving them what they needed and stop thinking about Talia wearing my shirt. Sadly, she'd have to change clothes.

Not even a 24-hour store would let the women inside in their present condition. After taking note of their sizes for both clothes and shoes, I went inside and purchased panties, knit dresses, and flip-flops for each of them. It wasn't perfect, but it would at least allow them to go into the store. I'd also bought some first-aid supplies for any with cuts, like Talia. They'd hastily changed clothes in the van and patched themselves up. While they went into the women's bathroom, I stood guard outside. I could hear the water running and the sound of splashing as they cleaned the dirt from their faces, and anywhere else they could reach without a shower.

I wasn't sure what my brothers would have waiting for them. To guarantee they had a comfortable night, I told them each to pick out something to sleep in as well as anything else they needed. A few cast longing looks at the magazine and book aisle.

"Why don't you each pick out one or two things to read? It's too dark to look at them in the car tonight, but you would have them for later."

I felt bad knowing they didn't have anything at all, aside from the few things I'd just purchased for them. A book or magazine might not seem like much, but at least it was something they owned that was theirs. There would be many more things they would need. For now, I just needed to get them through the night.

"Are you sure it's okay to pick something?" asked the youngest. She danced from foot to foot and twisted her fingers together in front of her. As much as I wanted to hug her and assure her everything would be fine, I worried I might scare her.

"Pick anything you want. I can't buy out the store for you, but I can do this much."

The younger girl hurried down the book aisle. Talia inched closer until she stood next to me. It didn't escape my notice she hadn't selected anything.

"What's her name?" I asked, nodding toward the teen.

"Riley."

I nodded, filing the information away. These women had been used and treated like objects. Using their names would make them feel more human. I'd learned that much while trying to save others over the years.

"There's something I should tell you," Talia said. "When you got rid of Vega and the others, I heard the women talking. There's an offshore account containing all the funds Vega received from his prostitution business. I'm not sure how you'd find it or even access it, but I thought you should know it was there."

"And exactly how do they know about it?" Was

one of them a mole? It was possible not all these women and girls were victims. What if one or more had been planted by Vega on the off chance someone tried to stop him?

"Heather mentioned it. The woman who drove the van. One of the times Vega gifted her to some men for a few hours, she heard them discussing it. On the ride here, she rambled about various things. Conversations she'd heard, her feelings and fears, and even worry over what would happen to her now. I probably learned more about her during the short ride than I've ever known about anyone else I've met."

It was something to consider. I might not know how to locate such an account, but it didn't mean Outlaw wouldn't. Badger had once told me the hacker's hands had been crushed. Even if he couldn't use a computer, perhaps he had other ways to look into things.

My thoughts strayed to Grizzly. There was something Badger hadn't told me. I knew it with a certainty. A gut-deep feeling that wouldn't go away. Since Grizzly had stepped down a while ago and already handed the club over to Badger, I didn't think it would have anything to do with that. No, something was going on with his girls.

I still had a few contacts outside of the Devil's Fury. It might be time to give them a call. No one liked walking blind into any situation, especially not me, even less so with others depending on me. I owed it to these women and girls to find out what was going on before we arrived at the compound.

I placed my hand on Talia's shoulder. "Can you keep an eye out for a few minutes? I need to step out front and make a call."

She shrugged. "Can't you just do it here? I think

they'd feel safer if they could see you."

"Fine. It's not necessarily something they need to hear. I'll move far enough away for my conversation to remain private yet close enough I can keep an eye on them." She immediately tensed. "Easy. It's nothing to do with any of you. I've been away from the club for quite a while, and I just want to check on a few things before we show up at the gates. A lot can change over the years."

She gave a quick nod and walked over to the women while I took several steps farther back. There was only one person I could think to call. An assassin I'd run into multiple times. I'd known him when we were younger, then we'd gone our separate ways, only to bump into each other years later. I'd never introduced him to my club, but he knew about them. He went by the name of Lock because once he'd locked onto his target there was no escaping him. But I had known him by a different name. Max Luton.

I pulled his name up in my contacts, and he answered almost immediately.

"Well, I'll be damned," Max said. "Just when I thought you must be dead. I'm going to assume this isn't a social call. What do you need, Ram?"

"Not even a hello? Well, fuck you too." Max chuckled on the other end of the line. "But you're right. I do need something. Information. I get the feeling I'm about to walk into a hornet's nest."

"You'll have to be a little more specific," Max said.

"I'm going home, back to the Devil's Fury. I know damn well you know every secret of every club on the eastern side of the US, and possibly the western side as well. Don't even try to deny it. Is there something I should know about Grizzly's death?"

Max sighed. "Yeah, there's some shit that went down when Grizzly passed. Not just with your club but it trickled over to the Dixie Reapers and the Savage Raptors. From what I've heard it started even before then. One of his daughters screwed up. Except it wasn't just her. The entire club was at fault, or most of it. Instead of learning how to get along, they made her feel unwelcome. In case you're wondering, she's now with Lynx at the Savage Raptors."

I let that digest for a moment. It was difficult for me to wrap my head around what could have possibly happened. Something told me it was a long story, one I didn't necessarily have time to hear right now.

"I'm taking a small group of women and teenage girls to the Devil's Fury. They need help, and I didn't know where else to go with them. Are they going to be safe there?"

Max let out a low whistle. Why did I get the feeling he thought I shouldn't take them there? Just what the hell had my club been up to while I've been gone? I'd relied on the random calls from Badger to keep me up to date. Now I wondered if that had been a mistake. Clearly he'd left quite a few things out.

"Are you saying I shouldn't take them there?" I asked.

"They should be fine, unless they try to hook up with one of your brothers. That's what started everything. Meredith wanted someone who didn't return her affection. Doolittle. When he found the woman he wanted, she managed to turn the club against them. I don't know the rest of the details except Grizzly sent her on a trip, one she never went back from."

I wasn't entirely certain how all of that figured into Grizzly's death or what was going on with the club now. As long as these women would be safe, nothing else mattered. If my brothers wanted to be a bunch of drama queens, I would treat them accordingly. It didn't matter if I'd been gone for more than ten years. Technically, I was still part of the club. Since Badger had known how to find me all along, I knew that even if my brothers were furious with me, it would eventually blow over. Unless they'd been emotionally reduced to eighth graders in my absence, which honestly seemed like it might be possible. Were they a bunch of hardened bikers or gossip-hungry teenage girls?

"Thanks for the info, Max. And thanks for your help several months back. I know you could have bumped me out of the way since the job was already yours, but I appreciate you letting me stick around. I think we worked well together."

"Anytime. If you need my help, you know how to find me. And Ram... don't let the club push you around or try to shove you out. There's plenty of dirt on most of them. It's yours if you want it."

Damn. Made me wonder what he had on me. Then again, I probably didn't want to know. "Thanks, Max. I have to go, but I'll be in touch."

I ended the call and went back to the women and girls. Each had at least one book or magazine in their hands. Riley had three and seemed conflicted over which two she wanted. Easy enough fix.

"Get all three," I told her. "It's fine."

She gave me a beaming smile, and even Talia seemed to thaw toward me a little. That one was as prickly as a porcupine, but damn if I didn't find her intriguing as hell. I wanted to know where she'd come from, what sort of life she'd led, and every single thing about her. And yeah, I could admit I wanted to know if her skin felt soft and what sounds she made when a man was balls-deep inside her. Probably better if I kept that last part to myself.

I should have gotten them some crackers or something while we were here, but they would probably prefer a hot meal. Not to mention, they might choke on the crackers if they tried eating them while the van was in motion. As hungry as they were, I wasn't sure they'd be able to eat slowly.

After I paid for their purchases, and they'd gotten back into the van, I pulled Talia aside. They seemed to listen to her, so I'd treat her like their leader for now. It was my hope, they'd slowly become more confident over the next few days, weeks, or even months. Until then, I'd speak to them through Talia unless they asked me to do otherwise.

"I don't plan to stop again until we reach the compound, unless one of you needs me to. Remind Heather to flash the lights if I need to pull over. I'm sure you're all hungry."

"I couldn't eat right now, but some of them haven't had food in a while."

I nodded, expecting as much. "If they eat fast food, which is all we'll have available, it will probably make them sick. It's better to wait until we reach the compound and eat there. I'll send Badger a text to have some hot food ready when we arrive, something that will be easy to digest."

"Thank you," she said.

I waited until she was in the van before getting on my bike. We had a few hours of travel ahead of us, and I wanted to start as soon as possible. Vega and his gang were unlikely to be reported missing. Eventually, a policeman would discover their bodies, and questions would arise. Fortunately, the gun I used hadn't been involved in any other illegal activities, so even if my bullets were traced back to it, there would be no connection to me. I was going to scratch up the inside of the barrel, wipe off any fingerprints, and get rid of it. Getting a new one wouldn't exactly be difficult.

Before pulling out onto the road, I paused long enough to text Badger as I'd said I would. Once we hit the highway again, I'd get us to the Devil's Fury as fast as I could. Even if I didn't know what sort of reception I'd receive, none of this was about me.

We ended up stopping twice more for bathroom breaks, and when we pulled up to the gates at the compound, the sky was starting to lighten. The Prospect standing guard, came out, hand on the gun at his hip as if he was just waiting for us to cause trouble. I remembered those days. Somewhat.

"Tell Badger Ram is here with the women," I said.

His eyebrows rose and he stared for a minute. "Where's your cut?"

"In my saddlebags. These women are tired, hungry, hurting, and most of all they're scared. They know I'm a biker but seeing me in the club colors probably wouldn't have soothed them any. Just open the fucking gate."

His gaze narrowed, but he did as I said. It seemed Badger had spread the word I was returning, or at least told this little shit to let us inside when we got here. *Off to a great start.*

I parked outside the clubhouse, then waited for the women and girls to get out of the van. I didn't hear any noise from the clubhouse, which meant if there'd been a party, it was over with. Just the same, I opened the doors to peek inside before letting the women in.

Once I saw Badger and two other brothers, and no one else, I stepped inside.

"Why the fuck have you been gone all this time?" Slash asked.

"Nice to see you too, VP. Had some shit to sort out."

He snorted. "You done?"

"Maybe. Guess that depends on how welcome I am around here."

"Look, we all know you went Nomad after something happened. If Badger knows the reason, he's never said. None of us will push you for answers, just know you're always welcome here," Demon said.

"Thanks." I eyed the club president. We'd spoken multiple times since I'd been gone, but this was my first time seeing him in person since the day I rode out of here. He'd aged quite a bit. So had I for that matter. I'd been a kid back then. Not so much anymore.

I introduced them to Talia, helped push two tables together and got the women situated with plates and drinks, then I went behind the bar to grab a cold beer. I didn't know how this was going to play out, but it looked like I'd be sticking around for a while. If they really meant it, and I was welcome here, then maybe it was time to put down some roots.

Chapter Four

Talia

We had arrived at the compound without any trouble. While the bikers seemed large and a bit scary, they had been kind to us. They had fed us soup with crackers and provided a variety of drinks. With our bellies full, the only thing we needed now was a place to shower and sleep. I didn't know where they planned to put us. It seemed best to let Ram take the lead.

The moment the men welcomed him, the tension seemed to leave Ram's body. They'd spoken of him being gone for a while. It only left me with lingering questions. We knew nothing about the man who had saved us, nor did we know anything about the place he'd brought us to. I could tell the others felt relieved and even safe. As much as I hoped they were right, part of me still feared this could be a trap.

Ram came over and pulled me to the side. His grip was firm yet not hard enough to hurt me. It reminded me he'd always been gentle with me, even when I'd been openly skeptical about his reasons for helping us. If none of this was an act, then he really was a good man. I hadn't realized those still existed.

"Without much notice, my club wasn't able to prepare very well for the six of you. There are two places they are calling apartments, each with two beds. That leaves two of you sleeping on the couch or floor in each unit. Unless the bravest of you wants to share the house they're giving me." I opened my mouth to tell him off, thinking this sounded far too much like he expected the sort of payment none of us wanted to give, but he lifted a hand to stop me. "It's not what you think. I've been told there is a three-bedroom house that's mine if I would like to stay. Since I don't plan to go anywhere, at least not right now, I'm claiming the house. You're welcome to use one of the extra bedrooms."

He'd taken me by surprise again. He seemed to be doing that frequently. Every time I expected the worst, he proved to be a kind and thoughtful person.

"Why me?" I asked.

He smiled. "Did you miss the part where I said the *bravest* of you could stay with me?"

As much as I didn't want them to, his words flattered me. I'd been called a lot of things in my life, but only Ram had ever used words like brave or fierce.

"And where is this house located?" I asked.

"I haven't seen it yet so I'm not certain, but it would be here at the compound inside the fence. Which means you'd be safe from the outside world. Several of my brothers have families now. The six of you will not be the only women, and I've heard there are also children. I've been gone for so long I haven't met any of them yet. Except for one. Adalia is Badger's woman, and she was the adopted daughter of Grizzly. I was told Grizzly passed away, so you won't be able to meet him."

"How is it that you know her but none of the others?" I asked.

"That's a story for Badger or Adalia to tell you. All I can say is that she's been here since she was close to Riley's age."

He was right about one thing. Knowing there were other women and even children here did make me feel a bit better, unless of course they were kept in cages like Vega had done to the others.

As if my thoughts had conjured them, two women entered the building. One walked over to Badger, and I assumed she was Adalia. The other approached the man named Slash. Each woman had a bag in their hands.

"If I had to guess, I'd say they brought a few things the six of you might need. Would you like to meet them?" Ram asked.

I gave a nod, even though I doubted those women would say if they were being hurt or not, with there being three big bikers in the room.

Calm down. Stop assuming the worst about everyone. I straightened my shoulders, stood a little taller, and followed Ram over to the two couples.

"It's nice to see you again, Adalia," Ram said. "This is Talia. she's one of the women I brought with me."

"You haven't changed at all," Adalia said. "You look exactly the same as when you left."

Badger folded his arms over his chest. "She's not entirely wrong. How is it that you look the same and I seem to have aged two decades?"

Ram shrugged. "I think the stress of being the club's president is what aged you."

Badger smirked. "No doubt."

The other woman gave us a smile and a slight wave from where she stood next to Slash. "I'm Shella. It's nice to meet you both."

"I don't mean to pull Ram away from this reunion, but I think the others would really like to rest now. Could someone show us where we'll be staying?" I fidgeted a little as apprehension filled me. Maybe I should have stayed quiet. Would these men be angry I'd interrupted?

Badger flashed me a quick smile, setting me at ease. "Sure thing. Sorry if we got a little caught up. Would you feel more comfortable if Adalia and Shella led the way?"

"I'd like to go with them as well," Ram said. "Unless Talia thinks that would be a bad idea."

As if I could tell the man no. For one, Riley seemed to really like him, and trusted him. And second, he was the only person we somewhat knew in this place. We might all still be strangers, but at least we'd experienced Ram's protectiveness.

"I think they would like that, especially Riley."

"Who is Riley?" Shella asked as she scanned the other women.

I pointed her out, which only drew Riley's attention. The moment she saw me standing with Ram, she got up and hurried over. The bright smile she gave him made my stomach knot. *Please don't betray her. Prove her trust in you is not misplaced.*

"Riley, this is Shella and Adalia. They're going to show us where all of you will be staying." Ram placed his hand on her shoulder, giving it a quick squeeze before letting go.

She looked like a kitten eager to lean into his touch. I didn't know how old Ram was, but I guessed he was in his late twenties to early thirties. Not quite old enough to be her father, but too old to be her boyfriend in my opinion. I didn't know if she saw him as a replacement for her dad, or if she'd fallen in love at first sight. I didn't think either option would bode well.

"We'll take you to the apartments," Adalia said. "Once you've had time to rest, make a list of anything all of you need. Even food preferences. Each apartment has a fully equipped kitchen. We've placed a pad of paper and pen on the counter in both kitchens. There's also a list of phone numbers on the fridge. We want to make your stay here as pleasant as possible."

"We appreciate your help," I said.

I motioned for the others to follow us. I took the lead of my small group, walking right behind Shella and Adalia. Ram brought up the rear. For some reason, it left me feeling reassured. I knew I had trust issues, but it felt like maybe I was beginning to open to him a little more. If he proved to be a liar, I'd deal with the fallout later.

The apartments were close by. It looked like they had more than two, but I assumed the ones they showed us were the only vacant units. Riley stuck beside Ram the entire time, and I noticed she grabbed his hand at some point. He let her, acting as if he hadn't even noticed. It seemed he was Riley's security blanket for the moment. I didn't know how that would work moving forward, but it didn't hurt anything for now.

Heather and a teen girl called Anna decided to take the first apartment. Marci looked from me to Riley as we toured the second apartment. I knew what she wanted to ask. Only two beds and four of us left.

"Where are you staying, Talia?" Riley asked.

I glanced at Ram. He waited patiently, letting me decide if I wanted to accept his offer. Being here with the women would be nice, but at the same time, if this really was a trap, then we'd all be cornered like rats. Staying somewhere else in the compound wasn't an entirely awful idea. Ram was a stranger to us, but he was at least a little familiar after what we'd been through tonight. If he'd wanted to hurt us, he'd have left us behind, right?

"I'm going to stay at Ram's house," I said. "In the guest room."

"There's a storage building at the compound. We don't store regular mattresses there, but we do have guests to the club often enough we've bought a

- 200 -

handful of air mattresses. If anyone would prefer one of those instead of a couch or the floor, we can grab some," Shella said.

Riley pressed closer to Ram and looked like she might cry at any moment. "Can't I go with the two of you?"

Ram arched an eyebrow and gave me a look that clearly said, *It's up to you.* Great. I didn't feel right inviting people to stay in his house. Didn't matter if he hadn't had it until this very moment. It was still *his*.

"There's only two bedrooms set up in the house right now," Adalia said. "We didn't think anyone would be staying with Ram and had to furnish the place quickly. There weren't a lot of options at the store so late at night. It's just those mattresses that come in a box, so we put a mattress cover on them to help mask the scent. They smelled really bad when we opened them. The Prospects let them air out as long as they could, but Shella and I finished setting up your house when we heard you were here."

"Oh!" Shella smiled. "Since we couldn't get a couch so last minute, we did get a futon at the store for you to have a spot to sit in the living room. It folds out into a bed."

Riley stared at me with big eyes and I knew that's where she wanted to sleep. I gave her a nod, and Ram flashed me a smile. It seemed I'd made both of them happy, even though I didn't understand why he wanted the young teen there. I'd ask about it later. Now wasn't the right time. And if I felt a teensy bit jealous, well, I'd keep that to myself. It was ridiculous. It's not like Riley wanted him to be her boyfriend or something. Ram made her feel safe, and that's all there was to it.

Why did I care anyway? I felt so conflicted. I

wanted to keep him at a distance, and yet, I also wondered what it would feel like to lean on him a little. Something told me he gave good hugs, and I couldn't remember the last time I'd had one of those.

"Then it looks like Marci and Renata will share the second apartment," I said. "Is there a phone at Ram's house? Can we add the number to the list?"

"There's not," Adalia said.

"They can call my cell phone." Ram went into the kitchen and wrote his number on the sheet stuck to the fridge. "Tomorrow, the four of you can see where the rest of us will be staying, and you can come over whenever you want."

"How long will we be here?" Heather asked.

"As long as you want to be," Adalia said. "If you decide to make this town your home, then you can use the apartments while you find jobs and save enough money to get a fresh start. But please don't feel like we're forcing you to stay here. You can leave whenever you want to."

"We need to get our things from the van," I said. "I'm sure they'd all like to shower and get some sleep. I know I would."

Adalia gave Shella a gentle shove out the door. "We'll leave you alone for now. Ram, to get to your house, just follow the road around the bend. It's a white clapboard with black shutters. When you see the large oak tree on the left, the house is just past it."

Ram walked them out, and I led the others back to the van. Once Ram and I saw they were secure in their apartments, he eyed his bike, then started walking down the road. It looked like he'd have to leave it behind since he couldn't very well fit three people on it.

"Wait," someone called out. I saw it was the man

called Demon. He scared me, in all honesty. Something about him felt incredibly menacing. He tossed a set of keys to Ram. "Take a club truck. You may need it later anyway. We just put the bare basics into your house. I'm sure Badger will want to call Church soon, so everyone can welcome you back properly."

"Thanks," Ram said.

We all got into the truck and drove to Ram's new house. It was easy to find and looked rather charming. I thought it would be really cute with some shrubs or flowers out front. I doubted a biker cared much about those sorts of things. I saw a barn not too far off, and wondered if they had livestock here. Just what sort of bikers were these?

We explored the house with Ram, set up the futon with blankets and sheets for Riley, then she and I took turns showering in the hall bathroom. By the time I'd dried off and dressed in my pajamas, I noticed Riley was sound asleep. Noise in the kitchen drew my attention, and I found Ram sitting at the table with a cup of coffee.

"Won't that just keep you up?" I asked.

"Not really. Makes me focus, but the caffeine doesn't keep me from sleeping."

I pulled out a chair and sat. It was a really small, square table with four chairs, but at least they'd made sure he had something. It looked nice, even if Ram did seem too big for it.

"May I ask you something?" He gave a nod. "Why did you agree to let Riley stay here?"

He leaned back and took another swallow of his coffee, seeming to contemplate the question for a moment. "Remember when I said Adalia came here when she was around Riley's age? She reminds me a bit of her from back then. Wounded. Not wanted.

Guess I just wanted her to feel safe, and like she had a place where she belonged. If being here with me gives that to her, then fine."

I should have known he'd give an answer like that. So far, everything he'd done had been for us. Well, maybe not killing Vega and his men. I hadn't asked his reasoning for it yet, and I wasn't sure I wanted to. Some things were better left shrouded in mystery.

"I'm going to bed," I said, standing and stretching a little. "Thanks for everything, Ram. I mean it."

"You're welcome." He drank more of his coffee and watched as I left the room.

No matter how long I stayed here with him, I wasn't sure I'd ever figure him out. And maybe that was all right.

Chapter Five

Ram

I had a house, a woman, and a teenage girl. None of which I'd ever expected, and I damn sure hadn't thought I'd be back with the Devil's Fury. Then again, I'd never gotten rid of my cut. I guess some part of me always considered the fact I'd return. It just hadn't been on my to-do list in the near future.

I had a feeling Talia would eventually leave. While I didn't know anything about her past, I knew she couldn't have had an easy life. The strength she had was the sort to be earned. It was clear she'd been through many battles before I'd met her yesterday. Even though I hoped Vega had been the worst of it, I doubted it to be true. I'd learned long ago just how cruel the world could be, and it liked to devour beautiful things like Talia.

Yes I could admit to myself that I not only found her intriguing but also alluring. The way she stared at me with defiant eyes, the thick mass of hair hanging down her back, and her full pouty lips, all made me want to reach out and grab her, hold on tight, and never let her go. I had to remind myself she was more like a wild mustang than a hissing kitten. Talia wasn't the type of woman to be easily tamed.

The house my brothers had given me was bigger than I'd expected. I didn't think it was more than 1600 square feet, but it was far larger than what I would need as a single man. It had been so long since I'd even been on a date, much less considered keeping a woman as my own. It didn't seem likely I'd settle down any time soon. Not unless I could gain Talia's trust and convince her she belonged with me.

Much like the women I'd brought here, I didn't

own much. Constantly being on the road meant I had to travel light. I only kept a small bag of toiletries, two pairs of basketball shorts, two tanks, one jacket for colder weather, and two changes of jeans and tees. My running shoes were in my saddlebags as well. When they made a list of the things they needed, I knew I'd have to make one for myself as well. The club might pay for the items the women and girls requested. I'd have to purchase my own.

I hadn't lied about having enough money for the things we'd bought along the way. It didn't mean my account was overflowing with cash. In order to pay for everything I'd need for both myself and the house, I'd have to talk to Badger about getting a few jobs assigned to me. Otherwise I'd be out of money within a few days.

Exhaustion pulled at me. Getting some sleep would be a good idea, except I had too much on my mind right now. I didn't know what to do with either Talia or Riley. One wanted to stay with me, and the other would be out the door without any hesitation. Talia was far too independent. Of course, that was one of the things I liked about her. I'd never been into meek and submissive women.

I had been telling Talia the truth when I said my cup of coffee wouldn't keep me awake. There was only one thing I knew for sure would give me the burst of energy I needed. A long run through the compound. When I had been a Prospect for the club, Grizzly had always told me to run it off whenever I had too many thoughts in my head. Over the years, I'd learned it was also a good way to stay awake. My feet pounding the pavement helped me center my thoughts, while the pumping of my heart gave me the adrenaline I needed to push through the day.

I'd left my bike at the clubhouse, which meant I didn't have easy access to my saddlebags. Not having access to my running clothes or tennis shoes meant I couldn't go on a jog. I could however walk to the clubhouse and ride my bike back. After making sure Talia and Riley were both okay, I quietly left the house.

I hadn't walked past more than three houses when I heard cursing and the sound of boots coming toward me fast. I didn't recognize the man, which meant he didn't know me either. The fact I wasn't wearing my cut wasn't going to make this any easier. It sounded as if he was right behind me, and anticipating him attempting to knock me down, I sidestepped at the last minute. The guy crashed onto the pavement and glared at me over his shoulder.

"I realize you're going to get up all pissed off no matter what I say, but I do belong here. In fact, I've been part of this club longer than you have. Just haven't been around for more than ten years."

The man stood up and dusted himself off. "Bullshit. Who the fuck are you?"

"My name is Ram, and if you'll let me continue on to the clubhouse, I'll get my cut out of my saddlebags. Or you can keep detaining me until my patience wears out. Then you'll be eating the pavement again." I noticed the patch on his cut said Dingo. I had heard about him from Badger. If I remembered right, he was one of the brothers with the family now. "Look, I get it. You have a family to protect and you saw some strange man walking by your house. If you really think I don't belong here, give Badger a call."

"If you're part of this club as you claim, why haven't I heard of you before?" Dingo asked.

I wasn't sure how to answer that question. As far as I knew, until last night, Badger was the only one aware I'd still been alive. He'd clearly spoken to Demon and Slash. He'd also mentioned needing to call Church to explain my presence here. Something told me Dingo wouldn't be the only man questioning whether I belonged here.

"Badger mentioned he'd called Church. I think he was giving me time to settle into my house and get some rest. To answer your question, I think everyone believed I was dead."

The skeptical look on his face made me wish I'd just stayed home. At this rate, I'd end up fighting him and possibly others before I even reached the clubhouse. All I'd wanted was to get my bike and go for a run. If it hadn't been for the women and girls, I wouldn't be here right now. And I was definitely second-guessing my decision to stay. It wasn't like I'd thought it would be easy, but I didn't feel like dealing with any of this bullshit right now. Where the fuck were the brothers who knew who I was?

"If you don't want to ask Badger, then give Demon or Slash a call. They both know I'm here. Adalia and Shella helped set up my house yesterday, so you could check with them too." I sighed and ran a hand through my hair. "Look, I just want to get my bike from the clubhouse. My clothes are in the saddlebags. If I'd have known it would have been such a hassle to leave my damn house, I'd have stayed home."

I heard someone approaching from behind and cursed my rotten luck. Was someone else coming to give me a hard time? This was getting to be more troublesome than it was worth. I didn't remember my brothers being this fucking annoying. Regardless, I held myself back. As much as I wanted to plant my fist in Dingo's face, I didn't think Badger would appreciate it much. And it certainly wouldn't earn me any points around here. Well, unless everyone else found this bastard annoying too.

"Are you kidding me right now?" I didn't even have to turn around. After ten years, I still recognized that voice. On the upside, maybe he could get Dingo to back the hell off. Then again, there was always a good chance Steel would just put me on my ass.

He stopped beside me, forcing me to turn and meet his gaze. It didn't seem like he'd aged as much as Badger had. He eyed me from the top of my head to the tip of my toes and back again.

"Yes, Steel, it's really me. It wasn't my intention to blindside everyone."

He pulled me in for a tight hug, slapping my back a few times. I had to admit it was good to see him. He was one of the few I'd truly missed while I was gone.

"Are you back for good?" he asked.

"I guess that depends on whether or not everyone wants me back. Badger gave me a house. It seemed like everything was a done deal, until I ran into this asshole who's been giving me shit." I motioned toward Dingo. "I just wanted to retrieve my bike from the clubhouse. Didn't think it was going to be such a big issue."

"Why am I the asshole?" Dingo asked. "I saw a stranger walking through the compound, no cut or bike in sight, and now I'm wrong for asking questions?"

"The fact you're still upright tells me he's not too pissed off. Yet." Steel smirked. "Because if he'd lost all patience with you, you'd not only be on the ground, but you'd also need a hospital. We didn't call him Ram for nothing."

Dingo threw his hands in the air and walked off. He called back over his shoulder. "I'd say it's nice to meet you, but I'm trying to teach my kids it's not nice to lie, and I lead by example."

Steel laughed hard enough he pressed a hand to his belly. It was nice to know someone was amused by this.

"That's right, laugh it up, asshole. I hope you choke on air."

If anything, my words only seemed to make him laugh harder. I rolled my eyes and walked off. Why did I get the feeling today was going to make me want a bottle of Fireball? At least I knew Badger, Demon, Slash, and Steel didn't have a problem with me coming back. Four down, and who knew how many to go. Judging by the number of houses, the club had grown a lot over the last decade. How many more new faces would I meet?

By the time I got the bike back to my new house, the urge to go for a run had long passed. Instead, I decided to check the cabinets and fridge and make a grocery list. I didn't think they'd have left the kitchen completely bare, but it didn't mean it would have everything I needed. I found a small package of paper plates and another of solo cups in a cabinet, as well as a box of plastic utensils. Thankfully, they'd provided a skillet, pot, baking sheet, and basic cooking utensils. At least I'd be able to fix us something to eat.

The food items were every bit as limited, but I found a package of chicken breasts, tater tots, and freshly made ice in the freezer. The fridge had half gallon of milk, orange juice, four bottles of beer, a small tub of butter, a carton of eggs, and a bag of shredded cheese. I certainly hoped they'd put more than this in the apartments. Opening a different cabinet, I found two boxes of macaroni, a few cans of soup, and some packs of ramen noodles. They'd also left some bananas and apples on the counter.

"Were they trying to feed a biker or a college student?" I muttered to myself. It was a good thing my mother had taught me to be resourceful in the kitchen. She might have passed before I'd turned eighteen, but she'd given me quite a few life lessons before then. I knew I'd had it better than some.

If only I had a baking dish, then I knew exactly what I'd cook for the three of us. I wondered if it was too early to call Badger's house. Surely Adalia would let me borrow one.

Instead of taking the chance of a ringing phone waking any of them up, I sent a quick text to ask about the baking dish. Of course, Badger's response made me wish I had Adalia's phone number instead.

A baking dish? Did you turn into fucking Betty Crocker while you were gone?

I pinched the bridge of my nose and took a breath before responding. It probably wasn't a good idea to start the day by calling my club president an asshole.

Can I borrow one or not?

It only took him a moment to reply. *Yeah. I'll have a Prospect leave it by your front door. I'd imagine your girls are still sleeping.*

I replied with a quick thank you and ignored his comment about *my* girls. While I waited for the baking dish, I decided to shower and change. Probably wouldn't hurt to go ahead and wear my cut as well. If I'd had it on earlier, maybe I wouldn't have had an issue with Dingo.

It didn't take me long to shower and pull on a clean pair of jeans and shirt, and I draped my cut over the back of a kitchen chair and left my boots by the front door. Checking the small porch, I found the baking dish and brought it inside. Since the Prospect had set it on the ground, I gave it a quick wash before setting it on the counter by the stove. I set the oven to preheat, then took the tater tots out of the freezer.

It took a minute as I pulled out different drawers, but I finally found some aluminum foil. It would take a few days before I remembered where to find everything. I spread it on the counter and placed the tots on top. After I put another sheet of foil over it, I pressed down hard and mashed the tots, then placed them in the bottom of the baking dish.

Some diced ham or chopped-up bacon would have been a perfect addition. Hell, I wouldn't have even minded some diced onion or even a little bell pepper. My mom always added those when she made this. Sometimes if she wanted to really spice things up, she'd use pepper jack cheese instead of cheddar, and add a can of Rotel. Getting the eggs, milk, and cheese out of the fridge, I cracked eight eggs into a bowl, added a splash of milk, then beat them with a fork. I poured the eggs over the tots, and topped it with shredded cheese, then baked it in the oven.

It might not be the most perfect breakfast in the world, but it would easily feed the three of us and would keep for several hours if Talia and Riley slept for a while longer. Although, I had improvised with the tots. My mom had always used frozen shredded hash browns.

I wondered what she would have thought of Talia and Riley. For that matter, I wanted to know what she'd think about the way I'd lived my life. Would she be proud of me? Or would it have broken her heart to know I wouldn't hesitate to take another life, even if it was in order to save others? Anytime I'd stayed in one area for too long, the papers would start to piece things together. I'd often been called a vigilante. They weren't exactly wrong.

I heard the sound of footsteps outside the kitchen. Turning to face the doorway, I saw Riley rubbing her eyes. She blinked at me like a sleepy little owl, and I couldn't help but smile. I didn't know why she didn't want to return home and I wouldn't pry. But one thing was for certain, if I'd ever had a kid like her, I'd have done anything to protect them and keep them safe. Of course, I'd never stayed with a woman for more than a few nights, not since high school. At this point in my life, I didn't think I'd ever be a father.

"Morning, Sunshine," I said. "You're up a lot earlier than I expected. Did you sleep okay?"

"I woke up a few times. I don't think I slept more than fifteen to twenty minutes before I'd jolt awake, thinking I was back in the cage."

I held my hand out to her, giving her the option to come to me or keep her distance. As much as I wanted to comfort her, I also worried I could do more harm than good. It surprised me when she not only came to me but wrapped her arms around my waist and snuggled against me. I closed my arm around her shoulders and gave her a hug.

"It will take some time to adjust. You have a lot of healing to do, and I don't just mean the physical kind. I'm not going to ask what you've been through, or why you didn't want to go home. But you can stay here for as long as you want to."

She took a step back and swiped her hands over her cheeks. I hadn't even realized she'd been crying. She gave me a tremulous smile before taking a seat at the kitchen table.

"I never knew my dad, not my real one. If I had, maybe he'd have been something like you. Kind. Generous. The type of man who would support his daughter and tell her everything would be okay no matter what she'd been through."

I walked over to the coffee maker, put in fresh grounds, and hit the start button. There was so much I wanted to say. Since Badger assured me I still had a place in this club, there was no logical reason I couldn't tell her what was on my mind. Fear held me back. It had been a long time since anyone depended on me. Was I even up to the task?

"My mom had me when she was really young. She'd gotten a fake ID to go to a bar, even though she was only sixteen. The only thing she knew about my dad was that he rode a motorcycle, and he'd told her his name was Montgomery. We lived in a trailer all my life, and she had a revolving door of boyfriends. Each one worse than the last."

I braced my hands on the counter, feeling as if my knees would give out. It had to be a coincidence, right? There were probably dozens of bikers in this country by the name of Montgomery. Just the same, I needed to know a little more.

"Riley, where did you grow up? I assumed Vega had found all of you not too far from the warehouse. Do you even know where I found you?"

"All I know is that they took me off the street, injected me with something, and I woke up in a cage. I'd been with those men even before I met Vega."

So there was a good chance some, if not all, of the women and girls weren't even from that area. We hadn't been too far outside of Birmingham, Alabama. Now we were in southern Georgia, near the Florida Panhandle. Had I taken her even farther from her home? She might not want to return, but the fact remained Riley was a minor. Was her mother even looking for her?

"What state are you from?" I asked.

"I grew up near Biloxi, Mississippi. I doubt my mom is looking for me. If you want to check, her name is Reba Carson."

I studied Riley's features, looking for anything familiar. From the shape of her eyes, to the color of her irises, and even the slope of her nose, I couldn't deny she looked like someone I knew. A much younger version of my mother. Her hair color and texture, the shape of her face and mouth, were all different. Fourteen years old. If I accounted for the months her mother would have been pregnant, then it would have meant she was conceived while I was in that area.

My heart pounded and my mouth went dry. I had thought about asking Riley if she wanted to stay here permanently, thinking I could adopt her. But if my new knowledge, and the math, were correct then she might very well be my daughter. The woman I'd hooked up with during those days hadn't been called Reba. Since Riley said her mother had used a fake ID, it was possible the name hadn't been real either.

"That fake ID your mother had, did she ever tell you what name she used on it? It wasn't by any chance Riva Carter, was it?"

Riley's eyes went wide, and she gave me a slow nod. "Mom ranted about it one night when she was drunk. How did you know that name?"

I swallowed hard and hoped I wasn't about to fuck up. She could take the news badly, thinking I'd abandoned her all these years. If I'd ever known about her, I would have made sure she was okay.

"Because I was in the Biloxi area roughly fifteen

years ago, and I met a woman named Riva at a bar." I moved closer to her and kneeled beside her chair. "I earned the name Ram when I patched into this club. When I left, I'd sometimes tell women my first name. I didn't really feel like part of the Devil's Fury anymore. My legal name is Montgomery Cash. Would you be willing to help me with a paternity test? There's a chance you might be my daughter."

Tears slipped down Riley's cheeks, and she flung her arms around me. I held her as she cried. As my gaze shifted to the kitchen doorway, I saw Talia. She paled a little and leaned against the door frame. I motioned for her to join us in the kitchen. She gave me a tight smile and came to sit down.

"Looks like we have something to celebrate," Talia said.

The timer on the stove dinged and I pulled away from Riley. After I fixed our plates, got us some drinks, and sat down I sent a quick text to Badger.

Any idea where I can get a paternity test done?

He didn't even bother texting back. Instead, he pounded on my front door about five minutes later.

Chapter Six

Talia

I couldn't quite process everything. Riley was Ram's daughter? They must have talked a lot this morning for him to piece that together. Now the club's president sat at the table with us. He seemed skeptical about the issue. As excited as Riley appeared, I hoped she really had found her father. As much as Riley adored Ram, it would crush her spirit to find out he wasn't really her dad.

The new development left me feeling even more conflicted. Something told me Ram might be attracted to me. Why else would he have asked me to stay here with him? The thought of trusting a man scared me, but part of me had wanted to give him a chance. Except now I wasn't sure how I would fit into his life. He and Riley had just found one another. Would there even be room for me in this new family?

"I'm going to need a DNA sample from both of you," Badger said. "Outlaw has connections at a lab to get it processed as quickly as possible. The guy he talked to said he should have results within twenty-four hours to seventy-two hours."

"Like hair or something?" Ram asked.

"You should probably swab the inside of your cheek," I said. "That's how they usually do it on those crime shows on TV. But you'd need a sterile swab."

Badger pinched the bridge of his nose and pulled out his phone. He pulled up a name in his contacts and hit the speaker button so we could all hear the conversation. I didn't know who he was calling, until I heard someone pick up and say *Outlaw*.

"Outlaw, we need a way to take the sample. Any ideas?" Badger asked.

"I'll send a Prospect over to my buddy's lab. He can get the items we need. Should have it within the hour," Outlaw said.

Badger ended the call and stood. "Looks like my work is done. I'll make sure they bring the test materials here. Give Outlaw a call once you're ready for the samples to go to the lab."

Without another word, he walked out of the room, and the front door opened and shut a moment later. I stared at Riley and Ram, uncertain what I should say. While Riley looked like she'd just received the greatest gift ever, Ram seemed a bit shell-shocked. Of course, if he'd had no clue he had a daughter, then it was understandable. Considering he'd risked his life to free the six of us, then brought us here when we had nowhere else to go, it told me had a strong sense of responsibility.

"Would the two of you like some time alone?" I asked. "I could always move into one of the apartments with the others."

"Stay," Ram said. His tone was low with a hint of gruffness to it. Yet I heard the command just the same. I wanted to bristle, fuss about men trying to tell women what to do, but... I wanted to stay here with him and Riley.

"Fine, but I think I should take the couch. If Riley is your daughter, then she needs a bedroom. It's her house too, after all." Ram scratched at his beard and studied me. I wished I knew what he was thinking, yet at the same time, I wondered if it was better for me not to know.

"Is there anyone here around my age?" Riley asked.

I wanted to thank her for breaking the building tension between me and Ram. I shot her a grateful smile, then stood to reheat my food in the microwave. I hadn't been able to eat once Badger arrived, and now my food was ice cold. Since Ram went to the trouble of making it, I felt like I should at least attempt to eat it.

"I'm not sure. It's been a long time since I was here," Ram said. "But we can certainly ask. I know there are families here now. There weren't any before. Only a bunch of single men. I'll send Outlaw a text and ask him. Eat your breakfast."

"Okay... Dad."

Riley's cheeks flushed when she said the word, and I saw how much she enjoyed being able to call Ram her father. Judging by his expression, he rather liked it too. Again, it left me feeling like I was intruding on the two of them. I'd offered to leave, but Ram said to stay. How did Riley feel about it? She might want him all to herself right now.

Ram stepped out of the room, and I took a chance to ask Riley how she felt. "Your dad said I should stay. What do you want, Riley?"

"You're not much older than me, are you?" she asked.

"I'm only six years older than you," I said. "Why? I promise I'm not trying to make Ram my dad too."

She took a bite of her food and watched me until I felt like squirming in my seat. When she spoke again, I was thankful I hadn't decided to take a sip of my drink or I'd have choked on it.

"Maybe you want to be his wife instead?" she asked.

"What? Why would you... Riley, I'm not trying to take Ram from you in any way. Not even as a wife. The two of you just found one another. I know how important this time is for you both."

She played with her food, shoving it around her plate with her fork. "My mom sucked as a parent. She always had loser boyfriends, and barely kept me fed or clothed. There were even times she'd get so mad she'd hit me, saying I'd ruined her life."

I didn't understand why she was telling me that? Was it a warning she didn't need a mom? Or did she really want one, but didn't know how to ask? Not that I was up for being one. I could barely take care of myself most days.

"I may have only met your dad, but I don't think he'd be the type to ever hit you," I said.

She shook her head, refusing to meet my gaze. "You wouldn't either. Right?"

Was she worried if Ram and I ended up together, which seemed farfetched to me, I would end up hurting her if I got angry? I did have a temper, and I hadn't exactly been nice.

"Riley, yesterday was really hard on all of us. So much happened in such a short amount of time. I don't know how long you were with those men. I might have only been there for a few hours, but they weren't the first ones to try and harm me. To say I have trust issues is putting it mildly. I'm scared that if I believe in someone, I'll end up getting hurt again."

"Isn't it lonely to live like that? You don't have anyone to rely on, no one to hold your hand when things get scary. I was so excited when Ram said he thinks he's my dad. Not only because I've always wanted to meet my real father, but I could tell he was the type who wouldn't abandon me." She finally looked over at me. "I think he'd stay by your side too, as long as you were willing to be here with us. To be part of the family."

This sweet girl was making my heart hurt. For

the longest time, I'd wanted exactly that. A family. The kind you saw on TV where kids got hugs, and everyone supported each other. I'd never had that. My mom was a distant memory. My father had been a gambling addict. He'd still been alive when I left, but I'd checked up on him a few times. Last time I'd asked around my hometown, they'd said he passed away.

"Riley, you may want me to stay here and be your mom, but life doesn't work like that. What if your dad and I don't get along?"

"What if we do?" Ram asked from behind me. I looked at him over my shoulder. He had his arms crossed, and a stern look on his face. "Do you have to assume the worst about everyone and every situation? Would it hurt to stay here for a while and give things a chance?"

No. It wouldn't. Not unless I fell for him, and he ended up breaking my heart. "I'll stay and see what happens, but it doesn't change the fact Riley needs her own room."

"I think the two of us should talk. Riley, would you like to go visit the apartments and see the others?" Ram asked.

"I can't stay here with the two of you?" she asked.

And it was already starting. She felt left out. This was why I'd suggested I leave the house and move in with the others. The glare Ram shot me said he knew exactly what I was thinking, and he didn't agree.

"I spoke with a friend. He has a daughter a year older than you. And I heard there's a little boy who's a few years younger. Would you like to meet either of them?" Ram asked. "The girl only lives a few houses away. Her name is Coral."

"What if she doesn't like me?" Riley asked.

Ram came closer and ran his hand over Riley's hair. "Honey, there's not a single person here who won't like you. If you want to wait a little bit before meeting anyone, that's fine. But I really need to speak with Talia about a few things."

"Can I sit in the living room and watch TV while you talk in here?" she asked.

"Sure. When we're finished, we'll make a list of everything we need so we can go shopping. Or do you want the pad and pen? You can start your list now," he said.

Riley nodded. Ram got the pad and pen off the counter and handed them to her. She jumped up from the table and rushed out of the room. I could see the excitement in her eyes. Last night, she'd been thrilled with the books he'd let her buy. I wondered what she'd put on her list for today.

Ram took Riley's vacant seat, shoving her plate aside. Then he stared at me, as if he wasn't quite sure what to say. He'd said he wanted to talk. Had I made him angry? Since he'd asked me to stay, he clearly wasn't going to throw me out.

"I kind of like your prickly side. Your sarcasm, defensiveness, and the way you glower at me are kind of cute. However, it tells me you've built some pretty high walls around yourself."

When he didn't continue, I figured he wanted me to say something. "What if I have?"

"You don't need to tell me everything in your past. All I want to know is what sort of trauma you've suffered and any triggers I should avoid. This isn't just my home, it's yours and Riley's too. For however long you want it to be. In order to make sure this is a safe place for you, it means I need to arm myself with knowledge. Otherwise I may say or do something that will scare you or cause a flashback to something you've tried to forget. So, help me, Talia. Give me the tools I need."

Why did he have to be so damn nice? When had anyone asked me for such a thing? Never, that's when. He'd been right about the high walls I'd built. Until now, no one had been able to penetrate them. Something told me Ram wouldn't break them down. He wouldn't have to. With his thoughtful yet persuasive words, and kindness, I'd rip the wall apart on my own.

"Fine. You want to know my triggers? Men. Every single one has to do with men. My father was a gambler. He lost the car, the house, and eventually his life. I ran away when I wasn't much older than Riley. Fell in with a bad crowd, thought I'd fallen in love, only for the bastard to turn on me. He sold me to some men for a few hours. When he came to pick me up, I was already gone. I was stupid and trusted two more men. Both taught me painful lessons. Happy now?" I asked.

He rubbed a finger over his lips, and I could practically see the wheels turning in his head. I'd dumped a lot on him, in a not so nice way. Sure, I knew I had an attitude. I also didn't like talking about anything in my past. It needed to stay behind me. Otherwise, I wasn't sure I could survive for much longer.

"You're angry. Not only at the people who hurt and betrayed you, but also at yourself. Until you learn to forgive *yourself*, I'm not sure you'll ever be able to fully trust someone or fall in love. You thought you loved those men. Or boys, I suppose. You don't look much older than Riley. I don't think it was love. You needed them in order to survive, so you convinced yourself you loved them."

How did this man see so much? It was like he could look straight through me. In all my life, I'd never met anyone like him. If I walked away, I didn't think I'd find someone like him ever again. No matter how scared I was, I needed to stay. He was right. I had some healing to do, and it was time I let people in again. And if I'd made yet another mistake, then I'd dust myself off and keep going, same as before.

Please be the man I think you are.

I might push everyone away, but it exhausted me. I needed someone to help me carry the load, to tell me things would be okay, and give me a shoulder to cry on. Not once did I ever dream of becoming an instant mom, and to a girl nearly the same age as me, but Riley wasn't a deal-breaker. If she was fine with me being part of her family, then the only thing standing in my way was… me.

Chapter Seven

Ram

It fascinated me to see the various expressions cross Talia's face. She didn't like what I'd had to say, yet she couldn't deny I was right, not even to herself. It was a start. I didn't only want her to let me in because I intended to make her mine. Even if I failed to convince her she belonged here, letting her leave without finding a way to make peace with herself and her past would only let her wounds fester. She'd be miserable her entire life, no matter where she went. We might have just met, but I still cared too much about her to let that happen.

The woman was a stranger. It shouldn't matter to me how she felt. I didn't believe in things like love at first sight. However, I did want more time to get to know her, and I had a feeling in my gut she was meant to be mine. Some guys let their dick lead them. For me, I needed a woman with some spark, someone who'd hold my interest. Curvy women were a dime a dozen. Same for beautiful ones. But someone like Talia who didn't hold back, and wasn't afraid to voice her opinions, those didn't come along nearly as often as I'd like.

It didn't take much to make me hard for a woman. Same was true for most men. The difference this time? I didn't want a quick fuck. Talia was the sort of woman I wanted to keep by my side indefinitely. To live with someone day after day, I needed more than sexual attraction. Something like that could fade over time. If I was going to take a chance on building a life with someone, then I needed a woman who kept me engaged when we spoke, or at least kept me on my toes with her antics. Once Talia settled in, I had a feeling I'd see even more of her fiery personality.

She wasn't the sort of woman you looked at and wondered if she was a model or actress. I wouldn't even have called her the next-door type of pretty. Yet, there was something about her that made me take a second and third look. I loved her eyes. They were expressive and fringed with thick lashes. I wouldn't mind staring into them the rest of my life. But the reason I wanted her had nothing to do with her appearance. It was her sassy attitude, and the way she'd decided to protect the others, even though she herself had also been a victim of Vega.

"I have a question for you," I said. "Have you ever slept with a man, and I mean *only* sleep. No sex. No kissing. Just lying beside each other all night."

"Of course not," she said. "What man would ever want to do something like that?"

"Me," I said. It wasn't entirely a lie. Did I want to do more than sleep beside her? Sure. But I had enough control over myself I wasn't going to take something she different offer. Nor would I try to convince her she wanted more. "Would you be willing to give it a try if I promise not to touch you without your permission?"

She narrowed her eyes at me, and I knew she was trying to figure out the catch, or wondering if I was about to show my "true" colors. It was clear she thought all men were like the scumbags she'd known, and yeah, I included her father in that. I'd already told her what I wanted. Now it was up to her to decide if she would be willing to take a chance. It was hard to earn her trust when she never gave me the opportunity to prove I wouldn't hurt her.

"What if you're lying and you touch me?" she asked.

"Then you can punch me, kick me in the balls, or

do anything else necessary to get away from me. Except I won't do anything you don't want me to, so I think I'm safe from being pummeled."

"For how long? How many nights am I supposed to sleep in the same bed as you?" she asked.

"Well, let's go one night first. If you think you can trust me beyond tonight, then you can sleep beside me for as long as you'd like. I thought we could let Riley move into the second bedroom today."

Mentioning Riley seemed to be the deciding factor. I saw the remaining fight drain from her, and she gave me a short nod. I felt like I'd at least found a foothold in the giant mountain I needed to climb. It was a cheap trick, but it worked. Although, I genuinely did want Talia in my bed, and wanted my daughter to feel like she belonged in this house.

"We should get the paper from Riley and add the things we need. I won't ask the club to buy things for the two of you. If we're going to be a family, then I should provide for you and Riley." She started to protest, and I held up a hand to keep her silent. "Hear me out. I didn't say we were running off to the courthouse to get married. Riley needs a family more than anything right now. If you decide that's not something you want, then we'll both move on, and the club will fill her need for a mother."

"You don't find it odd I'm not much older than her?" Talia asked. "I don't even know *your* age. If you can have a fourteen-year-old, are you in your fifties? And no, I'm not saying you look fifty. If anything, I'd say you're maybe thirty at the most."

She was certainly good for my ego. She wasn't far off, but I was halfway between thirty and forty. "I'm thirty-six. I was close to your age when I met Riley's mom."

Her brow furrowed and her nose scrunched a little. "You don't think her mother is looking for her? What if she wants her back? And I don't mean because she's suddenly become mother of the year, but she could see how happy Riley is now and decided she wants her just so you can't keep her. Or what if…"

She didn't have to finish her sentence. I'd essentially asked her to move in permanently and be Riley's mom, so it made sense she'd be concerned. There was always a chance Reba would come looking for Riley, but I didn't think it was likely.

"Reba could show up at the gates, and while I wouldn't have them run her off, I also wouldn't be welcoming her with open arms. Anyone can see Riley didn't have the best upbringing. Not to mention that bitch let her get kidnapped and doesn't seem to be looking for her. If she was, there'd be a missing child alert. If you're concerned I'll decide to move her into the house, you needn't be."

"You seem confident Riley is yours. Why even take the paternity test?" she asked.

"I think Riley needs that bit of reassurance. It's one thing for me to tell her she's mine, and another to have absolute proof. Plus, if Reba ever did show up, at least I'd have a legal right to keep Riley here with me." I ran my hand through my hair. "There's a possibility she's not my daughter. Not likely, though. Everything lines up a little too neatly."

"You're taking this awfully well. I'm not sure I'd react favorably in your shoes. First you save us from a monster who sold teenage girls, then you get the shock of having a daughter? And she's one of Vega's victims? I can't even imagine what's going through your mind right now," she said.

"Mostly, I'm wishing I'd made him suffer even

more." I gave her a slight smile. "At the time, I tried to end things quickly. I didn't want to traumatize everyone more than they already were. Seeing the things I wanted to do to Vega? It probably would have given all of you nightmares, and you definitely wouldn't have trusted me. You took your own revenge, but if I'd slaughtered him, tortured him for as long as I wanted, can you honestly say you'd be here now?"

She shook her head. "I think they're all tougher than you give them credit for. They survived, didn't they?"

"Yeah. All of you did."

We found Riley lying on her stomach on the futon. She'd set the paper and pen aside and had a movie playing on the TV. There wasn't Wi-Fi since I hadn't known about the house, so I assumed she was using the Blu-ray player. I'd noticed someone stocked a handful of movies for us, which I appreciated. Especially right now. There was so much to do.

"Talia and I are going to make our own lists, then we'll go over everything and figure out what's needed right away," I told her as I picked up the pad and pen. "It might take a few days, or longer, to get Wi-Fi or cable set up. We can get more movies while we're out."

"There's a Hulu gift card by the TV," Riley said. "Once we have Wi-Fi, we can sign up for an account."

Riley sat up and scooted to the end of the futon. I sat beside her, with Talia on my other side. While she watched her movie, I quickly made the list of personal items I'd need, then tore off a sheet of paper before giving the pad and pen to Talia. I'd noticed a pencil in one of the kitchen drawers earlier. I'd use it to make a grocery list and figure out what kitchen items we needed.

Talia and Riley came to find me right as I finished making a note of the basics. I had them list any foods or drinks they preferred, then waited while they showered and changed. I'd told Talia to use my bathroom, so they wouldn't have to take turns getting ready. Since she'd be staying in my room, it only made sense for her to use that one.

We'd take the club truck and get some necessities. I knew we should also check on the others and see if they were doing okay. Even though I'd brought them here, knowing they'd be safe, I had a feeling they were hiding in the apartments.

"Do you want to check on the others on our way out?" I asked Talia.

"Sounds good. Should we arrange for them to get the items they need?" she asked.

"The club has probably already been over there to get their lists. If they were smart, they sent one of the women. Wouldn't hurt to check on them, though. I don't want them to feel like I brought them here, then abandoned them."

She sighed. "You really are a good man, Ram."

"Only to those who deserve it." I really wanted her to stay, to make a life with me here at the Devil's Fury. She'd only met Badger, Slash, and Demon so far. Since Riley was my daughter, she'd need to meet everyone. There were a lot of new faces I hadn't met as well. "Would you be up for a club party? Not the wild kind with alcohol and sex. I mean more of a family type of get together. I'm not sure if that's something the club has ever done, but with old ladies and kids here now, I thought it wouldn't hurt to ask."

"Why are you asking?"

"The club needs to meet Riley, and there are new members I don't know. I'd like you to be there with us," I said.

"Then I'll attend."

I pulled out my phone and shot off a text to Badger. *Can we get the club together for a family type of party? I want everyone to meet Riley and Talia.*

It only took him a few seconds to respond.

Sure. After we've had Church.

I knew he'd be calling Church sooner or later. I only hoped he didn't send out the alert while I was gone. Only one way to make sure.

All right. Taking Talia and Riley out to buy some things we need.

There. Now he'd know we weren't going to be home for a little while. I'd like to treat the girls to lunch while we were out too. Not fast food, but somewhere a little nicer. None of us had the right clothes for anywhere fancy. I'd have to keep an eye on the main strip when we left and see what restaurants were still around, or what new ones popped up since I'd left.

Badger sent another response. *You're not making this easy. Text when you're back and I'll call Church, but I'll ask Adalia and Shella to help prepare something for tonight.*

I thanked him and started to shove my phone into my pocket, but it alerted me to another message. When I saw what looked like a text from Badger to the entire club, stating no club whores allowed at the compound today or tomorrow, I knew I'd have some pissed-off brothers.

Riley came into the kitchen in her new clothes and had her flip-flops on. She looked both excited and apprehensive. It was our first family outing, and I knew she'd take a while to adjust to her new life. Hell, anyone who'd been locked in a cage would be having issues right about now.

"If we're all ready, let's head out. Make sure we

have all the lists," I said.

Talia gathered them, and we went outside to the truck. I drove to a strip mall in town and let Talia and Riley shop for clothes and shoes before I got some things for myself in a different shop. When Riley saw a Five Below, she started bouncing on her toes, eager to look inside. I couldn't very well tell her no, so we went inside. I stuck close while they browsed. It didn't take long before I went to get a basket because Riley wanted nail polish, hair things, and even found some clothes and shoes she wanted. I had a hard time telling her she couldn't get the things she asked for. By the time we checked out, those five-dollar items came out to nearly two hundred dollars. Talia winced when she saw the total, but I pulled out my card and paid for it.

On the way to the next store, I received multiple alerts on my phone and stopped to check it. Now that I was back with the club, I had to be mindful of answering texts and calls on time. Badger might be welcoming me back without question, but it didn't mean I could ignore him or my brothers. For now, I needed to play it safe, especially since I needed to be at the compound for Riley's sake.

The fact I had an alert from my bank about a deposit was a bit shocking. I hadn't made one in over a week. Opening the app, I logged in and nearly choked when I saw my new balance. I couldn't tell where the money came from. Had someone made a mistake? Was it a banking error? I started to call them, then realized I had a few texts. I checked those first, and when I saw the one from Outlaw, I remembered what it meant to be part of the Devil's Fury.

Badger said there were funds Grizzly set aside for you the first year you were gone. I had them deposited into your account, and they should show up today or tomorrow.

Welcome back, Ram!

My throat felt tight, and I cleared it. I'd forgotten what it felt like to have people to rely on, to have brothers. I shot off a quick thank-you and moved on to the next shop. It took us three hours to get the personal things we needed, and then I decided we'd stop for lunch. I'd noticed a little café on a corner not too far from where we were. Driving over there, I found a place to park and led Talia and Riley inside.

"Are you sure we can eat here?" Riley whispered.

"Of course, we can. Get anything you want, sweetheart." The endearment slipped out and I wondered if I'd just fucked up. She smiled up at me, and I knew she'd liked it. At least it hadn't scared her or upset her in any way. I was adapting to fatherhood faster than I'd anticipated.

The hostess found a table for us and left after placing menus on the table. After we ate, we'd go to a store that carried kitchen items and linens. We needed more towels, bedding, and definitely needed more cookware. Not to mention we didn't have real cups, plates, or silverware. Today would be an expensive outing, but maybe the house would feel more like our home.

Thanks to Outlaw, I didn't have to worry about money. I couldn't believe Grizzly had set aside over thirty grand for me. It wouldn't last forever, especially since we'd also need furniture and better mattresses, but it did take off the immediate pressure I'd felt when I realized all the things we needed to buy. Up until now, I'd gotten paid in various ways. I'd taken a few bounties when I'd stayed in the State of California for a few years. Picked up odd jobs working on cars and bikes when cash was low. And yeah, whenever I took out someone like Vega, I made sure to empty their wallet. I'd done the same with Vega and his goons last night, but surprisingly, they hadn't had more than a few hundred on them.

When Riley ordered, I knew she'd asked for more food than she'd ever be able to eat. Talia kept cutting her eyes over toward me, probably wondering if I was going to stop my daughter. Nope. She could get whatever she wanted. Something told me she'd never eaten at a place like this. She'd been too concerned when we came in. If she wanted one of everything on the menu, then I'd get it for her. Yeah, I was going to spoil the hell out of her, at least for this first week. I'd reel her back in after that. Right now, I needed to show her she wasn't going to go hungry, or without new clothes. Did it mean I'd let her spend hundreds of dollars every week from this point forward? Of course not. Once she had a small collection of books and movies, and whatever she'd need for school and to feel like she fit in, then I'd stop unless it was a necessary item or I wanted to give her a special gift.

"Thank you... Dad." She gave me a shy smile and I reached across the table to hold her hand. One day, I wanted to know what she'd been through. When she was ready to talk about it. Until then, I'd support her any way I could. Be there for her, since it seemed her mother had sucked at being a parent. I refused to be the same. Whatever it took, I'd be the kind of dad she could be proud of, one she could lean on.

"You're good with her," Talia murmured.

"So are you." I'd watched as she helped Riley pick out nail polish and other items at the store. Riley had listened to everything Talia said, and it seemed like the two might have bonded a little. I hoped so.

"Thank you for staying with us. I think you're exactly what the two of us need, and I hope you need us too."

She didn't answer, but that was all right. I'd give her all the time she needed.

Chapter Eight

Talia

It wasn't my first time eating in a restaurant. I'd been a few times with a friend, or on my own when I'd had some extra money. Seeing the joy on Riley's face, made this time different from the others. She'd eaten so much, I'd thought she was going to make herself sick. Ram might have asked me to stay and give things a chance, but it didn't give me the right to tell his daughter what to do. I'd watched and waited for Riley to turn green and bolt from the room. Thankfully, the moment she started to feel queasy, she put the fork down.

Now she kept groaning as we walked the aisles of another store. Ram had a shopping cart and had asked me to push one as well. He kept placing the bathroom and bedroom linens into my cart, while shoving pots and pans into his, and anything else he thought we might need. Riley perked up a little when we reached the bedding.

"I'll order you a new mattress soon," Ram said. "But the bed will probably be the same size."

"I think it's a full," I said.

"So I can pick from the ones that have a sticker on them saying they're a full size?" Riley asked. "Any of them?"

"Find a set you really love, then one you at least like. It's better to have two in case something happens and you need to change your bed at night."

She glared at him. "I'm not small enough to wet the bed."

His cheeks flushed and he cleared his throat before speaking a low tone. "I was thinking more along the lines if you, um…"

He couldn't seem to stop, and I finally understood what he meant. I nearly snickered. Who knew the big, tough biker could be so endearing?

"Riley, have you started your period yet?" I asked. I knew stress could have prevented her from having one yet, even though most girls seemed to get theirs between the ages of nine and eleven.

"Oh! That's what he meant?" She peeked at her dad, a smile on her lips. "Yeah, two sets would be a good idea."

While she made her decision, I pulled Ram to the side. I whispered so Riley wouldn't hear us, but I couldn't help being concerned for her.

"Ram, I know you're probably happy to have Riley in your life and that you can get to know your daughter, but something's off. She's far too happy and bubbly after what she went through."

"What are you thinking?" he asked. "That's she's trying to suppress her real feelings?"

"Maybe."

He grunted. "I've been watching her. Right now, she wants to be treated like a normal teenage girl. From what she's said, I don't think she's ever had that before. I'll find a therapist for her, someone who can help her through the trauma she suffered. If it makes her feel better to put on a show, smile, and act like nothing's wrong, then I'll let her for the moment. You know how you get prickly and sarcastic? Well, being bright and bubbly is *her* defense mechanism."

I crossed my arms and stared at him. He'd killed those men without any hesitation. Helped all of us when he didn't have to. Came from a club of bikers, who looked like they'd rather kill a person than help them across the street... unless it was straight into oncoming traffic. So why did he seem to know so much about trauma responses, defense mechanisms, and that sort of thing?

"Who the hell are you?" I asked. "I mean really. What average biker knows this sort of stuff?"

He ran a finger over one eyebrow. "My mom taught me a lot. She was a great mother. Loving. Supportive. And she studied psychology in college. Unfortunately, she met my dad, got pregnant, and had me before she could graduate. However, she used that knowledge every day, and taught me the importance of not only a person's physical well-being, but their mental health as well."

Wow. I hadn't seen that one coming. I'd assumed he'd had a sucky childhood like me. Why else would he join a group of rough-looking bikers? Or go around killing people? It sounded like he had a normal, suburban upbringing. What happened?

"You, sir, are an enigma."

He smiled faintly. "Good. Maybe the curiosity will keep you around long enough for me to convince you to stay forever."

"Not sure I believe in forever," I said. "Never had proof that sort of relationship exists. Clearly, you haven't either, unless your dad took care of you and your mom? Maybe they got married and you had the perfect life."

He snorted. "Not hardly. If it weren't for Mom, I'm sure I'd have turned out much different. After she died, I felt lost. I decided to prospect for the Devil's Fury at the age of seventeen. The club helped me finish high school, and when I turned nineteen, they patched me in. Of course, I had some anger issues back then. Still do."

"Because of your mom dying?" I asked.

"That's why I was so mad back then. Now, I

mostly kick my own ass every day."

Something told me not to pry into what he meant by that. He'd tell me if and when he wanted me to know. For now, he'd shared quite a bit. I felt like I owed him something. A piece of my past. And not in a *let me dump all my shit on you* type of way.

"I don't remember my mom. She either died or left us when I was little. My dad always said she was dead, but sometimes I wondered if she couldn't handle living with him and just got up and walked out one day."

"And left her daughter behind?" he asked.

"I doubt she'd have been able to take care of me. I mean, if she couldn't stand up to my dad and felt her only recourse was to run away, would she have really had the means to feed me and clothe me? Dad sucked at it, but for the most part I didn't starve." I didn't want to go into the beatings when my dad lost big time. Or the times he'd rant I was too much like my mother. He wouldn't have won father of the year, but at least I hadn't been in the foster system. I'd met too many kids who'd been abused far worse than me, and by people who were paid to take care of them.

"If you want to find out whether she really died or if she's alive, I know someone who could either locate her or her grave. Just let me know," Ram said.

"Thanks. I'll think about it."

Not once had I ever wanted to see my mother. I'd always felt like she hadn't wanted me. No matter how many times my dad claimed she'd died, I'd never fully believed him. Why hadn't there been a funeral? Wouldn't the police have come by if she'd had an accident or something? Sure, I'd put on a brave face when telling Ram about her, but deep down, her leaving me behind had hurt. A lot. I wasn't sure I'd ever really forgive her, even if she stood in front of me and told me the reason. Unless, of course, Dad hadn't lied and she'd really died.

Riley finished making her selection. I'd noticed Ram put in two plain sets of bedding for his room. He'd asked me to stay, yet he didn't seem to want my opinion when it came to the sheets that went on the bed we'd be sharing. I eyed the set, and he noticed, his eyes twinkling with laughter. Asshole.

"Put the fangs away," he said. "Those are temporary. When I get us a new mattress, I'm ordering a larger bed frame too. They have a queen in there right now, and I think we'll need a California king to be comfortable. I'm not exactly short."

My cheeks warmed. I liked the playful side of him. He didn't show it often, from what I'd seen so far. It made me feel special to have him tease me like that. Riley ignored us as she checked out the items on practically every shelf in the store. Ram let her get a new shower curtain, bathmat, and the matching items for the counter. There wasn't anything wrong with the ones already at the house, but I could understand why he'd bought them for her. He wanted it to feel like her home, and this was a good place to start. It wouldn't surprise me if he'd paint her room and the hall bathroom if she asked him to.

He really was a good man, and an even better father. He'd only decided Riley was his daughter this morning, and already he'd done more for her than most dads did in their entire lives. Of course, most fathers didn't have to kill their daughter's abductors either.

"Did you do the paternity test?" I asked. I didn't remember seeing them use the ones Badger had delivered to the house.

"Yeah. We took care of it while you were in the shower. We did Riley's first, then I did mine while she got ready. Someone delivered it to the lab for us."

We finally found everything we needed and made our way to the register. The poor clerk's eyes went wide when she saw the two overflowing carts. I felt sorry for her, since she'd have to scan and bag everything.

"Did you buy a new house?" she asked, as she rang up the items.

"Just moved in yesterday," Ram said.

Riley grabbed some candy off the shelf under the register. "Dad, can I have this?"

He took it from her and placed it on the counter. The clerk scanned it, then handed it back to Riley. I had no idea where she planned to put it. Surely, she wasn't going to eat it right now? She'd just been moaning about how full she was.

"Riley, maybe you should save it for when we get home?" I suggested. "You don't want to get sick in the truck, right?"

Crap. Did Ram even realize the truck was already full? Where was Riley going to sit? I didn't see how all this would fit in the back seat with the other stuff we'd bought, and still leave room for the girl.

"You can ride up front between me and Talia," he said. "The armrest lifts up. You won't have a shoulder belt, though. I'll make sure I drive carefully."

"I think she should sit beside you, Dad," Riley said. That little devil. She grinned at me. Not only was her dad trying to talk me into staying and moving in permanently, but for some reason Riley really wanted me there too. One big happy family.

The clerk gave him the total and Ram handed over his bank card. Once he'd paid, we pushed the items outside and loaded them into the back seat. And sure enough, there wasn't a spot for Riley. Ram put up the armrest, which was wider than either me or Riley, and I found the lap belt underneath. I climbed in and buckled while Riley got into the passenger seat and Ram slid behind the steering wheel.

His thigh brushed against mine every time he pressed the pedal or shifted to the brake. By the time we got to the house, I felt like I was going to jump out of my skin. I'd never been so aware of a man before. My hand trembled as I unbuckled and got out of the vehicle, and my knees felt like jelly. Somehow, I managed to get inside, where I promptly went to the bathroom and splashed cold water on my face.

Get it together, Talia. You're stronger than this.

I saw Ram standing behind me, and my gaze met his in the mirror. "You all right?"

I nodded. "Just felt a little hot. I'll come help unload everything."

"Stay inside where it's cool. I'll bring in the bags. Badger needs me for a little while, so I'll let you and Riley sort everything into the correct rooms. We should probably wash the bedding and new towels before we use them. There's a laundry closet off the kitchen."

"Closet?" I asked.

"I can hardly call it a room when it's only deep enough for the door to open without hitting the washer and dryer, and there's no space on either side of the machines. Whoever designed this place clearly didn't wash clothes often. It would have been nice to have some cabinets and maybe a counter for sorting."

I pursed my lips and wondered why I found it so cute when he talked about things like laundry. It made him seem domesticated, while watching him ride his motorcycle had made him look wild and free. Which was the real Ram? Or were they both right, and he was just some odd mix that made him perfect husband material?

My cheeks flushed and I quickly looked away from him. *Husband material*? What the hell was I just thinking?

You're in so much trouble, Talia.

Chapter Nine

Ram

I'd anticipated a lot of questions, even hostility. However, the brothers who knew I was back and had already seen me in person were supportive. It didn't matter if they knew why I'd been gone or not. To them, I was family and I'd come home. It didn't mean everyone wasn't confused about my absence, or my return for that matter.

Badger introduced everyone I hadn't met before, or those who'd been Prospects and patched in after I'd left. There were more families than I'd realized. It was a good thing, though. Maybe it would make Riley and Talia feel more at ease. As much as Talia distrusted men, being at the club had to be hard on her. She hadn't complained. In fact, we'd had a great outing with Riley, and I thought the two of them would settle in nicely here at the Devil's Fury.

"How come some of us have never heard of you?" Dingo asked. "You don't find it odd the club never mentioned you?"

"Back off, son," Blades said. Dingo bristled, but kept his mouth shut. I wondered if the two had some connection aside from the club.

"It's a fair question," Badger said. "I contacted Ram periodically. Even though I knew he was alive, and Grizzly was aware as well, it was clear Ram needed time away. We didn't ask questions. I admit, I've been curious all this time. I can't imagine what could have sent you running, completely turning your back on your brothers."

"He wasn't even wearing his cut," Dingo said. "First time I saw him, I thought someone had broken into the compound."

I could tell this was going to be a long meeting. "You're right. I stopped wearing my cut years ago. It stayed in my saddlebags, as a reminder, but I thought it would be better if I never came back."

"Why?" Blades asked.

"Because my mistake cost people their lives," I said. "It was after Badger came back from prison. The last job I went on…"

Badger leaned back in his chair. "I wondered if that had anything to do with it. If I remember right, a few people died that day."

"Yeah. They did."

"Grizzly told you none of it was your fault," Badger said.

"Didn't make me feel any less responsible for what happened. Innocent people died because I got too anxious and made a move before I should have. They got caught in the crossfire, and nothing I do will ever make up for it. One of them was only nine years old. A little girl who had her entire life ahead of her. I should have turned myself in and gone to prison."

"No, you shouldn't have," Outlaw said. "You've done a lot of good since then, Ram. Sure, maybe you made a mistake and people got hurt and some died. It could have happened to anyone in the same situation. Since then, how many people have you saved?"

What the hell? Had he been keeping tabs on me all this time? Who else had known I was still around? When Badger said Outlaw was no longer able to work his computer magic, I'd thought it meant I'd been hidden all these years. Only reason Badger had managed to reach me was because I'd kept the same number. The first year, I'd ignored pretty much everyone. Badger was the only one I'd ever felt inclined to answer. Everyone knew Grizzly had a soft spot for him, and he'd been the first of us to settle down.

"Why don't you tell them what he's done?" Badger asked.

Outlaw tossed a thick file onto the table and I stared at it. Jesus. He really *had* kept tabs on me. Badger acted like he had no idea what I'd been doing those first few years, and later I could tell he wasn't completely blind to my activities. I still hadn't realized they'd have such detailed accounts. No way the file would be so thick otherwise.

"The first year Ram was gone, he saved a total of forty children and five women. The second year, he rescued more than one hundred people. Every single year he's been gone, he's taken down men the government set free. He's stopped human traffickers, taken out large drug operations, and even dismantled a slave auction all on his own." Outlaw shot a smirk at everyone around the table. "What the hell have you fuckers been doing? No offense, but there's not a single man here who has done as much as Ram, and he did it without the support of the club. No money from the Devil's Fury. No one at his back. Could you do the same?"

"Fuck," Slash muttered, his eyes going wide as he flipped through a few pages. "How the hell did you accomplish all this?"

"I wasn't one hundred percent on my own," I admitted. "Lock helped here and there, mostly with intel. Once or twice, we teamed up because we were after the same people."

"Lock? Who's that?" Frost asked.

"Assassin. You've heard of Casper VanHorne and Specter. He's on par with them, except even more tech savvy," Outlaw said. "And a bit more personable.

At least, to those he considers a friend."

"The point is Ram has been doing a lot of good out in the world. More than this club has done for anyone. Grizzly refused to take his patch. When I took over, I promised him I'd accept Ram if he ever came back. It's why I've tried to keep in touch here and there." Badger drummed his fingers on the table. "I didn't call Church to ask if you'd be okay with Ram coming back. He already has a house here. Far as I'm concerned, he's been one of us longer than quite a few of you. There's never been any question about his place in this club. If you don't like it, I'll be happy to let Ram hand your asses to you."

Frost held up his hands. "I have no problem with him."

"Like anyone is going to go up against someone who's done all that?" Smuggler asked, pointing to the file. "I don't think anyone here is that fucking stupid."

"The women and girls I brought with me may need some help for a little while. None of the girls wanted to go home. The older ones will be able to get jobs and sort their lives out. Not sure what to do with the ones under eighteen," I said. "I came here because I knew they'd be safe with my brothers."

"And the two in your house?" Demon asked. "Do I need to get a property cut for the mouthy one?"

I flipped him off. "Her name is Talia, asshole. And no, not yet. She's been hurt too many times. I need to show her I'm not like the other men she's known. Even her father was a piece of shit."

"And the other one?" Demon asked.

I glanced at Badger who gave me a slight nod. I didn't have the test results back yet, but I didn't really need them. My gut said Riley was mine. "She's my daughter."

"As in you're adopting her, or..." Blades' brow furrowed. "Where's her mom?"

"She's mine, genetically. As to her mother, I need to make sure Reba can't get her hands on Riley ever again. She's been a bad mother and has had a trail of assholes in her life. Riley refuses to go back there, and I can't blame her. She's going to live with me from now on. If Reba shows up, I'll hear her out. Doesn't mean she'll be moving into my house or getting a damn thing from me."

"Except maybe a boot print," Badger said. "You going to tell me you don't harbor some ill will toward the woman who mistreated your daughter, let her get kidnapped, and doesn't seem to give a shit what happened to her?"

"For Riley's sake, I'll let Reba walk away. At the end of the day, she's still Riley's mom."

"Which brings us to the next order of business," Badger said. "No whores here until after tomorrow. The Prospects are scrubbing the clubhouse. We're going to have a family night. Talia and Riley need to meet everyone, and I'm going to offer an invitation to the other women Ram brought with him. Even though there will be a lot of men packed into the room, I think it will do them some good to see how many women and kids we have here, and how happy they are."

I nodded. My thoughts exactly. Although, I had no idea how happy any of them were. Adalia and Shella were the only two I'd met, and I'd known Adalia before I left. It would certainly be good for Riley to meet the two kids closer to her age.

"I'll make sure I introduce myself to the women and girls," Outlaw said. "I'll bring Elena with me. I'm sure they're going to need documents like birth certificates, licenses, and possibly school files for the younger ones. I'll help track down what I can and ask Wire to create anything else we need."

"There's one more thing," I said. "One of the women, Heather, heard Vega talking about an offshore account. If there's a way to track down those funds and access them, I'm sure the money would prove useful. We could set up an account for each of Vega's victims, or at least the ones here at the compound. Feeling financially secure will go a long way to helping them feel less frightened."

"Jesus," Badger murmured. "What other insights do you have?"

"Is that a dig at my upbringing?" I asked. "Because President or not, I can still knock you on your ass."

He smirked. "You can try."

Fine. I'd let it go. I didn't need to openly challenge him like this, especially not in front of our brothers. If he thought I was going to undermine his authority, I knew he'd do whatever it took to put me in my place, as he should.

"Your upbringing?" Dragon asked.

"My mother was a psychology student when she got pregnant with me. She didn't get a chance to graduate, but she used what she learned to teach me how to observe people and give them what they need." I shrugged. "Kind of like with Talia. If I told her she was mine and I was keeping her, it would be detrimental to her mental health. She's independent, has put up walls so high there's no point trying to scale them, and uses sarcasm as a weapon."

"Then how are you going to convince her to stay?" Dragon asked. "Just curious. I didn't really go through that with Lilian."

Demon stared at him. "Really? You knocked-up

Grizzly's daughter, while he was still the president of this club, then she fucking ran and nearly died. All while being knocked-up with your kid. Maybe we should ask him to analyze *you*."

"You let her leave while she was pregnant with your kid?" I asked.

"*Let* is a bit misleading. Lilian is strong-willed. Everyone saw her as this weak, damaged woman. She's the one who pursued me, not the other way around."

"As for Talia, she needs to see I'm not going to hurt her, that I'll keep my promises, and I'll do what it takes to not only make her happy but give her the things she needs. I don't necessarily mean material objects, but things like stability, trust, friendship, and anything else she's lacked in her life so far. I don't need to scale that wall she's built because she's going to take it down herself."

Steel let out a long whistle. "Damn. Makes me scared to ask what you see when you look at me. You've only known that woman a day, right? And you already gleaned all that?"

I gave a nod. Everyone had issues, including me. As for Steel, he had a hero complex. Hell, most of us did. For him, it went to the extreme. Since he had a daughter now, I hoped he'd settled down some and didn't volunteer for so many dangerous jobs. Badger had been a stoic loner. I didn't think being with Adalia had changed him much. At the end of the day, I'd bet money he'd rather be home with his woman than hanging out with the club. And Demon… No, I wasn't even going there. The fucker was crazy, simple as that.

"Adalia already spoke with the women. Everyone is cooking or baking something to bring tonight. Since the Prospects are cleaning, I'm going to need two of you to make a drink run. We need sodas and juice for the kids, and anyone who doesn't want alcohol. Maybe bottled water too." Badger looked around the table. "Any volunteers?"

"I'll go," Bandit said.

"Me too." Hound raised his hand. "Want me to grab something like pretzels or chips with dip? I don't know what the women are making, but the kids might like some snacks."

"Lilian is making a Mexican casserole," Dragon said. "I'd thought it was for our dinner tonight, but now I know why she had two pans out on the counter when I left."

"I saw Minnie making sushki earlier," Doolittle said. "Uh, my wife is related to the Devil's Boneyard by blood. Her grandfather is Stripes, so she's been learning a lot of Russian recipes since discovering her ancestry."

"What the hell is sushki?" Dingo asked.

"It's a snack. They're hardened sweet dough rings. At home, Minnie lets the kids have them with jam, but I've seen her dunk hers in tea or coffee. Just give it a try. You've liked the other things she's made so far," Doolittle said.

"My China didn't think anyone would want traditional Chinese fare," Blades said. "I think she's helping Meiling make something."

"Meiling?" I asked.

"My woman," Dingo said. "Mei. After I claimed her, we found out she's Blades' daughter."

"Naturally, we had to get him out of prison," Outlaw said. "But that's a story for another day. Hell, there's so much you've missed. We could sit here for days and not cover everything."

"Should Talia and I bring something?" I asked.

"Just yourselves. Next time, we'll let Talia and Riley help with the food," Badger said. "Tonight is to welcome your family, and give you a chance to catch up with everyone."

"Anything else, Pres?" Slash asked. "If not, I'm going to run home and make sure Shella hasn't decided our kid would be better behind bars. Audrey has been a handful lately."

"Church dismissed," Badger said. "Everyone go home. Those of you who are single, if you wouldn't mind making sure the clubhouse is fit for women and kids, I'd appreciate it. Let the Prospects do most of the work, just keep an eye on them."

"You got it, Pres," Smuggler said.

"Kids like balloons. I'll run to the store and grab a helium tank and a few packs of multi-color balloons," Colorado said. "Maybe I'll get some party favor-type stuff for the smaller kids."

"I'll bring a few games from the house," Steel said. "We have some for all ages."

I stood and walked out, letting them figure out who was doing what. On my way back to the house, I stopped at the apartments and let the women and girls know about the gathering. I also made it clear they could leave if they felt uncomfortable at any time.

When I got to the house, I found Talia pulling things from the dryer. Riley had her room set up and had fallen asleep on the bed. The place was already looking more like a home than a temporary place to stay. Shit. I never even asked Talia where she'd been abducted, if she'd left things behind she needed, or anything along those lines. Did she have a car she'd want? Her purse? Any personal items that meant something to her?

"Hey," I said, since she hadn't noticed me yet. "I

never asked if you left anything behind that you'd want."

She shoved her hair out of her face. "Actually, you kind of did. I didn't have much. But it's been hectic. I'm not surprised you don't remember."

"What about a car?" I asked. "Do you have a license? If you didn't have a vehicle, we'll need to get one. I need one anyway so I can take Riley places."

She blinked at me, the linens clutched in her arms. Had I said something wrong? When she finally spoke again, I realized she'd just taken down another chunk of her wall.

"I'd like going car shopping with the two of you. A family car is a good idea, but maybe an SUV or truck? I think you'd need something bigger than a sedan. You don't seem like the type of man who'd get in and out of something low to the ground."

"All right. Tomorrow, then. We can check a few car lots and see what's available before we make a decision. Maybe test drive some different types and see what fits us best."

She gave me a warm smile, and I knew I was one step closer to Talia staying with us. Soon enough, she'd realize we needed her as much as she needed us. The three of us worked well together. Riley really liked Talia, and even seemed to be doing her best to convince the woman to be her stepmother. Between the two of us, we'd eventually convince her she belonged here. Sooner rather than later, I hoped.

Chapter Ten

Talia

Ram's version of a family gathering and mine were very different. Of course, I'd only had my father, and we hadn't exactly done things like this. But I'd watched families in our neighborhood or at the park. It seemed a little strange the bikers were letting their children run around a bar, though. Then again, maybe this was the only option they had without making everyone find a spot outside.

"So, you all come drinking here when the women and kids aren't around?" I asked, as Ram helped me find a table.

"Yeah." His cheeks flushed a little. Huh. Something told me they did more than drink in this place. I eyed the floors and the chair he pulled out for me. Someone hadn't been having sex on this recently, had they?

"Ram, if I ask you something, will you answer honestly?" I asked.

"As long as it's something I'm permitted to tell you."

"Do the men in this club have sex in here?" I asked. He froze in the middle of sitting down and stared at me. Yep. I'd just hit the nail on the head. "And they think this is a good place to bring their wives and children?"

"The women understand what they're signing up for. I know for a fact Badger would never cheat on Adalia, so he comes here to drink and that's it. The others who have paired off might be the same way. And if you're wondering, no, I wouldn't have sex with random women if I had someone at home waiting for me."

"But you have while you were single," I said. "Please tell me you've gotten tested."

He cleared his throat and looked away. "Not recently, but I'll get it taken care of tomorrow. If it makes a difference, I always used condoms."

I cast a subtle glance in Riley's direction. "I see how well that's worked. Of course, Riley is wonderful and I'm glad she's here. Think you have any other kids out there?"

"Jesus," he muttered. "I hope not."

"Why are we here? The people we brought with us are cowering in a corner. The men in your club are really loud, and a bit scary to be honest."

"I told you why they were having a family gathering. I'm giving you time to adjust, then I want to take you over to Adalia and Shella. They can introduce you to the other women. Riley already found Coral and seems to be doing fine."

I looked over at the table where Riley sat with Coral and a little boy. He looked younger than them, even though he was taller than both girls. They'd decided to play a board game and were getting it set up.

"Let's say I do stay here with you and Riley. What would I do every day? What would life look like as part of this club?" I asked.

"Sometimes I'll get sent out on jobs. Might be gone for an hour or two, and other times I could be away for days or even a week. I don't think I'd have to go farther than that. As for what you'd do, whatever you want. You could stay home, get a job, go to school. I'm not trying to lock you in a cage, Talia."

I nodded. I knew it, to some extent. I still had a hard time believing he wasn't like all the other men I'd ever met, and yet, he proved he was different every second of the day. Truth be told, I was scared. I felt antsy and wanted to run away. At first, I'd been terrified I'd fall for him and he'd break my heart. Now other things worried me. What if I didn't fit in with these people? What if no one liked me and it caused problems for Ram and Riley?

The biker's daughter was another issue. She wanted me to stay, for now. She could change her mind at a later time. If that happened, would Ram make me leave? I couldn't imagine him choosing me over his daughter, and I wouldn't want him to. Riley deserved to have her father in her life. Unlike me, she had a good one.

"Can you give these people a chance?" Ram asked. "I know I'm asking a lot. You've been hurt so many times before. I get it. I really do. But Riley isn't the only one who needs a support system. You do too, Talia. I think you could be friends with Adalia and the others, if you genuinely tried to get to know them."

"You're doing that thing again, aren't you? Where you try to guide me by asking questions, so you're not really telling me what I should do, but asking if trying something will harm me in some way. I hate it, mostly because it seems to work."

He smiled a little. "Good to know. How about I get you a drink and send Adalia over?"

"Fine. I'll take a soda. I'm not twenty-one yet, and I've never liked the taste of alcohol anyway. The few times I managed to sneak some, it either tasted bad or left me feeling awful."

"I'll be back. And, Talia, thank you. Whenever it's too much and you want to go back home, just tell me. We'll grab Riley and leave."

I watched him go and wondered why he had to be so damn nice and understanding all the time. It pissed me off. I couldn't stay angry with him because I knew he was trying to help me. At times, it felt like he was manipulating me. Then he'd give me that look, the one saying he worried about me. No one had ever cared about me before.

Adalia came over with Ram. He placed my drink in front of me, kissed the top of my head, which shocked the hell out of me, then walked off again. Adalia gave me a bright smile, except it looked a little forced.

"You don't have to pretend you want to sit here," I said. "I know Ram asked you to come over."

She sighed and slumped in her chair a little. "Sorry, it's not you. I haven't been feeling well tonight. Headache from hell, and all this noise isn't helping."

I wanted to ask why she was here if she felt so awful, but her husband was the club president. I imagined the job came with certain expectations. Kind of like someone marrying the president of a country. She'd have duties she'd be expected to handle, or places she needed to be. It must be the same for Adalia. Did Badger realize how much she was hurting right now?

"Can I get you anything? What helps when you get a headache?"

"Other than silence?" She shook her head. "There's nothing you can do, but I appreciate it. I'll stay a little while, then tell Badger I need to lie down. He'll probably worry himself to death and rush me home. Gunner and Luis are close, so our son may go to Dagger and Guardian's house for the night. And our Ivory really likes Slash's daughter, Audrey. They're cousins."

"Audrey and Ivory are? So, is Slash your brother or is Shella your sister?" I'd had so much thrown at me in twenty-four hours, I couldn't keep it all straight. I just knew I'd end up calling someone the wrong name before the night was over.

"Shella and I were both adopted by Grizzly. Same for Lilian and..." She pressed her lips together. "Meredith. You won't get to meet her anytime soon. Our fault, not hers."

It sounded like something she may not want to discuss, so I left it alone. Except now I wondered what happened between them. Ram had talked about Grizzly a few times. It sounded like he'd been a good man. It was a shame he'd passed away.

"Maybe things will get sorted out sometime."

"Someone might bring it up at some point, so I'll tell you this much. Doolittle and Minnie are together now. When she first came here, it wasn't pretty. She'd been a, um..." She froze, which only piqued my curiosity more. "I don't know what Ram has shared about the way the club works. The single guys need to blow off steam, so there are girls who come here to party with them. We call them club whores. Anyway, Minnie had been one at another club. Doolittle brought her here, and along the way, they fell for each other."

"I'm confused. What does that have to do with Meredith?" I asked.

"She had a crush on Doolittle. He'd told everyone for years he didn't feel the same about her. Anyway, Meredith acted out, made everyone turn on Minnie, and when it made Minnie run off, Doolittle went off on the entire club. He was so pissed. I never even knew that sweet man could be that mad." She shrugged. "We deserved his anger. Turns out Minnie was pregnant. When Doolittle brought her back home, Grizzly sent Meredith on a trip. We all thought it would be for the best. None of us considered she'd never come back."

"But she's still alive, right? Just doesn't live here?" I asked.

"She's with a man called Lynx at the Savage Raptors MC over in Oklahoma. She made peace with Grizzly before he died and got to spend a lot of his last days with him. At the time, it hurt me, Shella, and Lilian. It took a little time, but once the pain ebbed some, I realized we'd had so much more time with him than she did. I couldn't be angry about it anymore."

"But the others don't feel the same?" I asked.

"I think they're mostly over it, but Shella will never admit she might have been wrong. And Lilian... she'll probably reach out to Meredith before Shella will. I've spoken with Meredith a few times. I'm not angry with her, but it hasn't felt right to ask her to come visit either. With Grizzly gone, and her feeling so unwelcome here, there's no point. I don't want to ask her to do something that could end up hurting her again."

I leaned forward. "Maybe you should talk to Ram. This sounds like something he could help with."

Adalia gave a slight nod. "I'll bring it up to Badger later. Any questions about the club? Doubts? Fears? Hit me with it. I'll answer to the best of my ability."

I looked around the room and realized I didn't have the first clue what I should even ask. Everything seemed pretty straight forward. Alpha bikers. Club whores. A bar. I did notice the women all wore a cut like Ram had, except theirs claimed they were property of someone.

"You don't find it demeaning to be called Badger's property?" I asked.

"Not even a little, because I know he's just as

much mine as I am his. This property cut keeps me safe. When I leave the compound, it lets other people know the Devil's Fury are at my back. Someone fucks with me, Badger is going to destroy them and everyone they know. Think of it like… carrying around bear spray."

I choked on my swallow of soda. "Bear spray?"

"I couldn't think of a better analogy, but yeah. Instead of spraying someone in the face, they just take one look at the leather over your shoulders and know they have a choice to make. Be a dick and possibly lose their lives or keep walking."

"Huh. When you say it like that, it seems like something every woman should have."

"Right?" She gave me a soft smile. "I've enjoyed talking to you, and you're welcome to stop by the house anytime you want. I think I'm going to tell Badger I need to go."

"I hope you feel better."

Adalia got up and went to search for Badger. I saw Heather and the others sitting nearby and decided to go visit with them. I noticed most of the bikers were keeping their distance. Probably a good idea. I didn't think Heather would run away, but some of the others might. They looked ready to bolt at any moment. Even though they'd let Ram help them, being in room with so many men was completely different. Especially big, gruff-looking ones.

"Everyone doing okay?" I asked.

"I think so," Heather said. "Someone came by this morning and got our lists. A few hours later, we had groceries, clothes, and anything else we'd need for the next week or more. I think most of us are still feeling a little lost and woke up this morning expecting to see bars surrounding us."

"If I can help with anything, let me know. Even though I'm not staying with all of you, I'm only down the street."

She leaned in closer. "What's it like living with Ram?"

"He's really nice, thoughtful, and genuinely wants to help people. We haven't had an argument or anything, if that's what you're asking. He actually wants me to stay. Indefinitely."

Heather nodded. "I kind of got that feeling when he hauled us out of that warehouse. He couldn't seem to stop watching you. Even at the store, he might have kept an eye on all of us, but his gaze was constantly flicking over to you, as if he needed to make sure you were still there."

Really? I hadn't noticed. I felt a hand on my shoulder and looked up at the man in question. He leaned down and spoke low near my ear. "I thought you were supposed to meet all the women from the club?"

"Adalia wasn't feeling well and went to find Badger. It's fine, Ram. I know her and Shella."

"Wait here. I'll bring over Farrah and Mariah. They're sisters. One is with Demon and the other is with Savage. I've heard they can be... difficult, but since they've lived with two clubs, they might have useful information for you." He drew back and returned a few minutes later with two women in tow. After a quick introduction, the women joined us at the table.

The two looked at each of us sitting at the table, and I couldn't quite tell what they were thinking. Although, the look in Farrah's eyes made me think we fell short of her expectations. Ram did give me a warning of sorts. Was he sure he wanted me to meet these women if he was trying to convince me to stay?

"So, you're the one staying with Ram?" Farrah asked, looking right at me.

"Yes. And Riley," I gave a nod toward the girl in question. "She's Ram's daughter."

"Have you ever been around bikers before?" Mariah asked. "They aren't like most men."

"Ram is the first I've spent time with," I admitted. "I have no idea how this club thing works, even though Adalia did give me a little information. Ram mentioned you've lived with two clubs."

Farrah nodded. "We both grew up in the Dixie Reapers MC. Our dad was their VP until recently. For us, this is a normal way of life."

"Farrah is with Demon. He's the Sergeant-at-Arms here, and I'm with Savage. Although, I didn't come here voluntarily. My dad wanted to get me away from a bad situation, even though I was stubborn and insisted I was in love with a man who ended up being a monster. Savage agreed I could be his. He's the club Treasurer. So we're both with officers."

Uh-huh. Did that mean they felt they were better than me? Because their dad and their men were all officers, or had been in the case of their father? I didn't give a crap about any of it. The hierarchy here didn't mean anything to me. The way Farrah lifted her chin a little, with a slight smile on her lips, said yeah, she was a pampered princess who thought her shit didn't stink. I couldn't stand women like her.

"All right," I said, refusing to play into their hands. With my lackluster response, they both sobered and looked at me like I'd just sprouted horns. Clearly, people tended to react more favorably to their bragging. "My dad was a gambler who beat me, stole my money, and could barely keep the lights on or food on the table. I've been taking care of myself for a very long time."

"Is that why the kidnapping and what Vega did to you seemed like it didn't even bother you?" Heather asked. "I thought you were acting so strong and brave for all of us."

"The first guy I trusted ended up raping me, then he let his friends have a turn. The second guy took everything I had, knocked me unconscious and left me for dead. The third... Well, you get the picture. Anytime I've put my faith in someone, or tried to take their proffered hand, it's come back to bite me in the ass."

Heather's eyes went wide, and she reached over to give my hand a squeeze. "Well, for what it's worth, I'll be your friend if you'll let me. If it weren't for you, I'm not sure how things would have turned out for us. The way you went toe to toe with Ram, it showed me he wasn't a bad man. If he were, he'd have hit you or even killed you. You were so brave, and it gave me the courage to step up and hot-wire that van."

"You haven't realized what a good thing you have," Farrah said. "I may not know Ram, but if he's part of this club and he wants you to be his, then he'll do anything to protect you. You'll never have to work, worry about starving, or whether you'll have a roof over your head. Shouldn't you be more grateful to him?"

I couldn't tell if she was trying to sell me on Ram and the club, or if she was picking at me. Perhaps it was a little of both. I did think she came off as a little stuck-up. As for her sister, I think she tried to emulate Farrah, which wasn't necessarily a good thing. Looking at her, I imagined her to have a sweeter nature.

"I don't mind working for the things I have or

need. It's what most people do. I'm not the type to sit at home like a pampered pet. And no offense, but if the two of you are supposed to convince me to stay, you're doing a piss-poor job of it."

Farrah gaped at me. Before she could respond, Demon came over, grabbed her, and tossed her over his shoulder. "If you'll excuse us, ladies, I believe my wife needs another lesson on manners."

"She didn't do anything wrong," Heather said, going pale.

Demon paused. "I'm not going to hurt her, although she might not want to sit down for a day or two. There's a lot you still don't know about all of us, including some family issues that haven't been completely dealt with yet. So don't take this as a club thing. It's personal."

He left, with Farrah beating on his back and calling him names. Mariah stared after them before scanning the room. She must have found her man because she shrank in her seat, as if hoping he wouldn't notice her. It didn't take long for Savage to come get her.

"She didn't cause trouble, right?" he asked.

"From what I hear, you're just as bad as her," Ram said. "Did you seriously go to the Dixie Reapers and treat Ridley's sister-in-law like shit? You, Mariah, and Farrah should all be ashamed. What the hell would Grizzly think of how all this played out? And yeah, Badger told me tonight. He worried Farrah and Mariah might not behave themselves around Talia. If I hadn't thought they might give her better insight to how clubs work, I would have kept them away from her."

Savage muttered something I didn't catch. Did this have to do with the story Adalia was telling me?

Or was it some other drama that happened? Maybe I didn't want to stay with this club. Were they tough bikers, or toddlers throwing tantrums?

I wanted to go home. I'd had enough of these people for the night. I'd liked Adalia, but the others... Truthfully, I hadn't met enough of them to form an opinion. Were there others like Adalia? Or was everyone else like Farrah and Mariah? I'd had enough drama to last me a lifetime.

Two more ladies came over and took the empty seats Farrah and Mariah left behind. One of them smiled brightly. "I'm Lilian, and this is Elena. I'm with Dragon, and she's Outlaw's wife."

"Farrah and Mariah can be a little much, especially after coming back from their last trip home. It's a long story, but essentially, their parents told them to leave and not come back until they grew up. They didn't behave well while they were there, and their attitudes haven't gotten any better since they came back to the Devil's Fury." Elena shrugged a shoulder. "If it's any consolation, the rest of us don't bite."

Lilian pointed across the room to two Asian women. "That's Mei and her mom, China. Well, Mei's full name is Meiling, and I can never pronounce China's real name without butchering it, so I don't try. I feel like I offend her every time I get it wrong."

"Neither of our children are close to Riley's age," Elena said. "But you're welcome to come over and talk, or we can find a movie everyone will like. It's important for Riley to bond with people here, and I'm betting you could use some friends too."

Lilian tapped her finger on the table. "I'm sure this is all a bit too much, and maybe even scary. But for what it's worth, I'm glad you're here. I haven't heard about Ram before, and only met him for the first time tonight, but he seems like a sweetheart. I think being back with the club will be good for him, as well as for you and Riley. If you can give us a chance."

The women stood and walked off, leaving me with Heather and the others. They'd remained quiet during the exchange. In fact, it almost seemed like they wanted to disappear. This was probably a lot for them to handle, but Heather had a thoughtful look on her face. She scanned the room, and I noticed her gaze stopped on a biker. From here, I couldn't see what his name was, but he didn't give off a menacing vibe. Had she met him already? Or had he just caught her eye during the party tonight?

I had a lot to think about. I liked Adalia, Lilian, and Elena. Shella had seemed nice too. If I wanted to stay with Ram, then I needed to get to know these people. I hadn't ever really had friends. Not since I was a child. What would it be like to have an entire group of people I could rely on? Someone I could talk to when things were bothering me?

Ram made his way back over to me, placing his hand on my shoulder. Until this get-together, he'd been careful not to touch me. I really did need to talk about my past with him and let him know he didn't scare me. Not in the way he thought anyway.

"Ram, do you think we could go home? I think I've had enough for today," I said.

"I'll get Riley. Meet me out front in a few minutes." He kissed the top of my head again and hurried over to Riley. Heather leaned in close to whisper to me.

"If you give him up, you're stupid. Just saying."

Yeah, I was beginning to have that same thought. Ram wasn't like any man I'd ever met before, and even in this room full of bikers, he still stood out. He wasn't quite the same as them.

And I'm the lucky bitch who gets to live with him.

Fine. I'd deal with the club in my own way. I wouldn't embarrass Ram, but I wouldn't take anyone's shit either. Farrah and Mariah had said and done everything to appear nice, unless you looked deeper, or studied their words more. Arrogance was only the beginning with those two, but it looked like maybe they were going to be taken down a few pegs by the end of the night. Good. They clearly needed the attitude adjustment. If what Lilian and Elena said was true, then others in the club thought so as well.

"Goodnight, everyone," I said before heading to the front door.

Was it wrong I hoped we didn't have to do this again anytime soon? All of them in one room was far too much for me to handle. I'd be better off meeting people two or three at a time. I'd mention it to Ram and see what he had to say. Tomorrow. For tonight, I just wanted to put on my pajamas and go to bed. It had been the longest day ever.

Chapter Eleven

Ram

I'd had two reasons for leaving Farrah and Mariah with Talia. First, I'd hoped they could give her insight without being complete bitches. In the event they couldn't hold back, the second thing I had hoped to achieve was to give Talia a chance to stand up for herself and show she couldn't be pushed around. There was only one way to get respect around here. She needed to stand her ground and protect what she thought of as hers. Yeah, I'd essentially thrown her to the wolves, and I felt like an asshole for doing it.

Riley went to bed and was asleep within minutes. I'd let Talia get ready for bed first. I had some pent-up frustration I needed to handle before I went to bed. I grabbed a clean pair of basketball shorts from the dresser and carried them into the bathroom, making sure I shut the door all the way. It only took a moment for the water to warm up. I stripped down and got into the shower.

Bowing my head, I let the hot water cascade over me. I braced a hand on the wall and closed my eyes. It had been good being with the club again. I'd enjoyed talking to everyone and getting to know the men who'd joined since I'd been gone. The entire time, I'd kept an eye on Talia and Riley. My daughter seemed to settle in with the kids faster than Talia was with the women. Although, she'd spoken for a bit with Adalia, and seemed to get along with Lilian and Elena.

If things were different between us, we'd have come home, made sure Riley was asleep, and then we'd have spent the next hour pleasuring each other. I'd told her I'd get tested tomorrow, and I would. Depending on the lab, I could have results by the next day. Of course, I didn't think Talia would open up to me quite so easily. I could very well have blue balls for a while.

Soaping my hand, I slicked my cock and started stroking. The thought of being inside Talia, of feeling her hot, wet pussy gripping me, was nearly enough to make me come. I worked my shaft faster, groaning a little as I felt my orgasm building. My balls drew up, and I bit my lip to keep silent as I came, spraying my release on the shower wall. I opened my eyes and cleaned up. As I turned, I caught sight of Talia outside the shower, her jaw dropped and eyes wide.

"Um. I had the door shut for a reason." And now my cock was getting hard again. The way she stared at it meant the damn thing wouldn't go soft anytime soon. "Talia? Honey, can you go back to the bedroom and shut the door behind you?"

"I guess that depends," she said.

"On what?" I seriously felt like I was going to lose what was left of my sanity if she didn't leave.

"Who you were thinking about while you did that."

I closed my eyes and prayed for patience. "You, Talia. I was thinking about you, all right?"

"Then... would you like some help?"

I had to have heard her wrong. "Excuse me?"

She motioned to my cock. "I'm not saying we should have sex, but I could use my hand to get you off."

I couldn't say a damn word. Did I want her to get in here with me and touch me? I wasn't a fucking saint, so yeah, I did. However, it probably wasn't the right move to make. I'd been working hard to show her she had nothing to fear from me, could take her time easing into this relationship, and now... The second I felt her hand on my cock, I wasn't sure I'd be able to put on the brakes. I'd want to go full steam ahead.

"Unless you don't really want me," she said.

"It's not that. Talia, I told you to take your time, get to know me, and I wanted to prove to you we could share a bed without me touching you. Now you're in here, asking to get me off?"

"I'm a not a virgin, Ram."

"Have you ever willingly been with a man?" I asked.

She pressed her lips together and shook her head. "That's part of why I want to do this. I know you won't hurt me. Not in this way. You've done and said too many things to prove you aren't that sort of man. I may not be ready for sex, but I'd like to do this much, as long as it's okay with you."

"You going to be all right getting naked and joining me in the shower? Or do you want me to dry off and lie down on the bed?"

"I can... join you." She slowly removed her clothes, her cheeks flushing a bright pink. I opened the shower door and took two steps back, giving her room to either get in, or run away. I saw the hesitation in her eyes, and the moment she decided she was going to do this. With her chin tipped at a determined angle, she entered the shower and closed the door behind her.

"Anytime you want to stop, just back away and get out of the shower. I won't follow you, grab you, or try to restrain you in any way. All right?"

She nodded and slowly reached out a hand. She pressed her palm to the center of my chest, slid it over my pecs, then down my abdomen. I couldn't remember a time I'd ever been so turned-on. When her fingers wrapped around my cock, I sucked in a breath. It took everything in me not to come immediately.

"How do you like it?" she asked.

"Tighten your grip a little, then just... stroke me however you want. If you need to adjust something, I'll let you know."

She moved slowly. Long pulls of her hand to the head of my cock, then the same slow drag back to the base. A shiver raked my spine. It was absolute torture, but the best kind. Talia came a little closer, and I could feel her breath against my skin. It was enough to push me over the edge. I came, my release hitting her stomach and spraying across her breasts. Panting, I tried to catch my breath. My heart hammered in my chest like I'd just run a marathon.

"If you weren't worried about scaring me, what would you do right now?" she asked.

I swallowed hard, and wondered if I should be honest or not. Fuck it. She didn't deserve a lie, even if the truth made her run from me. "I'd run my fingers through the cum on your skin, then push them inside you. I'd make you beg me, leave you whimpering with need, and then I'd let you come."

"I'm not on birth control. I'd possibly get pregnant."

My cock started getting hard again at the thought of Talia giving birth to my kid. "I know. If you were mine, I'd do whatever I could to knock you up. Sneak up behind you in the kitchen, lift your nightgown, and slide deep inside you. Fuck you until you had cum running down your thighs. Pin you face down on the bed and ride you so hard we'd need a new one after I broke the frame. I'd sit you on the bathroom counter, spread your thighs, and watch your tits bounce with every stroke of my cock."

"Oh, Jesus," she whispered, her cheeks flushing. I noticed the way she pressed her thighs together. Had my words turned her on? Yeah. Her nipples were starting to pucker, and I saw the rapid rise and fall of her chest.

"You should clean up. I've never caught anything, and I promise I'll get tested tomorrow but just to be safe…" I couldn't bring myself to tell her the last woman I'd fucked had been a prostitute.

We traded places and she stood under the water. Then she shocked the hell out of me by taking my hand and placing it on her breast.

"Can you help me clean it off?" she asked.

I let the water rinse most of it away, then soaped my hands and ran them over her soft skin. I cupped her breasts, letting my fingers slide across her nipples. Her breath caught, and her lips parted. I took my time exploring her body, ready to back off the moment she seemed uncomfortable.

After I helped her wash the soap off, I backed her to the wall, leaving a little space between us. "Tell me if this is too much."

She slowly shook her head. "No, but… I ache."

"You need to come," I said. I slid my hand between her legs, not quite touching her pussy. "You can use me to get off."

"Is there a way we could, um… I mean, could we both…"

"Come together without me being inside you?" She nodded. "Get on your hands and knees. I'll show you how we can play together."

She did as I said, and I kneeled behind her. Draping myself over her back, I put my hand against her pussy again. This time, I eased my first two fingers inside her, and used my thumb to stroke her clit. She gasped and rocked against me.

"That's it," I murmured. "Just like that. Fuck my

hand. Make yourself come."

"Wh-what about you?"

I adjusted so my cock was nestled against the crack of her ass. "You keep doing what feels good. You'll see how this works."

She rode my fingers, her ass sliding against my cock. I felt the heat of her release, and it made me come as well. But my little Talia didn't seem to be done. She kept rocking against me. I wanted to watch as she got herself off.

"Hang on, honey. Let's change positions."

I sat on the floor of the shower and motioned for her to straddle my thighs. I slipped my fingers inside her again and toyed with her clit some more. After a few experimental movements, she leaned back, placing her hands on my knees, and took what she needed. Watching her expressions, and the way her tits bounced, made me want to remember this moment for the rest of my life. I'd never seen anyone so sexy or gorgeous in my life.

She came and paused for a moment, trying to catch her breath. I didn't get a chance to remove my fingers from inside her before she was riding me again. My little Talia came another three times before she couldn't hold herself up anymore. She twitched and moaned, her hips still shifting a little.

Damn. I'd never met anyone like her before.

"Are you still not done?" I asked.

"More. It feels so good."

Since she hadn't voluntarily been with a man before, I wondered if she'd never bothered trying to get herself off. Had tonight been the first time she'd ever had an orgasm? I could see why she'd be addicted and want to keep going.

"I think we should stop for tonight. But

tomorrow, when I go to get tested, I'll stop at a special store and bring home some things for us to use after Riley goes to sleep. Then you can come as many times as you want."

"You must think I'm a whore or something."

I shook my head. No, I would never think that of her. She'd discovered something new and wasn't ready to stop. Nothing wrong with that. If I'd already been tested, I'd let her ride my cock all night if she wanted. Well, if that's something she wanted to try. I hadn't expected this much from her so soon. Better not push my luck.

"I'll get you off as much as you want, without putting my dick inside you. But there's one thing I need to make clear."

"What?" she asked.

"The day you agree to let me fuck you, you become mine. No leaving if you decide you can't take it anymore. You'll get a property cut like the other ladies, and I'll marry you if that's what you want."

"It's too much, I..." I pressed a finger to her lips. I didn't mean right this second, but she needed to be aware of what would happen if we took that last step. She nipped my finger. "Fine. I understand. But... can you make me come again?"

I smiled and pulled her onto my lap, her back flush against my chest. Pressing her thighs apart, I got her off with my hand another three times before the water ran cold and we had no choice but to get out.

The more I thought about her reaction tonight, the more I realized Talia hadn't just put up a wall to keep people out. She used it as a way to control everything in her life. Those orgasms had given her a way to maintain the upper hand, since I hadn't taken charge and only offered my fingers, while feeling more pleasure than she'd ever experienced before. Once she fully let me in, I had a feeling I'd have a naughty little nymph in my bed.

I couldn't wait.

I shut off the water and wrapped a towel around my waist, then grabbed one for her. I helped Talia dry off and she pulled her pajamas back on. I put on my basketball shorts and climbed into bed beside her. She rolled to her side to study me, and I wondered what the hell she was thinking. Nothing in her eyes gave her thoughts away. She licked her lips, her gaze trailing over my bare chest.

"I still want more," she said. "Is something wrong with me?"

"No, honey. I do have a question, though. Is it by any chance getting close to that time of the month for you?"

She narrowed her eyes. "What does that have to do with anything?"

"You may be ovulating. You know how animals go into heat? Consider it the human version. Not all women crave sex the way you seem to, but I bet that's what's going on. So no, there's nothing wrong with you. Are you sure you won't be sore in the morning?"

"I don't care," she said.

"Lie on your stomach, then pull your knees up under you. Put your ass in the air."

She only paused for a second before obeying. I got up and went to the bathroom, grabbing the lube I'd bought when neither of my girls had been paying attention. When I got back to the bedroom, I kneeled on the bed beside her. I tugged her pajama shorts and panties down as far as I could. Running my hand over her ass cheek, I lightly teased her slit with my fingers. She tried to spread her thighs, but the shorts had her trapped.

I slicked my fingers with the lube and liberally coated her pussy, even sliding my fingers inside her. She jerked and trembled, but she didn't pull away. I wished like hell we had some toys. Having my fingers inside her was driving me mad. I wanted to fuck her so bad my balls ached. Even though I'd come twice, my dick was already hard again. I'd never recuperated this fast before.

I teased her clit with light circles. "I wish you knew how beautiful you look. I'm so fucking hard right now. Do you want to see what you do to me?"

She nodded her gaze focused on the front of my shorts. I took them off, tossing them aside. My dick bobbed and a bead of precum formed on the head.

"I'm going to buy a vibrator for you tomorrow. Maybe more than one. There's one that will buzz against your clit as well as inside you. I think I'd fucking come right now if I had one of those toys and watched you fuck yourself with it. Or maybe I'd keep you like this, slide it in deep, and fuck you with it until you screamed in pleasure."

"Oh, God." She closed her eyes and I felt her trembling. Oh, ho! She liked that, did she? Good to know. Now I really wished I had one of those damn toys.

"I'd get you off so many times, you'd have cum running down your thighs. Your little clit would be so sensitive I'd barely have to touch it and you'd orgasm."

"Ram, please. I need to…"

I pressed a little tighter against the hard bud, circling it faster. She was close. I hoped like hell this didn't come back to bite me in the ass. Tomorrow, she could wake up and decide this had been a horrible mistake. Then I knew without a doubt she'd take off and I'd probably never see her again. But I found her so damn addicting.

"What do you want, Talia?" I asked. "Tell me."

"More of what you're doing, and… I want your fingers inside me."

I shifted on the bed, kneeling behind her. Pre-cum now dribbled onto the bedding, but I couldn't exactly make it stop.

"You want me to stuff this pretty pussy with my fingers?" I asked.

"Yes! God, Ram. Stop teasing me. I feel like I'm going to die if you don't make me come again."

Yeah. I was now certain she had to be starting soon. I'd heard some women turned into absolute little whores right before their period hit. I'd also get a toy she could wear. One she could set off with an app on her phone, or a remote or something. Then every time the urge hit, she could quietly excuse herself to the bathroom and come as many times as she needed to take the edge off. Then even if I wasn't around, she could still have as many orgasms as she wanted.

I pinched her clit between my thumb and forefinger, rubbing it, while I slid three fingers from my other hand inside her. I found that special spot inside her and made sure I rubbed against it with every thrust in and out of her pussy. She cried and screamed, bucked, and thrashed. I made her come so much, her pajamas were soaked, and our sheets would be wet too.

I finally left her sated enough she could fall asleep, and I went back to the bathroom to jerk my cock again.

I left the door open and watched her. If I closed my eyes, I could picture her on her knees, shorts shoved down, pussy on display. It only took three pumps before I was coming.

"You're going to be the death of me, Talia," I murmured. If she ever left, I'd lose my damn mind. Now that I'd had a taste of what things would be like with her, I knew no one else would ever compare. She'd just ruined me for every woman on the planet.

Chapter Twelve

Talia

What the hell had I done? My cheeks burned with mortification. I'd not only put my hands on him, gotten him off, but I'd begged him to make me come for over an hour. *I'm such a slut!* I'd never realized an orgasm would feel so incredible. Hearing about it, or reading it, was entirely different from experiencing it myself.

Even now, my body hummed, and I knew if Ram slid his hand into my panties, I'd be pleading with him again. Was he right about me acting like this because it was so close to being that time of the month? I'd never felt like this before. Why now and not the other eight years I'd had a period? If I asked Ram, he'd probably say it was something psychological, and he might be right. Until last night, I'd always equated sex with something degrading and painful. Now I knew how good it could feel, as long as the person you were with made sure you were comfortable and willing.

Ram had been gone when I'd woken up, and Riley had still been in bed. I'd found a note on the kitchen counter letting me know he'd gone to get tested and pick up a few things on his way home. I wanted to hide my face when I remember exactly what he'd said he wanted to buy. Would he really bring home a vibrator? I'd never used one. What if I hated it?

Since I had a feeling Riley would be hungry when she woke, and I was starving, I pulled out the ingredients to make eggs, sausage, and biscuits. Within thirty minutes, I had everything done and on plates. I still hadn't heard a peep out of Riley and decided to wake her up. Going into her room, I gently shook her shoulder.

"Riley, it's time for breakfast."

She mumbled something but didn't seem inclined to get out of bed. Gripping the covers, I yanked them off her. She gasped and bolted upright in bed. The terror in her eyes made my heart nearly stop. I hadn't meant to scare her.

"I'm sorry, Riley. I didn't…"

She focused on me, and slowly seemed to remember where she was. "Oh, Talia. Is it morning?"

"Yeah." I sat on the edge of the bed. "Who used to wake you up like this?"

She brought her knees up to her chest and wrapped her arms around her legs. She stared at the wall across from her. "When I turned twelve, my mom's boyfriend started getting me up in the mornings. He'd yank the covers off the bed, then grab me."

"Grab you?" I had a feeling I knew what she meant, but I wanted to be certain. My gut told me Riley was hiding a lot of pain and abuse. If she didn't let some of it out, she'd eventually either erupt or break down.

"I don't have much up top, but for a twelve-year-old, my breasts were bigger than most girls my age. He'd grab them, give them a squeeze, or do the same to my butt. I stopped wearing a nightgown after he…" A tear slipped down her cheek, and I pulled her into my arms. She cried and clung to me. Her dad found us like that about ten minutes later.

Ram didn't say a word, just quietly entered the room and sat on the other side of Riley. She sniffled and refused to meet his gaze.

"Riley, I think you should tell your dad what you shared with me. Except, don't hold anything back. He needs to know what happened when you lived with your mom. It could make a big difference in you being able to stay with him legally." Of course, I didn't know that for sure, but I didn't think a judge would give her back to a woman who allowed her to be molested. "I'll be in the kitchen when the two of you are ready to eat something. Ram, I'll fix a plate for you."

I stopped in the hall, just out of sight. Listening to them, I made sure Riley was going to be honest with him. My heart broke as she confided in her dad, and even told him the things she hadn't shared with me. I pressed a hand to my mouth and felt tears prick my eyes. That poor little girl.

I tiptoed away and set the table. By the time they joined me, I'd re-heated our food and poured some drinks. Riley's eyes were red and puffy as she took her seat. Ram squeezed my shoulder as he passed me and sat down across from me. It put Riley between us, and it wasn't the first time he'd done that. I had to wonder if it was on purpose. Was it his subtle way of telling her she'd be protected here?

"Badger texted me on the way home. They're holding Church again in a little bit, so I'll have to head over to the clubhouse. The two of you can stay here, or he said you were welcome to go to his place. Adalia was going to bake cookies today."

"Cookies?" Riley asked.

"If Riley is up for it, then we'll go say hi to Adalia," I said. "Can you come pick us up on the way home? I don't think I'm comfortable driving that big truck, and I don't know how far of a walk it will be."

"I can drop you off and pick you up." Ram reached out and ran his hand over Riley's hair. "My brave girl. I'm going to make sure your mother will never have custody of you again. All right?"

"Thank you, Dad," she murmured.

"I don't know what sorts of things you like for breakfast. I've never had the opportunity to do much in the kitchen. Money was tight, so I mostly lived off ramen, hot dogs, and spaghetti because it was cheap and filling." I took a bite of my eggs, thinking they didn't taste as good as what Ram had made for us yesterday. "I wouldn't mind learning to cook more meals. I'm sure I could follow a recipe."

"We can get a few books," Ram said. "What about you, Riley? Is there anything you want to learn? If not cooking, then maybe a craft or something?"

"I don't know what I'd like," she said.

"Then you can try some different things. I asked Badger who everyone used for Internet and cable, then stopped by the company's office while I was out. They have us scheduled for next week to get service. The house already has the proper cables run, so it shouldn't take them long to set it up." He patted Riley's hand. "Once we have Wi-Fi, you can watch some different videos to see what you find interesting."

"I know I don't need a job to pay for anything here, but I also don't like sitting around doing nothing all day," I said. "Does your club ever do volunteer work in the community?"

"Adalia would be the one to ask," he said. "And if there's not something already set up, then I'm sure she'd have a few suggestions."

We finished breakfast and I went to shower and change. Riley got ready too, since we were both leaving with Ram. He dropped us off at Badger's house on his way to the clubhouse, and Adalia welcomed us with a warm smile.

"Sorry I bailed early last night," she said. "That was one of my worst headaches ever."

"I hope you're feeling better today," I said.

"I am. Riley, the kids are in the living room watching Disney movies. I know you're a little old for that kind of thing, but you're welcome to join them. Or you can sit in the kitchen with me and Talia. Whatever makes you feel most comfortable," Adalia said.

Riley went to sit with the kids, and I followed Adalia to the kitchen, where she already had snacks and drinks set out. "The kids have sodas and cookies. I made sure to set out enough for Riley in case she decided to go in there with them."

"I appreciate you letting us drop in like this. Ram said you'd be the best person to answer the question I had this morning. It's about what to do with my free time. I'm not used to being idle."

"Hmm. Well, the club runs an underground clinic for women who were raped, or who are trying to escape abusive relationships. The front side is a small bookstore. If you don't have medical knowledge, you could always help out in the store. Or if you're good at making things, there's a small section there where we offer handmade items, and all proceeds are donated to a different charity every quarter."

"Wow. I didn't realize the club did so much for the town." The more I learned about this place, and about Ram, the more certain I became that I was in the right place.

"We didn't used to. Wolf's woman actually helped us with the clinic. She'd been raped in college, and her school swept it under the rug. She wanted a way to help women in her situation."

"She sounds like an amazing woman."

Adalia nodded. "You didn't get to meet her last night? Her name is Glory."

"No, I only spoke with you, Farrah, Mariah, Lilian, and Elena. I have to admit, I could have done without the conversation with the two sisters."

Adalia sighed. "I don't know what to do with those two. I'm not sure Badger does either. So far, he's letting their men handle it. The problem is Savage would do anything for Mariah. I'm not sure he could give her tough love. Demon, on the hand, won't let Farrah get away with anything."

"Riley wants to learn a craft. Maybe I'll learn one too. We could make things to sell in the shop." I hated turning the conversation so abruptly, but I really didn't want to discuss Farrah and Mariah. It would ruin my good mood. "What sort of things do the other women here make?"

"Hmm. Instead of telling you, why don't we use that as a way for you to meet the other women here? We could have a crafting day once or twice a week. Each of us could take turns hosting it, until you've had a chance to try a little of everything. Riley would be welcome too, if she wanted to attend."

I had to admit it sounded fun. I'd never been able to do something like that before. Then again, I hadn't had a lot of friends in my life, and none in the last seven or eight years. Was this the sort of thing friends did together?

"A few get together for a book club too," she said. "If you enjoy reading, you might like meeting with them. I think they pick a new book every week."

I'd never really had the time to read. Buying books had been a luxury, one I couldn't afford. I didn't even have a cell phone anymore. The one I'd had was a cheap one I paid by month. It wasn't a great loss.

I heard the kids giggling in the other room and smiled. This was good for Riley. I hoped she was having a nice time, even though the children were younger than her. Maybe that actually made things easier for her. Although, she'd gotten along well with Coral last night.

"I think Ram said Coral was Steel's daughter. Who's her mother?" I asked.

"Rachel. She's a quiet, sweet woman. I think you'll like her. You've probably noticed most of us are younger than our men. Steel and Rachel probably have the biggest age gap, but it works for them. He treats her really well, and I'm pretty sure she sees him as her savior."

"There's sixteen years difference between me and Ram," I said. "I still can't believe he's thirty-six. He doesn't look it."

The kids raced into the kitchen, with Riley bringing up the rear. She stood uncertainly in the doorway, and I held my hand out to her. Rushing over, she grasped my fingers and held on tight. Had something happened?

"Mom, Riley said she's never played a video game before. Can I show her how to play the Switch?" Gunner asked.

"I'm not sure you have the sort of games a girl would like," Adalia said.

"Please," he begged. "Besides, Dad got me the Nintendo Pass, so there's all kinds of games on there. She can pick whatever she wants."

I glanced up at Riley, and I could tell immediately she really wanted to play yet felt embarrassed over not having done so before. Poor girl probably hadn't had access to a gaming system. The way her mother treated her, it wouldn't have surprised me if she'd been starving most days. Something like a video game wouldn't have even been possible for Riley. Not before. Now? The moment Ram heard she wanted one, he'd get it for her. I really needed to pull him back or he was going to spoil her rotten. I understood why he wanted to. Didn't make it right. One day, it might come back to haunt us.

"Ivory, let her use your headphones. That way she can sit in the living room with the two of you, and the movies don't have to stop. I know it's boring watching someone else play." Adalia shooed them away, but Riley hung back.

"It's okay, Riley. Go wait in the living room and Gunner will show you how the games work. As long as he's fine with you using his game system, I don't see an issue with it. But if he asks for it back, hand it over."

"All right." She hesitated another moment. "If I like it, do you think maybe Dad would get me one?"

"When is your birthday?" I asked.

"Not until next year. I just turned fourteen a few months ago," she said.

"Hmm. Then you may need to wait for Christmas, but if you tell him that's what you really want, then I'm sure he'll get one for you."

She smiled and hurried from the room. Good. Now I could tell Ram she didn't expect one until the holidays.

"You're good with her," Adalia said. "And that was smart, bringing up birthday and Christmas. If Ram is anything like the other guys around here, he's a total sucker for his kid. I swear mine would have so much crap it wouldn't fit into this house if I didn't tell Badger to wait every time they said they wanted something. Especially Ivory. At her age, she changes her mind every other day."

"I'm glad to see Riley getting along with them. She broke down this morning. I accidentally scared her, and once she told me why, the floodgates opened up. My heart hurts for her. I may not have had a great life, but it could have been worse."

Adalia cleared her throat and lowered her voice. "Pretty much every woman here has been abused one way or another. Elena's adopted parents were going to marry her off to a man who sold women to brothels. Lilian's past is so horrific none of us thought she'd ever heal from it. When I was a teenager, a man dragged me into an alley to rape me. Badger heard me crying for help and killed the guy. Spent a lot of time in prison for it. I told you about Glory. About the only ones who weren't physically hurt were Farrah and Mariah, because they were little princesses at the Dixie Reapers."

In other words, Riley and I were in good company, and so were the women and teens we'd brought here with us. It was a good thing we'd come here with Ram. This place was exactly what we all needed. And in the end, it gave Riley the father she'd wanted.

"Oh, crap. I forgot Ram was supposed to get the paternity test results today. Do you think he has? He didn't say anything before he dropped us off," I said.

"I believe that's part of what Church is about," Adalia said. "They tend to keep club business from the women and kids. However, I overheard him talking to Outlaw and Riley's name came up. They're probably brainstorming ways to keep her out of her mother's hands."

"Ram said he'd pick us up on his way home. We won't be in your way until then, will we?"

Adalia shook her head. "Not at all. Come on. We can go watch the movies with the kids if you want? Or we can keep talking."

"No, I think I'm all out of questions right now and have a lot to process."

I followed Adalia to the living room, where Gunner and Ivory were watching the live action version of Aladdin, while Riley played on the Switch. I settled on the couch with Adalia and had to admit it was the most relaxed I'd felt in a while. Almost like... I was finally home.

Chapter Thirteen

Ram

I'd had mixed feelings when I'd left Talia and Riley at Badger's house. It wasn't that I thought Adalia would be rude to them or anything. She was too sweet for something like that. What worried me was Riley's breakdown this morning, although it armed me with the knowledge I needed to make sure Reba never had custody of our daughter again.

Badger leaned back in his chair, looking tired as hell. "I'm going to let Outlaw run point on this one because he and Wire did all the work."

"Right, so…" Outlaw set the papers on the table and everyone took a set. He'd been so damn organized, he'd stapled a packet for each of us. "Ram and Riley had a paternity test done, just to verify she's his kid. Spoiler alert, she is. The problem is that he's not been part of her life, and not having known about her until now, he's never paid child support."

"I would have if I'd known I had a daughter," I said, feeling a little defensive.

"From what I was able to track down online about Riley, and the conversation I had with Ram on the way in, I can say with absolute certainty we can get a judge to grant him custody. However, to make things as smooth as possible, there's two things you need to do, Ram. First, we need to get Riley into school. We need to show she's established here, has friends, and lives in a safe, nurturing environment. Which brings me to point two. She needs a mother."

"Um." Slash tipped his head and stared at Outlaw. "I thought the problem was the fact she has one."

"A stepmother," Outlaw said. "And we'd need

to backdate the marriage. A judge will want to see a stable relationship before he grants you custody. I know things have been rocky with Talia. Making any progress?"

"Yeah. I think things are going well. But if I tell her we need to be married, and it needed to happen months ago, then she may take issue with it," I said.

"Then tell her it's for Riley," Badger suggested. "If you make it about your daughter and not you getting into her pants, then Talia may give in. You get the woman you want, and you get to keep your daughter."

"I can talk to her, feel her out." She'd either agree or smack the shit out of me before packing up and moving into the apartments, if she didn't go even further and leave the compound.

"Next, Ram mentioned an offshore account for Vega. We haven't been able to find any other victims. None who are alive anyway. Which means that money will be divided however we decide. Wire already transferred it into an account and gave me access to it." Outlaw cleared his throat. "I agree with what Ram said before. The victims living here do need a sizable portion to feel secure and be confident in starting their lives over. However, no one realized how much money was in there. We aren't talking a few hundred thousand, or even a few million."

"Then how much was in there?" Demon asked.

"A little over three billion," Outlaw said. "I thought we could give each victim one million dollars. That includes Talia and Riley. They can do whatever they want with the money. In the case of the underage girls, I suggest we take another million and divide it equally, then invest it for them. We can let it mature and in twenty years, they could earn out dividends."

"Is this Church or an investment meeting?" Dingo asked. "You're making my fucking head hurt."

"Mine too," Blades said. "And I'm not agreeing with him just because he's the father of my granddaughter."

"Any objections to what Outlaw said about the money so far?" Badger asked.

"I'd like to know why, if there's a few billion dollars, we're only giving the victims one million each. Seems like a paltry sum in comparison to what they've been through. Why is the club keeping the rest?" I asked.

Wolf leaned forward. "Glory would be over the moon if she could even have half a million to help fund the clinic. I know we've had to shut it down here and there for various reasons. That money could go toward security upgrades, medical supplies, and anything else the women will need."

"Unless some of you want to take in more pets, I could use about ten thousand. It would offset the cost of supplies for the rescues I take in," Doolittle said.

"Could we donate some of it to various local programs?" Steel asked. "Food pantry and maybe the community center?"

I sighed and leaned back in my chair. "Before Badger gets any more pissed, because I see the steam coming out of his ears, I want to say one thing. I think the women and teens I brought here should get at least three million each. Although, I wouldn't tell Riley about hers. I'd keep it safe, and when she's ready to move out, she can have access to the funds."

"I'm fine with that suggestion, as well as the requests from Wolf, Doolittle, and Steel. If anyone else has a charity in mind for a donation, let Outlaw know. We could also use some of the funds to start a clothing donation for the schools. I know the elementary school is always asking for gently used clothes in case someone has an accident." Badger shifted his weight and looked around the table. "Now, no more talk about the money. Is there anything we need to discuss aside from Ram's issue with Riley?"

"Wire said he hasn't noticed any movement with Vega's people. Either they haven't found the body yet, or he's not missed even by his own goons," Outlaw said. "But I'm going to keep an eye on the situation. If his death somehow gets tied to Ram and this club, it could cause trouble later. For now, I don't see anything happening so we should be fine."

"All right. I do have one other issue to bring up. As you know the apartments aren't very far from the clubhouse," Badger said. "I know I said I was only banning the club whores for two days, with today being the final one, but I think we need to discuss this a bit more. We still have a lot of single men, and I don't want to keep you from partying, or hooking up with anyone. However, I also don't want our guests to feel scared. Between the loud music, the way you get rowdy when you party, and the barely clothed women going in and out, it could be damaging to them. They've suffered sexual abuse, and I don't want to take that lightly."

Smuggler cleared his throat. "Personally, I'm fine with not having any parties for a little while. Might be good for us. I mean, we aren't exactly thirteen-year-old boys. I think we can handle not getting laid for a week or even a month."

Frost cursed. "A month? I don't know about you, but I'd rather not get blue balls."

"Figure it out," Badger said. "Or I'll let you explain to those women and girls that getting your dick wet is more important than their well-being."

Frost winced. "When you put it that way…"

"If there's nothing else, then I think we're done here." Badger brought his fist down on the table like Grizzly used to do, and it reminded me of something.

"Wait, Pres…" I stood so I could see everyone clearly. "I know I was gone for a long time, and I wasn't here when Grizzly died. I've heard what happened with Doolittle's woman, and that Farrah and Mariah pissed off the Dixie Reapers over the situation as well. From what I've gathered, this club damn near imploded, and you still aren't the cohesive brotherhood you were when I left."

"What's your point?" Badger asked.

"I think it would be good to have Farrah, Mariah, and Grizzly's daughters all sit down with a mediator. Until those women heal the rift between them, things are going to be strained around here. Even I can feel the tension. And it's not just them. Savage, you're tense as fuck, and I'm sure what happened is a large part of it. Do you dislike Doolittle's woman?"

"No," he said. "Minnie is a nice woman, and she's a good mom."

"Then the problem you have is with the sister who married into the Savage Raptors?" I asked.

He shrugged.

"There's a lot of people who still aren't happy with Meredith," Badger said. "And when Grizzly knew he was dying, he wanted to spend those last days with Meredith. I can't blame him. She'd been gone for a while."

"All I know is I can feel there's something wrong in this club, and I'm sure Talia and Riley can tell as well. Find the root of the problem and fix it. Otherwise, it's going to snowball until it's so big it's going to blow up in everyone's face at the worst possible time."

Badger smirked. "Did your woman talk to you? I think she mentioned something to Adalia about you talking to everyone."

"No, she didn't. But I'm glad she has that much faith in me."

"All right. *Now* we're done," Badger said. "Everyone get the hell out of here. Go home to your families, or go down some beers. Whatever makes you happy."

I left and waited for the Pres. Since I was going to his house anyway, might as well walk out with him. I pulled the truck keys from my pocket and stared at them. Talia and I had discussed looking at vehicles, but we hadn't been able to get to it today.

"Something wrong?" Badger asked, slapping me on the back.

"I still have the club truck. I'll need to buy something for Talia and Riley to ride in," I said.

"Just take care of your family right now. You can keep the truck as long as you need it. Don't rush into buying something because you feel like you need to. The three of you need to bond, and you need to convince Talia to be Riley's stepmom."

Right. This was going to be a fun day. So much for making Talia scream my name in pleasure. Now she'd be yelling at me in anger instead. Of course, she could surprise me.

"Thanks, Pres. I'm going to go pick them up from your house and go home."

"If Riley is having fun, let her stay a little longer. She won't be in the way."

"I'll see what she wants to do." I got into the truck and pulled away from the clubhouse. Badger zipped past me on his motorcycle, pulling into his driveway as I neared his house. I stopped on the street and turned the engine off.

He left the front door open for me, so I let myself into his house. Riley sat on the floor with Gunner showing her something on a handheld game. Adalia, Talia, and Ivory were on the couch watching a movie. Everything seemed peaceful, and they were getting along nicely. Good.

"Is it time to go home?" Riley asked.

"Only if you want to. Badger said you could stay longer. Totally up to you," I said.

"Can I really?" she asked, looking from me to the Pres and back again.

"You bet. Just let Badger or Adalia know when you're ready to come home. They can text me, and I'll come pick you up."

Talia stood up and came over to me. I took her hand and led her outside, waving bye to everyone in the living room. It only took a few minutes to get home and let ourselves into our house. There was so much to tell her, and I didn't even know where to start.

"So... is this so we can have some alone time?" she asked.

"Yeah, but not for the reason I'd hoped. There's something I need to discuss with you, and I'm not sure how you'll take it."

She crossed her arms and looked away. "If it's something that will piss me off, maybe you should make sure I'm *really happy* first."

I tried damn hard not to laugh. And failed. It looked like that need hadn't calmed any, and she still wanted to come multiple times. At least I had some toys to help us out this time.

"As much as I want to give in to that demand, we really do need to talk about Riley. Or rather, your role in her life. Outlaw brought up some good points today if I want to keep my daughter the legal way."

"What's the illegal way?" she asked.

"Kill Reba and her boyfriend, which sounds mighty fine to me. But I don't want to tell Riley the reason her mom vanished is because I decided to remove her from this world."

She sighed. "Fine. And the legal way requires what?"

"For us to be married." Shit. I hadn't meant to blurt that out. She stared at me a moment before turning and walking away. Damnit. I'd been worried this might happen. She didn't leave the house, so I gave her some space. After fifteen minutes she came back, sat down, and let out a long sigh.

"Tell me everything. I can't promise to make a decision right this second, but at least give me the information I need in order to make a proper decision."

And that's what I did for the next thirty minutes. By the time I'd finished, Riley was back home, and our playtime was on hold.

Chapter Fourteen

Talia

It had been one week since Ram dropped the bomb on me. Marry him in order to keep Riley safe. It had cooled things between us considerably. Even though we'd had an incredible night before, after that discussion, I hadn't been able to even think about having orgasms. But now I'd pretty much made up my mind.

Riley was off playing with Coral, so we had the house to ourselves. I'd stripped out of my clothes and lay stretched out on the bed, waiting for Ram. We hadn't had a chance to use the toys he'd bought, and I was more than a little curious. I also felt both excited and nervous. It wasn't like he hadn't already seen me naked or made me come. So why did it feel like this was our first time?

And the toys... I'd never used any before. What if it hurt? Having his fingers inside me was one thing. The toys would probably be shaped more like a man's dick, and part of me worried I might freak out or something. Although, I'd gotten Ram off without panicking.

He'd taken the sack with the mystery items into the bathroom to clean them, so I hadn't had a chance to see them yet. When he came back, he'd removed his clothes, except for his underwear. The fact he'd left them on made me feel warm and fuzzy inside. If he'd come out with his hard cock bobbing in front of him, I might have changed my mind about this.

He hadn't done anything last time we'd been naked together, not anything I hadn't wanted. Why did it feel a little different in the light of day?

"You sure you still want to do this?" he asked,

apparently seeing my hesitation.

"Yeah, just… go slow?" I asked. "This is new for me."

"Same rules as before, honey. You want me to stop, say so. If something hurts or doesn't feel good, tell me."

I stared at the toys in his hands, and wondered what they'd feel like. He'd gotten the one he'd mentioned, where it had a part that went inside me and a smaller piece that would vibrate over my clit. I hadn't expected it to have a tiny butterfly for that part though. It made it seem less scary. The other one looked like a thick cock.

Ram got the lube from the drawer. He held the two toys up. "Which do you want to try first?"

"The smaller one," I said.

He nodded and set the larger cock aside. With the click of a button, he turned on the vibrator. Ram slicked it with lube, then put more on his fingers. I tensed for a brief moment when he spread my legs open, then relaxed as he lightly swiped the lube onto my pussy. Closing my eyes, I remembered all the things he'd done to me last time. He'd made me feel so incredibly good and that had only been with his fingers.

"Do you want to lie on your back for this one?" he asked. "We can do this in any position you want."

"I want to stay like this," I said.

"Does it make you feel vulnerable to be open?" I slowly nodded. Without another word, he closed my legs, bent my knees, then gently pressed them to my chest. "Then let's try this."

I felt the toy slide up and down my pussy. It bumped my clit a few times, sending little sparks of pleasure through me. When he eased it inside me, it slid right in. The second the little butterfly settled into place, I thought I'd died and gone to heaven. He managed to drag the toy in and out of me, while keeping the smaller part over my clit. The slight pressure and friction soon had me curling my toes.

"Ram, it feels so good." He shifted so that he kneeled in front of me. I released my legs and splayed them on either side of him. "Does sex always feel like this?"

"I'd like to think it gets better." He winked at me. "The day you tell me you want my cock inside you instead of these toys, I'll be able to die a happy man."

My breath caught as I stared at him. It was in that moment I realized something. He didn't just look at me with affection. He genuinely wanted me to stay by his side. Not only as a mom for Riley, but as the woman who shared his bed and every other aspect of his life. And I thought I might actually be ready to give it a try. No more doubts or hesitation.

"Ram... when do you get your test results back?" I asked.

"I got them back the next day. I'm clean."

Was I brave enough to ask for more? "Then, after you make me come, can we try some of those things you whispered to me in the shower?"

"If I take you bare, there's no going back, Talia. Even the chance you could be pregnant would be enough for me to hold on tight and never let you go."

"I know," I said softly.

"Is this you agreeing to marry me?" he asked.

I nodded. Until right now, I hadn't realized it wasn't only what I wanted, but also what I needed. No, it was what we all needed. I could be Riley's mom, Ram's wife, and together, we'd be a family. Something I'd never really had. Riley hadn't either.

He flipped me onto my stomach and yanked me up onto my knees. I gripped the covers, and pressed back, eager for whatever was coming next. Hopefully me!

I felt the bed shift and looked over my shoulder in time to see Ram remove his underwear. I'd been right about him being hard. The moment he worked the toy inside me, I closed my eyes and moaned. It felt so wonderful.

"Yes, Ram. Please don't stop."

"Not going to," he promised. "Come for me, Talia. Show me how much you want to feel my dick inside you."

His words turned me on even more. I thrust back against the toy, and it didn't take long to make me come. I'd thought he'd only make me come once, but I should have known better. Ram didn't stop teasing me with the toy until I'd had multiple orgasms. My thighs were soaked with my release by the time he stopped.

He came down over my back, pressing my cheek to the mattress. I felt his cock slide along the lips of my pussy. The slow drag and pull was making me feel crazy. I needed more! I wanted him inside me.

"I'm ready," I told him. "You don't have to keep waiting."

"Remember the scenario where I pinned you to the bed and fucked you until my cum was overflowing from your pussy?"

"Y-Yeah."

"You better hold on tight because I'm going to come inside you again and again. I'll make you scream my name, beg for more, and I'll take you every which way I can. Are you ready?"

"I'm ready! I'm so ready," I said.

The head of his cock split me open, and he used

shallow thrusts to enter me. He was far larger than his fingers or the toy. It burned as I stretched to take him. Adjusting his position, he started fucking me, but his cock kept hitting just the right spot inside me. It made me see stars, and I felt such an intense orgasm building, it nearly scared me.

When I came, I felt my release flooding the bed. Ram growled, and his control seemed to snap. He drove into me with long, deep strokes, not slowing for even a moment. His hips slammed against me and I felt his cock swell. The heat of his cum filled me up, and still he kept going.

My knees trembled and I didn't think they'd hold me up much longer. Ram slammed into me one last time, staying deep inside me.

"Please tell me I didn't hurt you," he said.

"No, it was wonderful," I murmured, barely able to stay awake. It felt like he'd sapped all my energy.

"We're not done yet, honey. You came nearly nonstop for an hour last week. I want to make you do it again."

"Did you want to marry me, or kill me?" I asked. "Because I think that many orgasms might do me in right now. I don't think I could move if I tried."

He chuckled softly. "All right. You get a short break, then I'm going to do my best to give Riley a little brother or sister."

"Do you think we're going too fast?" I asked.

"Ask some of the other women here how long their men waited to claim them. I bet some of those relationships happened faster than ours, and they're still together all these years later."

Ram pulled out and stretched out on his side. I'd started to drift off to sleep when he tugged me against his body and wrapped his arms around me. I'd never been held while I slept. Not even Ram had done it. It made me feel safer than I'd ever felt before, and I let sleep pull me under.

* * *

When I woke up, I was in the bed alone. I heard Riley and Ram in another room, and lazily stretched. I couldn't help but smile. If anyone had ever told me I'd enjoy sex, and even want a husband and baby, I'd have told them they were insane. And yet, here I was. Had he told Riley yet? What would she think about it?

I still felt bad about the morning I'd scared the crap out of her. It never occurred to me yanking the covers off her would remind of her something so awful. Since that morning, I'd been careful to stand in the doorway and call her name. If that didn't get her up, then I'd lightly shake her shoulder. I'd also apologized countless times for what happened.

I shoved the covers off me and got out of bed. After using the bathroom and taking a quick shower, I put on my pajamas and went to find Riley and Ram. The fact the sun no longer shone through the window told me I'd been out for quite a while. I found the two of them in the kitchen making dinner. Standing just inside the doorway, I watched them for a few minutes. Riley looked so happy. I wondered if I should go back to the bedroom so they could have more time together.

Riley turned and saw me. Her eyes lit up and she ran over to me, hugging me tight. "Mom!"

Uh… I awkwardly hugged her back. It seemed Ram had told her the news, and she'd taken it better than I'd thought. Then again, she'd tried to push the two of us together from the start.

"I see your dad told you we're getting married."

She released me and led me over to the table. She pulled out a chair, motioning for me to sit. I did, feeling a little bemused. Ram saw me and winked before facing the stove again.

"Stay right here. We're making something special for you," Riley said.

"Oh, really? Then should I leave the kitchen so I won't get any hints as to what it is?" I asked.

"No, you can stay. It's almost ready, right, Dad?"

"Right," Ram said. "Riley, why don't you set the table?"

She took down plates and got out the silverware. She even folded some paper towels to use as napkins. I couldn't remember seeing her quite this animated, not even when we'd had our big shopping trip.

Ram brought over a plate of steaks, placing one on each of our plates. While he put the pan in the sink, Riley carried a bowl of mashed potatoes to the table. She set it in the middle, and Ram added a basket of rolls beside it. I knew Ram had bought steaks, but he'd said they were for a special occasion. Looked like that was today.

"I helped Dad make the mashed potatoes," she said. "And I put the rolls in the oven."

Ram and Riley took a seat. Once we each had the potatoes and rolls on our plates, it was time to taste the masterpiece they'd put together. I had to admit it was really good.

"Riley wanted a nice dinner since we're going to officially be a family. She was talking about dresses and flowers, but I explained we had to do things differently to make sure she could stay here with us."

I looked from him to Riley. "And you're all right with that? Knowing this is to keep you away from your mom?"

"You're my mom," she said, taking a bite of her food.

Well, all right, then. If Ram wasn't going to say anything about it, neither was I. Besides, I may not have ever raised so much as a plant, but I couldn't fuck up nearly as much as Reba had.

"Don't you start school tomorrow?" I asked.

She nodded. "Coral said I could ride with her, since we'll both be going to the same school. Is that okay?"

"It's fine with me. Do I need to pick you up, or will you be coming home with her too?"

"I don't know," she said. "We can ask Ms. Rachel when they come to get me before school."

It was hard to believe she was already doing normal things like going to school and making friends. She'd gone from being held captive by Vega and living in a cage, to having a nice home, a dad who adored her, and a good life. I hoped she always found things to smile about. If anyone deserved to have lots of happy moments, it was Riley.

After dinner, we watched a movie, then I helped Riley prepare her things for school. They were simple tasks. Things a million other families had done before. And yet, they were special to me, because it was my first time experiencing them. Sure, I'd eaten dinner with Riley and Ram every night since he brought us here, but being an official family made it different this time.

Whatever it took, I'd make sure I was the best mom for Riley. She already had an amazing dad. I didn't know what the future would hold for us, but I did know we'd make a lot of good memories.

So this is what it's like. If I'd known sooner, I wouldn't have fought against Ram so much. I'd have agreed to stay right away. Well, maybe not. I was stubborn, after all. Always had been.

We tucked Riley into bed, then retired to our own room. I'd thought Ram might want to play some more. Instead, he held me and we talked a little. Mostly about Riley, and how our marriage would be handled. By the time my eyes felt heavy again, I realized I was more content than I'd ever been.

I think I love you, Ram. One day I'd say the words out loud. When I felt braver.

Chapter Fifteen

Ram

The day I'd dreaded had finally arrived. I knew things had been too quiet. Everything with Vega went too smoothly, which meant the proverbial shoe was going to drop elsewhere. Right at the damn gate in the form of Riley's birth mother, Reba. I crossed my arms and glared at her.

"You're not going to let me in to see my daughter?" she asked.

"Nope."

"Seriously? I came all this way to take her home," Reba said.

Yeah. Sure. What she most likely came for was money, and I'd be happy to give her some, as long as she signed a contract stating she'd never contact my family again. She'd never been a true mother to Riley. I refused to let her destroy the happiness my daughter had found.

It had been five months since we came to the Devil's Fury. Riley had been in therapy for a little over four months now, and she'd made a lot of progress. I worried seeing Reba would crush everything she'd accomplished so far. No fucking way would I let that happen.

Reba's eyes zeroed in on my finger. The one with the gold wedding band on it. Outlaw had asked Wire to backdate any files for our marriage, even though he'd had to hack into several places to make it happen. To anyone snooping, it would look like Talia and I were married three months before I found Riley locked in a cage. The counselor also had documentation of the abuse Riley suffered while living with her mother. And he'd been paid well to keep his mouth shut about certain things. There were records a judge could access through a subpoena, and those he kept locked up in a private area no one knew about.

"How did you find us, Reba? I didn't exactly leave a note for you, and it's not like you were searching very hard for Riley," I said.

"That's not true! I've been worried about her the last three months."

Was she shitting me right now? Had she not even realized our daughter was gone before that? I'd known she'd been a fucking awful parent, but this... I had no words.

"Reba, she's been with me for a little over five months, and you only noticed she was gone *three* months ago? Not to mention where I found her. She'd been kidnapped and gone from your house for who knows how long. What does that say about your parenting skills?" I asked.

She pursed her lips, looking like she'd sucked on a lemon. How had I ever found her attractive? If she'd once been pretty, the years hadn't been kind to her. She had a lot of wrinkles, her skin looked like she'd baked in the sun every day for five decades, and her hair had thinned and appeared brittle. Looked like she'd been doing a lot of drugs. I couldn't think of another explanation. This went beyond a poor diet and living conditions.

"I need to see Riley. You can't keep her from me."

"Actually, I can. Is that how you found us? You finally read the papers the judge sent? Your custody has been revoked, Reba. You have no rights to our daughter. None."

I heard a hiss behind me and turned to see Talia. Shit.

"*Our* daughter?" She glared at the woman. "Is that the piece of shit who let her boyfriend molest our sweet Riley?"

"It is. What are you doing here, Talia?" I asked.

"I went looking for you. Badger said you were on garbage duty, which didn't make any sense. Now I see what he meant."

"You can't talk to me like that," Reba said.

"She's my wife, Reba. She can talk to you however she wants. Now, I won't tell you again. Get the fuck away from here and never come back."

Reba straightened her spine. "You owe me! Do you know how expensive it was to take care of that girl on my own?"

Not very since she hardly ever fed her, barely clothed her, and wasn't a parent in any way imaginable to Riley. I wasn't going to say as much, though. Instead, I took out my wallet, pulled out the few hundred I had inside, and tossed it through the gate. As it fell to the ground, she scrambled to pick it up.

"Is this all? It's not enough," Reba said.

"It's more than you deserve. I meant what I said. Never come back here." I moved closer to the gate and leaned toward Reba, lowering my voice. "Because if you do, I'll make sure you disappear for good. Do you think anyone will look for you? I doubt it. No one would miss you, would they?"

"My daughter certainly wouldn't," Talia said. "If Ram doesn't make you vanish, I'll be happy to do it. Or I'll pay someone to take care of you."

I looked at the Prospect and pointed to Reba. "Make sure she's gone. If she comes back, let me know, then make sure there's no trace she was ever here. You get me?"

He nodded. "Got it, Ram."

I watched Reba slink away like a beaten dog with her tail between her legs. Something told me she'd come back, but I hoped I was wrong. I didn't want to deal with the headache of killing her. Riley might ask about her one day, and I didn't want to tell her I'd slit the woman's throat.

"Think she'll stay away?" Talia asked.

"Not sure. She'll probably use Riley as an excuse to get more money from me. I think I'd have needed at least five grand to shut her up permanently. Maybe more. It's not like she knows how much money the club has access to. She always thought I was a broke-ass biker. Doubt that's changed."

"Should we tell Riley?" Talia asked.

"As much as I want to say no, I think we should. If Reba decides to stick around town, she may run into Riley at some point. The last thing I want is for our daughter to be blindsided by that parasite."

Talia nodded. "All right. We can talk to her when she gets in from school."

"Aren't you supposed to be resting?" I asked. We'd thought Talia might be pregnant. She'd missed her period and kept throwing up. Unfortunately, it was a false alarm. Instead, she'd picked up a really nasty bug and the stress on her body had kept her from starting. I'd been disappointed, but if we were meant to have more kids, it would happen one day.

"I don't like lying around the house," she said.

I was all too aware of that fact. For someone who hadn't had a true home in her entire life, she sure didn't stay in ours for very long. I never knew where I'd find her. She volunteered sometimes at the bookstore, visited Rachel, Adalia, Glory, Lilian, Shella, and Elena rather frequently. She hadn't grown as close to the others, but I wasn't going to push her. Sometimes people just didn't get along.

"Why don't we go visit Badger and Adalia? I should tell him about Reba, and you can ask Adalia about possible ways to help the club or places in town to volunteer," I said.

"Badger knows Reba was here. Besides, I think now would be a really bad time to stop by his house," she said. "He went home. Adalia said she had something to tell him, and she looked really stressed about it."

Great. Just what we needed. When it came to Adalia, Badger didn't handle bad news well. She'd always been his weak spot. I couldn't imagine what she'd need to tell him that would be so upsetting, though. Not my business, not unless it affected me somehow. Doubtful.

"All right. Then let's go home. You know, where you were supposed to be already," I said.

She took my hand, rolling her eyes. I'd ridden my bike to the clubhouse, so I got on and waited for her to climb on back. She wrapped her arms around my waist and pressed her cheek between my shoulder blades. We didn't get to go for rides very often. There seemed to always be something to do, or we'd have to take Riley with us.

I pulled up to the house and stared at the SUV in the driveway. I still couldn't believe Badger had used part of the funds from Vega's account to buy us a Tahoe. Brand-new at that. It had taken over a month to convince Talia to drive the damn thing. She'd insisted it was too big and she'd wreck it.

Before I could get off the bike, she stood and wrapped her arms around my neck. Leaning in, she pressed her lips to mine. Talia didn't like to give kisses very often, so when she offered one up freely, I greedily accepted. She drew back, a little smile on her lips.

"What was that for?" I asked.

"I just love you."

I shook my head. Crazy-ass woman. She told me that all the damn time, but I could count on two hands the number of times she'd kissed me in five months. Every time I started to ask her about it, something held me back. I had a feeling it was a traumatic memory for her, so I tried not to push. One day, she'd confide in me. The wound might be too raw right now. While I didn't like her bottling things up, I also knew forcing her to talk about something was the wrong thing to do. Which was why she now saw a counselor as well.

I heard what sounded like an explosion, even though I didn't feel so much as a tremor through the ground. When Dingo, Steel, and two other brothers rushed past us and looked like they were heading for Badger's house, I decided I'd better go too.

"Go inside and lock the doors," I said, not having any idea what I was about to walk into.

Talia quickly did as I said. The moment Badger's house came into view, I came to a screeching halt. What the fuck? He'd taken a baseball bat to Adalia's car, and it looked like it had been smashed by some superhuman freak of nature. I knew he had a temper, but I couldn't imagine what happened to drive him to do this.

"Any idea what's going on?" I asked Steel.

"No idea." Adalia stood on the porch, her hand over her mouth and her eyes wide. When she realized she had an audience, she went to Badger, placing her hand on his chest.

Since he seemed to be calming a little, I decided

I'd be the brave one and find out what was going on.

"You all right, Pres?" I asked.

"No, I'm not fucking all right."

I looked to Adalia for help. The words that came out of her mouth had me seeing red, just like Badger. Now I understood why he wanted to destroy something, because what he really wanted to do was kill a bastard.

"One of the kids in Gunner's class asked what it was like to have a whore for a mother," Adalia said. "Apparently, he overheard his mother say some disparaging things about me and the other women who live here."

"They called *my* wife a whore?" Steel asked.

"I have to second that question," I said.

"All of our women," Badger said. "And apparently our daughters are whores in training. What the fucking hell? Gunner is only in sixth grade. What kind of children speak that way?"

"Did he say who the kid was?" Dingo asked. His voice was so quiet I did a double take. The rage in his eyes had me taking a step away from him. Yeah, calling his woman a whore was definitely the wrong thing to do. I wanted to rip a motherfucker apart for it, but Dingo looked like he might keep them alive for a few months and torture them daily.

Steel leaned in closer to me and whispered. "Mei was prostituted when she was just a kid. When she got older, she slept with men in order to survive. It's a hot button for Dingo."

Good to know. I wondered if any other women had similar stories here. Aside from the ones I'd brought with me... I already knew those had been forced into prostitution.

"May I make a suggestion?" I asked. "My

daughter isn't at the middle school, so I can't exactly barge in there and demand answers. But some of you can, like you, Pres. Take down every detail from Gunner, then call the principal for a meeting. If they refuse, threaten him with the media. The school will do anything to avoid being on the news if it's for something bad like this."

"Then what?" Steel asked.

"Either the school disciplines the kid, or they try to cover it up. In which case, the club can handle things our own way with a face-to-face with that little shit's parents. But I think we should try the nice way first." I glanced at Adalia's car. "And buy your woman a new vehicle since you destroyed that one."

"I'm going to ask Coral if she's heard anything at the high school," Steel said. "If your daughter hears that shit, it may derail the progress she's made so far."

He wasn't wrong, and if that happened, I'd gut the asshole responsible.

"I'm going home. Talia is probably worried." I walked off, wondering why things couldn't be quiet. First Reba, and now this shit with the schools. I didn't even know how to go about this particular fight. If the school administrators wouldn't do anything, and it wasn't likely they would, then we couldn't exactly make the parents disappear. It was a worry for another day.

I knocked on the door when I got home. "Talia, it's me."

I used my key to let myself in, now that I'd made sure she knew who was on the other side. After running off the way I had, if I'd gone inside unannounced, it could have scared her. She sat on the sofa with a cup of hot tea in her hands.

"Everything all right?" she asked.

I told her what happened, then decided to put it out of my mind for now. I could only tackle one thing at a time, and first, I needed to make sure Reba would stay gone. There was no way she'd left town.

"Would you be all right with me taking some cash out of the bank and paying off Reba?" I asked.

"It's your money," she said.

"No. You're my wife and it's *our* money. So would you be all right with me doing that?"

"Depends," she said. "Are you going to make her sign something to guarantee she'll stay away?"

"Yes. That will be the condition of her getting the money."

"Then go do what you need to do. I'll wait here for Riley to get home from school. Oh, and make sure there's a clause in there that says she can't contact her by mail, phone, or any other means. Make sure she can't find a loophole."

I kissed the top of her head. "I'll take care of it. Love you, Talia."

She smiled up at me. "Love you too. Now go. The sooner that woman leaves, the better I'll feel."

She wasn't the only one. I quickly texted Outlaw, asking him to draft a contract for me, then went to his house. He tracked Reba through her bank card. I'd been right about her sticking around. She'd gotten a room at a motel in the shady part of town. I took the contract with me, along with a pen so she couldn't use that as an excuse not to sign, then ran to the bank for the money.

When I approached her motel room, I had a cashier's check in my hand for ten grand and the papers she'd have to sign before I gave her the money. The moment she opened the door, I smelled the pot she'd been smoking. Looked like she'd already spent the money I gave her earlier.

"I have a proposition for you," I said. "I'll give you ten thousand dollars to stay out of Riley's life forever. All you have to do is sign a paper agreeing to the terms."

She snorted. "What's a stupid piece of paper mean anyway?"

"Well, if you break the terms of the contract at any time, I won't sue you, have you arrested, or anything else that would allow you to keep breathing." I gave her a smile guaranteed to chill her blood. "What I *will* do is slit your throat, watch you bleed out, then dispose of your body like unwanted trash. Do you understand?"

I was done with Reba. Life was too damn short to deal with this kind of shit. I had a wife and daughter at home who needed me, and I wasn't going to waste another second thinking of Reba.

Epilogue

Talia

Paying Reba off had worked, and she'd been out of our lives the last six months. I hoped it would last forever. The only issue we faced now was a battle with the school system. The child who'd called Adalia and the rest of us whores had only gotten a slap on the wrist with a strongly worded *don't do it again*. The entire club hadn't liked the school's answer. They'd tried going over the principal's head to the school board. Not much luck there either.

So now, I was going to step in. I hadn't told anyone I was coming here, not even Ram. I had a feeling I'd be in trouble later. Sometimes, you had to take a chance on doing something wrong in order to make something else right. At least, that's how I was going to view it.

Outlaw had given me the account information for the money I'd received out of Vega's funds. At first, Ram had been worried I'd run if I had it, and at the time, maybe I would have. Now I loved the stubborn-ass man, and I enjoyed being part of the Devil's Fury. Although, I still wanted to yank out the broom handles from Farrah's and Mariah's asses. They hadn't warmed up to me even a little, and that was fine. I'd never thought I'd easily make friends with one person, so having only two sneer at me wasn't a big deal. To me. Ram, on the other hand, wanted to beat their asses every time he saw them.

I got out of the brand-new Tahoe Badger had insisted on buying for our family vehicle. He'd used the funds stolen from Vega's account, so I didn't feel quite so guilty about the cost. It still scared me a little to drive something so large, but I'd gotten the hang of it. Holding onto my purse strap, I walked up to the main doors of the school and pressed the intercom button.

"May I help you?" a woman asked.

"I'd like to meet with the principal, please," I said.

"Are you a parent?" she asked.

"No. I'm the wife of one of the Devil's Fury members. Our daughter goes to the high school, but I think I have a way to resolve the issue without things escalating further."

"Just a moment," she said.

I waited about ten minutes before someone opened the door. It was an older man, balding, with a belly that hung over his belt. Was this the man giving Badger and the others such a hard time?

"I'm Mr. Lewis," he said. "Vice Principal. Our principal, Mr. Andrews, asked me to take you to the conference room over in the guidance area. If you'll follow me, please?"

I nodded and made my way through the front office, where I had to stop and sign in, as well as have my photo taken. Security measures. I was fine with it. Anything to keep the kids safe. When we reached the conference room, I saw a woman and another man already waiting.

"I'm Mr. Andrews," the man said, standing and offering me his hand. He was tall, thin, but not the least bit attractive. His wire-rim glasses slid down a blade-thin nose, and his lips were nearly non-existent. "This is my assistant, Miss Linden."

"It's nice to meet you both. I'm Talia Cash."

He eyed the property cut over my shoulders as he took his seat again. Mr. Lewis pulled out a chair for me, and I gave him a grateful smile as I sat. Once I had everyone's attention, I decided to take charge and not let these people steamroll me.

"I understand the issue with Gunner's classmate and the things said haven't been resolved to the satisfaction of the Devil's Fury. And before you interrupt, give me excuses, or say one damn word, I want to ask you something. Do you understand *why* they're so upset over this?" I asked.

The three shared a look and Mr. Andrews shook his head. "I assumed they were being difficult."

"Several of the children go to this school. So when Gunner comes home and says something he heard, it spreads like wildfire through our compound. We have women who have come from horrific backgrounds. Kidnapped as children and forced into prostitution, raped, beaten, abused, and they've suffered so much already. The words of that child have hurt a lot of people deeply. Not only the women he labeled whores because of something his parents said, but also those of us who love them. I'm not sure if you're married, Mr. Andrews, but if your wife had suffered any of those things and your child came home and said someone at school called her a whore, what would your reaction be? How would you feel when you saw the devastation on her face, and all those old wounds reopened for her?"

The three remained silent. It seemed they either hadn't known about the fates of some of the women at the compound, or they'd chosen to ignore it. Perhaps they didn't see them as victims, and in my eyes they weren't. They were survivors. It didn't make this issue any less painful for them.

"My daughter was kidnapped by a man who used her however he wanted. He sold her to other men." I took a breath and watched their expressions.

The woman paled a few shades and looked truly remorseful. Mr. Andrews had his nose wrinkled as if he smelled something foul. And Mr. Lewis... holy crap! Were those tears in his eyes? At least two of these people had a heart. "I have a proposition for you. I'm willing to write you a check, here and now, for twenty-five thousand dollars to be used by the school in any way it deems necessary. However, I want to write another check for ten thousand dollars with a very specific purpose. To teach these children what it means to be a bully. I'd imagine the man who took my daughter started out as a little boy who got away with too much because of who his parents were, or because his teachers thought he was a star student. And he turned into a monster when he became an adult."

"What's the catch?" Mr. Andrews asked.

"The club has full approval over the program you use to educate these students on bullying. Specifically, the mothers who are hurting because of that child's words and your inability to properly discipline them. That's not negotiable."

"Anything else?" he asked.

"Yes. I want a proper apology from that child, *and* his parents. In writing, and to be read in front of the entire school, explaining why those words were wrong and hurtful. If you don't teach these children now, who's going to correct them later? You can pass this issue off and think someone at the high school will do a better job sorting them out. Except they don't. They pass them along to the professors at their colleges, for those who even attend. And guess what happens? Nothing. Those children become filled with hatred, think they can say and do whatever they want, because *you* have told them it's okay."

Miss Linden shifted in her seat and Mr. Lewis

cleared his throat. Good. At least those two were paying attention, and I didn't think they disagreed with me.

"I can't force the parents to do something like that," Mr. Andrews said.

"Well, you also can't force me to write you two checks totaling thirty-five thousand dollars. You don't get the money until our club receives an apology. A genuine one." I stood. "I've said everything I came to say. I'll leave my number at the front desk. Call me when you make a decision."

Without another word, I walked out. I checked out at the desk, leaving my information as promised, then got back into my car and left the school. I'd need to tell Badger what I did and explain why. Ram needed to know too. Those people pissed me off so much!

I'd visited the school website the other day. Their anti-bullying policy was a fucking joke. I read over it, three times, and not once had they followed the rules they'd set for their own institution. I didn't know if Badger followed through on threatening them with media coverage. If they didn't accept my terms for the money, then I'd draft something and let the club officers read it over. My friends and family were hurting, and I wasn't about to sit back and do nothing. The school clearly wanted a fight, and I wasn't going to let them win.

When I got back to the compound, I noticed Ram's bike, as well as a dozen others were outside the clubhouse. He'd warned me what I would find if I ever went inside when it wasn't scheduled for a family day. I didn't want to wait until he got home, so I parked and went inside. Smoke hung heavy in the air, along with cheap perfume. I waved a hand in front of my face and looked around. I saw a few women who were mostly naked. The men they were entertaining saw me and quickly looked away. I wondered if this was about on par with being caught by your mother? Grinning, I moved farther into the room, looking for Ram.

I saw him coming out of the back area, along with Badger, Steel, Dingo, Slash, and the other officers. Unfortunately, I wasn't the only one who saw them. A flash of red hair caught my eye as a woman hurled herself toward the men, her bare breasts bouncing. I folded my arms and watched for a moment. Ram hadn't even seen me yet, but the moment she tried to touch him, he gave her a shove and a nasty look.

"I told you and the other bitches here, I'm already taken."

"So? You can do whatever you want." She smiled. "And I'll let you put it wherever you want."

I rolled my eyes. Did that shit really work on these guys? Ram glared at her and pushed her away again. The moment she grabbed hold of his arm, pressing her breasts against him, I decided he was too nice to put her on her ass. So I'd lend a hand.

I strode forward, reached out and grabbed a handful of her hair, then yanked her back and down. She shrieked and fell on her ass.

"I believe my *husband* said he wasn't interested in having your nasty hands all over him. Now be a good little slut and find someone single and willing." I released her and she immediately came at me, her fingers hooked into claws as she aimed for my face.

I smacked her hands away, then punched her in the nose. I heard the *crunch* and saw the blood spurt. Good. Looked like I had probably broken it. None of the men did a thing to intervene. If anything, Ram looked concerned for me. I waved him off and advanced on the little would-be home-wrecker. I'd stabbed a man before. But Vega was different from this woman. Something told me I'd cross a line if I went after her full force. But the way she eyed the men she damn well knew had families, made me want to rip her apart. My friends deserved better than this.

Still… no one had to *know* I wasn't going to actually stab her. I reached over to the pocketknife I noticed in Badger's pocket and yanked it free. His eyebrows arched, but he didn't bother to stop me. I flipped it open and placed a knee on the woman's stomach before leaning down closer. I put the blade against her right breast and pressed just hard enough to draw a little blood.

She screamed and cried, and the fear in her eyes made me want to smile. This woman had the balls to go after men who didn't want her, who had women and children waiting for them at home, but she didn't have what it took to stand up to someone who would fight back.

"I'm not sure how much you paid for these, but unless you want me to pop them like unwanted birthday balloons, you'd better keep your hands off the men behind me. Understood?" I asked.

Two of the other women came closer, eyeing Badger. "You going to let her treat us like this, Pres?"

Badger snorted. "You're not part of my club, so I'm not your president. Call me Badger. Better yet, don't call me anything and leave me the fuck alone. As for Talia, she's defending her territory. I don't see a problem with it."

I felt a presence behind me, and by the scent I knew it was Ram. He hunkered down and put his chest to my back, then slowly reached for my hand wrapped around the knife handle.

"Honey, she's not like Vega. You can't stab her,"

Ram said.

"Wait. Your woman really has stabbed someone?" Dingo asked.

"Yeah. She went a little nuts on Vega after I freed her and the others," Ram said. "Made me damn proud of her. Just like I am now. But I don't want her to do something she might regret later. This stupid bitch crossed a line. I can agree with that much. I'm not sure it's a stabbing offense, though."

"Really?" I looked at him over my shoulder. "What if this was a man and he'd grabbed hold of me that way, shirtless, and was trying to get me to fuck him? Would it be a stabbing offense for you then?"

Ram didn't say anything. It didn't take long for him to release me and back away. "Fair enough. Do what you want with her."

The woman started shrieking again, and she was giving me a damn headache. I stood up and handed the knife back to Badger, but he waved me off.

"Keep it. Since it seems you know how to use one, it might come in handy someday." He patted me on the shoulder. "Good work."

The men went outside, including Ram. I stared down at the woman who now lay crying on the floor. "I realize you serve a purpose here. For the *single* men. Touch my husband again, or any man who belongs to one of my friends, and I will fuck you up so bad no one will recognize you. Got it?"

The woman nodded and I decided I'd made my point. I went outside where the men were waiting. Now it was confession time.

"Um, Badger. I sort of went to the middle school and spoke with the administrators."

He sighed and a ran a hand through his hair. "All right. Let's hear it."

I spent the next fifteen minutes outlining what I'd said and promised, and when I'd finished, the man was smiling. The others seemed to be in agreement as well, and I had the green light to draft a press release about the incident, just in case we needed it.

I followed Ram home and sank onto the couch when we got inside. I needed coffee. Or maybe a donut. No… I wanted both.

"What's wrong?" he asked.

"Are you mad? About what I did at the school and at the clubhouse?"

"Said I was proud of you, didn't I? Like Badger said, you were defending what was yours. In this case, you were marking your territory, and I'm eternally grateful it didn't require you to pee on me."

I smirked. "Fine. I'll remember that the next time someone does something stupid."

"Pretty sure they all got the hint," he said. He pressed a hand to my belly, and I knew what he was thinking about. We'd thought I might be pregnant twice now. The first time, I'd missed my period due to stress. The second it had been nearly two weeks late. Also due to stress.

"One day," I said. "The doctor said I can have children. It's just not the right time."

He nodded. "I know. Besides, Riley is enough for now. If we time this right, by the time she's asking me if she can date, she'll have a little brother or sister to distract her."

I smacked him on the thigh. "That was rotten of you. But I like it. Not sure she'll appreciate it, though."

"Come on. Let's go take a shower and lie down."

"Is that a new code for having sex?" I asked.

"No. You look like you're ready to drop from exhaustion. But if you decide to get frisky while we're in there, I won't push you away."

He leaned down to kiss me, and I melted a little. It had taken a while for me to be ready for kisses. Now that I knew how much I loved him, it was the one thing I wanted to do all the time. I loved the way his lips felt against mine, and the flutter of butterfly wings I felt in my stomach each time he kissed me.

"I love you, Ram."

"Love you too, Talia. More than you'll ever know."

I wouldn't say I'd become more trusting since meeting Ram, but he'd definitely made me pull down the walls I'd built around myself. Now I had friends and family, and I was happier than I'd ever been before. Who'd have thought what I needed was a big, sexy biker to make me realize life was so much sweeter when you had someone to share it with?

Harley Wylde

Harley Wylde is an accomplished author known for her captivating MC Romances. With an unwavering commitment to sensual storytelling, Wylde immerses her readers in an exciting world of fierce men and irresistible women. Her works exude passion, danger, and gritty realism, while still managing to end on a satisfying note each time.

When not crafting her tales, Wylde spends her time brainstorming new plotlines, indulging in a hot cup of Starbucks, or delving into a good book. She has a particular affinity for supernatural horror literature and movies. Visit Wylde's website to learn more about her works and upcoming events, and don't forget to sign up for her newsletter to receive exclusive discounts and other exciting perks.

Harley at Changeling: changelingpress.com/harley-wylde-a-196

Bad Boys Multiverse

A Bad Boy Romance
Dixie Reapers MC
Devil's Boneyard MC
Hades Abyss MC
Devil's Fury MC
Bryson Corners
Owned by the Mob
Reckless Kings MC
Savage Raptors MC
Devoted Guardians MC
Dixie Reapers MC Print
Dixie Reapers MC Audio
Devil's Boneyard MC Audio
Hades Abyss MC Audio

Changeling Press E-Books

More Sci-Fi, Fantasy, Paranormal, and BDSM adventures available in e-book format for immediate download at ChangelingPress.com -- Werewolves, Vampires, Dragons, Shapeshifters and more -- Erotic Tales from the edge of your imagination.

What are E-Books?

E-books, or electronic books, are books designed to be read in digital format -- on your desktop or laptop computer, notebook, tablet, Smart Phone, or any electronic e-book reader.

Where can I get Changeling Press E-Books?

Changeling Press e-books are available at ChangelingPress.com, Amazon, Apple Books, Barnes & Noble, and Kobo.

ChangelingPress.com